Beyond The Aether

By

Peter Oxley

Book Three in the Infernal Aether Series

Burning Chair Limited, Trading As Burning Chair Publishing
61 Bridge Street, Kington HR5 3DJ
www.burningchairpublishing.com

Published by Burning Chair Publishing, 2023

Edited by: Ben Way
Cover: Burning Chair

ISBN: 978-1-912946-36-5

For Jess, Tom and Sam

Prologue

From the Almadite Book of Worlds

In the beginning, Ahriman held dominion over all of the realms, and He and He alone held the power to travel between realms…

Of all of the creatures in all of the realms, the children of our world were his favourites and they pleased Him in their worship. So pleased was He with his children that He left them so that He may stand in judgement over the other realms…

After many years of wandering, Ahriman returned to our world to find that His children had become plentiful, spreading to every corner of their realm. However, He saw that they were weak and divided in His absence. Where before there had been one strong race, now there was a multitude, all growing fat and complacent across the land.

And so Ahriman came down to His children and told them that He would bestow His gifts on only one of the tribes, but they had to defeat all others to win His favour.

And so it came to pass that a great leader named Almadel took charge of his tribe and cut a swathe across the land, defeating all who lay before him. And thus it was that Almadel and his people stood supreme in the realm.

And Almadel spoke to Ahriman, saying: "Look, Father, at what we have done. We have cast aside all of our enemies and now stand utmost before you as your very own master race."

And Ahriman was most pleased and gave Almadel and his people the gift of long life as well as the five runes to the Aether, the runes that Ahriman had used to travel across all of the realms.

Almadel founded a great land onto which he bestowed his name, and great was the fear that all other creatures felt as they beheld this fierce majesty.

And so Almadel and his fearsome warriors set forth from their land to subjugate all others, to cleanse all of the realms and ensure that only the children of Ahriman could rule supreme, as is only right and just.

And Ahriman saw this and was most pleased.

But Ahriman's brother Ormazd also saw this, and in His jealousy sought to put an end to Almadel's ambitions. Thus he came down and took four of the runes from Almadel, casting them to the other realms, and to Heaven and Hell, in His folly ensuring that no one race could ever be supreme above all others. Almadel, his heart broken, swore that he would not rest until he had united the runes and disappeared, forever hunting the runes.

Ahriman saw all of this and was enraged. He entered into battle with Ormazd. The fighting lasted for thousands of cycles, and the Heavens were aflame, until they could stand no more and they rent asunder, opening a doorway to the Druj, where both brothers were interred to battle on to this day…

Chapter One

The rough sand collected beneath my shirt as I crawled forwards, trying to keep the tall rocks between myself and the demons as I squinted against the light from the second, brighter sun high in the sky. If there were any doubts in my mind that we were in another realm, the three suns circling overhead banished them.

I reached the nearest rock and pressed myself against the hard-red stone. I edged my body upwards into a standing position, holding my breath as I peered round it to see a group of five demons engrossed in their tasks. I looked back to check that Joshua, Kate and the Pooka demon Byron were in position and then held up my hand and counted down with my fingers: three, two, one.

We darted round the rocks and ran at the demons, shouting as we closed in on them. Byron and I threw ourselves at the three Berserkers, which were clearly in attendance as bodyguards-cum-porters. Kate dropped to a knee and fired her LeMat pistol at the remaining two, the Warlock demons. In doing so, she provided Joshua with precious time to work his magic.

I swung my runic sword at a roaring Berserker, exulting as I did so in the animalistic joy that came from being in perfect harmony with the weapon. The beast attempted a clumsy swing at me but I parried with ease and brought an end to its challenge with a swift uppercut of my blade that scythed its head asunder. Wrenching the steel free, I twisted out of the path of an axe swung by another demon, arching my back and feeling the rush of wind as it passed me by a mere whisker and buried itself in the ground. Before my attacker could pull it free I kicked hard at the beast's chest and followed up with a swing of my own. That one hit home and the demon fell to the ground, extinguished.

I turned to see Byron still locked in battle with the remaining Berserker and looking as though he was gaining the upper hand. Joshua was struggling with the two Warlocks, and so it was this engagement upon which I focused my attentions.

I ran over to Kate, where she was attempting to help Joshua by firing at the Warlocks with grim determination. I nodded to her as she stopped to reload. "Everything all right?" I asked.

"I'm fine," she said, "although it'd be nice if they looked even a bit bothered by me shooting at them." She snapped the chamber of the pistol closed and opened fire again.

The bullets bounced off the Warlocks, earning little more than irritated glances from them as they engaged in a battle with Joshua that defied all of my senses.

He faced them from across the sandy plain, his face screwed up in intense concentration. The Warlocks' mouths opened and closed to form words and sounds that, while nowhere near intelligible to my untutored ears, conjured up images and feelings in my mind that were nothing short of breath-taking. Thankfully, I was not the target of their utterances, for the demonic invocations were being hurled directly at Joshua. For his part, our friend was repelling and returning them with equal vigour, his mouth twisting to form a guttural flow of consonants.

As for the forms of the invocations themselves, they were streams of fire plucked straight from the sun and directed with malevolent intensity, furious dragons arrowing towards their foe. Then again it were as though the cold light of the most distant stars had been wrenched down and flung outward like spears of piercing light. The sight was agonising, not only to my eyes but also my mind and my very soul; every projectile wrenched at the fibre of my being, even though I was a mere onlooker.

The Warlocks were incredibly powerful, and I could not tell how long Joshua's resolve could withstand their onslaught. Kate's gunshots were stopping the demons from focusing all of their ire on him, but surely it was only a matter of time before he was overcome.

"He needs help," I muttered.

"What?" shouted back Kate, straining to hear my words over the discharge of her pistol.

"I'm going to help him," I said.

She raised her eyebrow at me. "You plannin' something stupid?"

I grinned. "But of course." My mind made up, I charged straight towards the demons, ignoring Kate's curses and Byron's shout of alarm.

The Warlock did not see me until it was too late and I shouted with joy as my sword cleaved through its neck and torso with lethal intent. Then I blinked: there was nothing there. Before I could refocus on where the Warlock had gone, my world exploded into a red-hot Hell.

It were as though I had been thrust up into the burning sky, the land receding leagues beneath me. Everything around me twisted and turned as I realised that I was slowly and agonisingly being unmade.

At this point it is customary to say that my life flashed before my eyes, but even that cliché was denied me; perhaps a blessing given the many trials and terrors I would have been forced to relive. I instead stared into an abyss born of fire, housing at its centre a being I had seen before, a swirling red angry mass that wanted nothing more than my total annihilation. *Who are you?* a distant part of me shouted once more into this hideous, seething hatred.

Your doom, came the reply in a cavernous voice that would

have snatched away my breath had I any to steal.

Why?

You… are repugnant, an abomination. You do not belong here; none of you do. I will destroy you all.

Once again, a million shadowy crows attacked me, gnawing into my soul, an insane flashback to the time when Maxwell sought to cure me of my demonic tendencies by forcing me to inhale his strange gaseous Compound inside his laboratory. But then my attackers exploded in a shower of jagged silhouettes and I fell to my knees, my hands buried in the coarse sand as I listened to the Warlock scream his last. I looked up to see Byron and Kate running over to me while Joshua glowered from where he had just torn the demons to pieces.

"You fool," Joshua said. "You could have been killed."

I coughed as I tried a laugh. "I managed to distract him for long enough so you could do your thing, did I not?"

The young man glared at me and then stomped away.

*

Byron and I stood on the edge of a cliff, looking over the cracked alien landscape of the world that we had nicknamed the 'Red Desert' The three suns hung in a blood-red sky that was dotted with at least five moons moving across the firmament in a perverse dance as dizzying to witness as it was surely impossible.

Below and around us, red sand and rocks stretched out to the horizon, interspersed with twisting towers of rubicund stone reaching up to the heavens, so high it seemed they would snag the celestial bodies whirling overhead. Nothing lived in that wasteland aside from us and our two friends, who were busy examining the demons' work.

"Beautiful, isn't it?" asked Byron.

I grunted. "Not quite the word I would use. A bit too desolate for my tastes."

He gestured to the sky and expansive landscape. "Does all of this not astound you?"

"Makes me seasick, more like." I turned to look at the Pooka, noting the way the hairs on his elongated ears rippled in the breeze. "Is this what your world was like?"

"A little. I have certainly missed having something interesting to look up at. The sky in your world is so… pedestrian. No wonder you haven't explored the heavens: there's bugger-all up there to inspire you."

"It's your world too now," I pointed out.

Byron and his fellow Pooka demons had played a vital role in helping to repel the Almadite invasion of Earth six months previously. For that service they had earned the gratitude of the Queen and her government, who were moved to grant them citizenship of the British Empire if only to ensure that we kept such strong allies to hand in case they were needed again. For their part, the Pooka were happy to have somewhere they could at last call home, having lost their own realm to the Almadites a long time before. While they had been on Earth for many centuries, giving rise to a multitude of legends and lores, it was not until they stepped into the light to fight at our side that they found true acceptance.

"Yes, it is my world too," he conceded. "Doesn't make it any more interesting though, does it?"

"We could make Earth more interesting if you like," I said. "For instance, we could reopen the portal and let the Almadites come back through—would fighting them excite you?" I grinned at him.

"That's all right, thank you all the same." He shuddered and looked at me. "Your kind have a bizarre sense of humour, you know?"

"It is the only way to stay sane in the face of all this madness," I said. "Speaking of which, how is your prodigy getting on? He seemed to acquit himself quite well back there."

Byron glanced at Joshua, who was busy examining the Warlocks' device, Kate stood over him like a watchful angel.

"Yes, he did. He is powerful, there is no doubting it, and we are only just beginning to tap into what he is capable of. But…"

I raised an eyebrow. "But what?"

Byron grabbed my elbow and led me away. When we were far enough to ensure that we could not be overheard, he continued in a low voice: "I am scared by what he is capable of. There is so much pain and sorrow there. I fear that his bitterness is what's really driving him."

A cold chill ran over me. "Lexie?"

He nodded. "He has not yet recovered from her death. It is as though there is a void where his humanity should be, if that makes sense."

I shook my head. "He is the most human of us all," I said. "He is grieving; that is only natural."

"It has been six months, Gus, and he has shown precious little emotion aside from anger and a single-minded focus."

"Well, that's good, isn't it? Letting his magical studies distract him from his grief and sadness?"

"Ordinarily I can see how it would be beneficial, perhaps. But I know something about it from personal experience, and I can tell you that the worst thing you can do is refuse to talk to anyone about how you are feeling."

I tensed up with the instinctive reaction of a true Englishman discussing such alien things as emotions. I had lost my parents when I was a child and, in spite of how I had felt about them, I could not deny that their loss had affected me, throwing me down into a rebellious funk that shaped my formative years. It sent me spiralling from the potential for a respectable life into a chaotic ramble around the world as I tried to run from my problems. Indeed, my brother Maxwell had often pointed out that my tendency towards an overreliance on alcohol and laudanum no doubt stemmed from my seeking release from the feelings I sought to repress over the years. No doubt my addiction to the runic sword had its roots in my troubled past as well.

It was somewhat ironic, therefore, that I should have found release and purpose thanks to the one creature that was truly responsible for the loss of my parents: the demon Andras. In driving Maxwell towards creating the portals to the Aether, Andras had also inadvertently pushed me into a position of responsibility, one where I was a key driving force in the battle against the evil Almadites.

Byron, on the other hand, had not only lost his parents but also his entire dominion. In a hideous foreshadowing of what they intended to do to our world, the Almadites had invaded the Pooka's homeland when their defences were down. They had done this by constructing an elaborate bluff that led them to believe that the intended target of their invasion was the valuable Eternal Mines and its seemingly endless supply of power and resources. While the Pooka army had readied themselves to defend the Mines, the Almadites, led by Andras, had swept into their realm and enslaved their people, stripping them of everything so that they were nothing more than mindless slaves, unable and unwilling to do anything but serve their new masters.

By the time the Pooka army had realised their mistake it was too late, and their attempts to mount a counterattack fell flat in the face of the superior numbers of Almadite warriors.

I knew from many nights speaking with Byron that he never stopped dwelling on those he had lost and the destruction of his culture, but he and his people had learnt to move on and now had finally established a home once more.

"I take it he has not talked to you about his sister?" I asked.

"No. Nor has he spoken to Kate or indeed anyone else."

"It could be that he does not wish to think about it just yet."

Byron shook his head. "His every waking moment is directed by her memory." I shot him a questioning glance and he tapped his forehead. "I am experienced in such matters, as you know. I wonder whether I should stop teaching him for a time."

"No," I said. "We need all the powerful individuals we can get, especially now. If anything, you should be considering how you can *accelerate* his training."

"Normally I would agree with you, but his aims and yours are not truly in alignment. You see, you believe he is learning how to create portals and fight Warlocks so he can help in the defence of Earth."

"Of course…" I said slowly.

"But his real motivation is to find his sister."

I blinked. "But she's dead; we watched her die. Does he not accept—?"

"Don't worry, he is not delusional. But he is focused on learning everything he can so he can travel to the spirit world."

I could not help but laugh in disbelief. "Max proved a long time ago that the Aether is not the spirit world, that the creatures there just prey on those desperate to believe. Even you have told me that there's no such place…"

"No," he said. "I have said that I have never encountered such a place. But I'm just a plain old soldier who sometimes acts as a tutor to desperate humans. What do I know about the mysteries of the universes?"

I paced back and forth for a moment, trying to consider the implications. "As long as our interests are aligned, then surely it is not a bad thing that he explores this other option?"

"Unless he gets distracted at a crucial moment. A rifle is only useful if it fires when you need it to."

I glared at him. "He is not a weapon. He is…"

"What? Do not tell me you are intimately concerned for his welfare as a person and a friend: you have hardly spoken to him over the past few months."

"Well, I shall remedy that." I folded my arms.

Byron chuckled. "No offence, Gus, but maybe you should ask Kate to make the first move. A woman's touch may be better than you blundering in."

"Have you met Kate?" I asked with a half-smile. "She is probably the least empathetic out of all of us."

"Regardless, I think she should try speaking to him first.

Before it is too late."

"What, before he disappears on some wild goose chase trying to find heaven so he can resurrect his dear departed sister?"

"Possibly," mused Byron. "Or before he gets himself killed trying. I have noticed a rather reckless arrogance about him in recent weeks. For instance, back then—attacking two Warlocks on his own. He is powerful, but not *that* powerful. He took quite a risk."

"He still managed to defeat them, though."

"Yes, but only because you nearly sacrificed yourself as a distraction. Do you fancy doing that every time he gets himself in a tight spot?"

I rubbed my head, remembering the horror of that formless voice that had bellowed at me: alien and yet somehow familiar. "Not really," I said with a wry smile. "I don't like him *that* much."

A shout from behind made us spin round to see Kate in the grip of a Warlock, the demon holding her in front of him like a shield. Joshua was slowly rising to his feet as we ran over.

"No one thought to check there were any others around, then?" shouted Kate.

"Be quiet!" snarled the Warlock, making her cry out in pain as it squeezed her closer.

"Impossible," muttered Joshua. "I didn't sense it—"

"Time for that later," I said, then louder to the demon: "Release her and we will let you go unharmed."

The Warlock cackled. "Do you really think I am so stupid as to trust the likes of you? Do not make any moves or I will kill her."

"What do you want?" asked Byron.

"Exactly what you have given us," said the Warlock. A swirling vortex appeared behind the demon and he stepped through before any of us could react, taking Kate with him.

We all shouted as one, charging forwards, but the portal sealed shut with a pop a moment later.

Chapter Two

All three of us ran over to the space where the portal had been mere seconds before. I cast around, hoping in vain that some vestige of the demon's spell remained that we could hitch on the back of.

"No-no-no-no!" shouted Byron, his cheeks flushed with rage.

"Open it," I said to Joshua. "We need to go after her. Do it now."

Joshua shook his head, running his fingers through his hair. "I cannot."

I stomped over to him, jabbing my finger at his chest. "You transported us all here single-handed. One more portal. *Now* please."

"It is not as simple as that," he said. "I do not know where the demon has gone."

"Almadel would be a fair bet, wouldn't you agree?"

"Yes, but… I don't know where Almadel is."

I expelled a puff of air and turned to Byron for support, but the Pooka just nodded. "He is right. You can only conjure a portal if you know exactly where to point it. So far we have not been able to pinpoint the location of Almadel."

"But all these years of you fighting the Almadites…"

"Strangely enough," Byron said, "I have always been keen to

keep as much distance as I could between me and the beasts. Finding out the location of their home has been right at the bottom of my list of priorities."

"But the amount of Almadites who have been summoned to Earth," I tried again, turning to Joshua, "including by you. How did you…?"

"They came from the Aether," said Joshua. "We have never needed to reach into their homeland to summon them. Not that we would ever want to." He shuddered.

I clenched and unclenched my fists, the helplessness of our situation making my skin itch. "We have to do something," I said. "We cannot leave her with them…" An image flashed across my mind's eye of Kate surrounded by demons in their own realm, of the unspeakable things that they were doing to her.

Byron looked down at the equipment the Warlocks had been assembling prior to our attack. "Anything here that could help us?" he asked.

Joshua shook his head. "From what I can tell they were constructing some form of divination spell."

"Divination?" I asked. "So not trying to form a portal?"

"No. It would appear that they were trying to find something."

"Any idea what?" asked Byron.

I threw my hands in the air. "Should we not be focusing instead on the more pressing matter at hand?"

"If we know what they were looking for it might give us a clue as to how to find them, or at least it might give us something to bargain with," Byron said, as though he was speaking to a small and somewhat hysterical child.

"Difficult to tell," said Joshua in answer to Byron's initial question. "We should take it back to Maxwell: he may have some insights."

"Agreed," said Byron. "It is pointless us remaining here."

"So we go back to Earth. And in the meantime, what about Kate?" I asked as they gathered up the equipment.

"There is someone there who can help us. Someone who knows where Almadel is. Remember?" Byron watched as the realisation dawned on me. "Good. Now help us to get all of this back into the capsule."

*

The Aether is a vast and dangerous place, and travel through it is not for the faint-hearted. My own experiences of that terrible void had been enough to populate a lifetime's worth of nightmares. As such, when it came to voyaging through the Aether to other realms, we were keen to take as many precautions as possible.

Given that our original incursion into the Aether had nigh on resulted in us falling victim to the grasping hands of the undead creatures trapped there, we had all agreed that we would feel a lot better if we had a protective barrier between us and any potential attackers.

Maxwell had therefore designed for us a machine that was, true to form, as functional and effective as it was dispiritingly ugly. The best way to describe the ingenious craft that conveyed us across the Aetheric wastelands on adventures to fantastic worlds was that it resembled a simple wardrobe. When Maxwell had shown me his original sketches I had been naïve enough to hope that he would adorn the cabinet-like contraption with at least a few ornamental flourishes to pique the imagination and hint at the vehicle's amazing potential. However, once again he had rejected anything that did not add to its utility.

We were therefore reduced to travailing in a tall, rectangular box that had been painted a rather dull blue colour, the only features of interest on its exterior being the doors through which we entered it and a narrow slitted window. Inside it was cramped, with just about enough room for six people as long as they did not mind being pressed together in an overly friendly fashion.

Two tubes ran the length of the wall from balloons stored in the ceiling cavity, supplying air to the interior in the event that the vehicle found itself in a vacuum. Other than those, a couple of dials and a few strategically placed runes were all that was included within, with the main propulsive force being provided by our friend Joshua.

I stepped in and closed the door behind me, helping Byron to stow away the Warlocks' equipment while Joshua readied himself for the spells and incantations that would transport us back home.

After checking that we were all in place and the equipment was stowed, the young man closed his eyes and started chanting. The runic sword strapped to my back vibrated in response to the words, a reaction that was becoming increasingly common when it was around kindred magical phenomena. While it was at first alarming, I had grown used to the sensation over the past few months and now found it almost reassuring, acting as an early indication that Joshua's spells were working.

His abilities had grown in impressive fashion since we first met him, helped by a single-mindedness in his devotion to study and practice following his sister's unfortunate death. I had assumed that he was using that focus as a way of coping with his grief and stemming the flood of emotions that would overwhelm him if he stopped to think about what he had lost, although Byron's words had made me wonder whether there was a darker motive to all of this. Joshua would not be the first person to attempt to cheat death and bring back a loved one; I feared, though, that he might well be the first to actually be in a position to make it possible.

My sword's vibrations increased in intensity as I peered through the slitted window and saw the world disappear, replaced by an all-pervading blackness. I tried not to focus too much on what was now beyond the fragile walls that encased us, for to do so was to invite my imagination to run riot. A wisp of mist floated by, and I fancied that I saw the shape of a face within it, hungry eyes and probing teeth seeking a way into our miniscule safe haven.

The mist dissipated, replaced with shuffling and moaning sounds that in turn receded quickly. I breathed a sigh of relief at this sign of our travelling at speed through that inhospitable place. Thankfully, any breeze making its way into our confined space was minimal, ensuring that our small lantern was still lit, a small mercy that saved us from the terrors of our imaginations. I shared a nod with Byron and we both looked to Joshua as his chanting increased in volume. The young man's face was taut with focus and effort, the veins standing out in his neck as he made the final push to punch a hole through the Aether and back to our own world.

I held my breath, never enjoying that moment when we were at the mercy of so many elements, when the merest miscalculation or lack of focus could end with us being deposited on another alien land. Or worse: trapped in the Aether forever.

We stumbled as the vehicle landed with a jolt, sunlight streaming in through the narrow window. Joshua slumped to the floor, his face pale and his limbs shaking as the effort took its toll on him. We helped him back to his feet. "We're back," he said simply.

"Well done," I said, feeling foolish and patronising even as the words left my lips. Joshua did not seem to notice or mind, instead taking a few deep breaths to recover his poise before nodding to us.

I opened the door and stepped out into the warm Hertfordshire sunshine, to be faced by a dozen rifle barrels pointed at me.

Chapter Three

I paced the cold stone floor of my cell, pausing only to kick at the damp walls at either end.

"Stupid, stupid, stupid!" I bellowed, turning to bang on the solid wooden door with my fist. The sound of my hammering echoed down the hall outside and I listened in vain for any response.

"Mindless automatons!" I yelled at no one and everyone in particular. "Do you have any idea what you are allowing them to do? And how did you get to St Albans so quickly? Who tipped you off?"

If anyone could hear me they neither cared nor wished to reply, leaving me with just the distant echoes of my voice for company. With a snarl, I turned to recommence my pacing.

I wiped sweat from my brow with a shaking hand and stamped my feet in an effort to stabilise my feverish mind and weakening body. A shadow in the corner thickened and congealed in the half-light, and I fancied that I could hear a distant cackling.

I took a deep breath and squeezed my eyes shut for a moment, gritting my teeth against the wave of helpless nausea that threatened to overwhelm me. I was damned if I would give them the satisfaction of finding me in a vomit-splattered cell.

"Who is incurring the wrath of the great Augustus Potts this time?" asked an improbable voice from the corner.

I turned and marched away from the hallucination, hoping that ignoring it would hasten its dissipation.

"After all we've been through, and you won't even give me the time of day?" tutted the vision of Andras, his harsh and demonic features off-set by a formal jacket, trousers and top hat. "Would it be more pleasing for you if I adopted this form instead?" His face shifted and solidified until it was that of my old friend N'yotsu.

The sight of that long-vanished figure stopped me in my tracks, the vision of the man Andras could be when he was stripped of his demonic elements and allowed to be human. I shook my head. "Do not do this," I muttered, clenching my hands into fists. "Not him."

"Too soon?" Andras again. "Wounds still somewhat raw?"

"You are not really here," I said through clenched teeth. "You are not here, you are not him…"

"Correct," said Andras, bending forwards to examine his clawed hands in a weak shaft of sunlight. "Although I will credit you this: the quality and detail of your hallucinations are second-to-none."

I barked a short, sharp laugh and slapped my hand against the wall. "I am clearly going mad."

Andras eyed me. "If you ask me, that happened a long time ago." He tapped his finger on his pursed lips. "But what if this is a rare moment of lucidity, a flimsy raft of sanity after a lifetime adrift in a sea of madness? What if everything you believe you have experienced over the past few years was just a hallucination?"

"And I've been living in an asylum all this time?" I shook my head. "This is not an asylum; there's not enough shit and screaming."

"Not all asylums are the same," he replied, wagging a finger at me.

"Just leave me be." I turned to commence my stomping once more.

Andras watched me for a few moments, arms folded and a wry grin on his face. "You know, it is a lot healthier to discuss these things rather than just bottle them up."

"So I should talk to my visions to stop myself from going mad? Is this an attempt at irony?"

He shrugged and then peered at me. "If you don't mind me saying, you don't look very well. Is everything all right?"

"You know full well it is not," I muttered. "Kate is in the hands of the Almadites, and we are stuck here thanks to the stupidity of our pathetic excuse for a Prime Minister."

"It seems to me that you are the authors of your own misfortune. After all, you disobeyed a direct order."

"It was a stupid order," I shot back. "Ordering us not to engage with the demons, refusing permission for us to travel through the Aether—"

"But if you had not gone over there, Kate would not have been taken…"

"Don't you think I don't know that?" I shouted, smashing my palm against the stone wall and wincing at the sharp pain before looking up, hoping that the sensation had driven away the hallucination.

I was sadly disappointed.

"Touchy, aren't we?" grinned Andras. "Maybe chaos such as that which you have managed to cause was exactly what Prime Minister Gladstone was intending to avoid when he banned all travel into the Aether."

Gladstone. I spat at the name as I mulled over my many misfortunes. Time was that we were fêted as the heroes of the hour, the only ones who could truly help to drive back the threats from the demons of Almadel. But then the Prime Minister Benjamin Disraeli and Queen Victoria had been exposed as having been—for a brief time—under the control of the demons. That was enough for the politicians to do what they did best: paralyse the country in endless debates and back-stabbing.

Disraeli had had precious little time to recover from the demons' attempted invasion through the portal at St Albans—which I had helped to stop, dammit!—when he was unceremoniously ousted through a vote of no confidence, forcing the Queen to turn to the Leader of the Opposition, William Ewart Gladstone.

I remembered what Disraeli had said when someone had asked him to define the difference between a misfortune and a calamity. "If Gladstone fell into the Thames," Disraeli had said, "that would be a misfortune; and if anybody were to pull him out, that would be a calamity." Those were sentiments with which I wholeheartedly agreed.

Andras chuckled. "You still have not warmed to your new Prime Minister, have you?"

I glared at him. "He is an uptight prig who is more concerned with process, procedure and religion than dealing with the threats right under his nose."

"Spoken like a true friend of Disraeli's."

"I grant you that my views are no doubt coloured by my association with Disraeli, but no one can doubt that life was a lot simpler when he was in charge rather than this… wet fish."

"A bit harsh."

I laughed. "Ever since Gladstone became Prime Minister, everything has ground to a halt. Nothing can happen without endless committee meetings, papers and discussions; anyone who shows even a *mote* of initiative is locked up."

Andras chuckled. "It never pays to be one of the dangerous intellectuals, coming up with unwanted things like ideas, does it?"

"Certainly not these days." I patted the wall with my hand, softer this time to avoid hurting myself again, and then sighed. "I would not mind, but arresting us for the simple act of going to the Aether, when we are the only ones standing between this world and the demons…" I drew in a shallow breath; it felt as though the air was being sucked out of the room.

"What makes you think you are the only ones who can fight demons?" Andras said.

"Do you see anyone else who could do it?" I asked, blinking to clear my vision. "The army's movements are just as restricted as ours and you're… well…"

He shrugged. "Maybe Gladstone has a higher plan, one to which you are not privy."

I barked a short laugh. "The only higher plan he seems to have is that of boring the demons into submission." I looked around in vain for some form of ventilation; the walls seemed to be closing in on me.

"Even so, if you had listened to your brother's advice and not indulged in your pleasure cruise to the Aether, then Kate would not be kidnapped and you would not be under arrest for disobeying the Prime Minister's direct orders, vis-à-vis travel to the Aether."

I frowned through the fog at the hallucination. "If you are here to torture me with my own miscalculations…" I muttered.

The image before me shifted, and for a moment Kate was there, frowning at me with hands on her hips. "What's the matter, Gus?" she asked. "Feelin' guilty about summink?"

Then Andras was before me once more as I leant back against the wall to relieve the pressure on my shaking legs. "You really are looking slightly peaky," he observed. "If I didn't know better, I would say you are sickening for something."

"I'm fine," I managed, sliding to the floor and the welcoming coldness of the flagstones.

"Or suffering the withdrawal symptoms from an addiction, perhaps? Tell me, when was the last time you were separated from your sword?"

The runic sword. Just the mention of the weapon made my heart skip a beat in frustrated desire. For a long time it had been as much a part of me as my own hands, the first thing I reached for every morning even before my clothing. I frowned as I tried to recall a time when it was not strapped to my back or at least within arm's reach.

"Poor man," came a voice from far away. I looked up to see a huddle of white-coated men peering down at me, their faces blurred and obscured as though I were viewing them through a glass bowl. "He clearly does not have much time left. The attachment is too far advanced to allow him to operate without it for any length of time…"

"No!" I shouted, flailing my arms at these assailants before they condemned me as a lost cause. "Leave me alone! I don't need you…!"

Rough hands grabbed me under the armpits and picked me up. "Gus," barked a voice. "Gus!"

The world swam back into focus as another voice, to my right this time, opined: "If you ask me, he's gone bonkers, sir."

"I did not ask you, Private," snapped a familiar voice.

I shook my head and blinked. "Albert. Captain Pearce," I managed. "You are a sight for sore eyes." I stared at his shoulder where he had slung a brown canvas bag. I felt the familiar pull of the runic sword from within the material, even from that distance giving me enough sustenance to rouse me from my fever. I looked round to see that the hallucination of Andras had disappeared.

"Don't get your hopes up," Pearce said, as a pair of manacles were clapped painfully over my wrists. "You're coming with me for questioning. You're in big trouble." He nodded to the two soldiers who were propping me up. "Bring him."

*

Captain Pearce refused to say another word as I was half-marched, half-dragged along dark corridors and down vertiginous flights of stairs. The chains that bound my wrists clinked and rattled as I walked, heaping further indignity upon me. I asked to at least be allowed to walk unaided but was rewarded with a hard shove in my back. This unjust treatment continued until we stepped through a large oak door and I emerged, blinking, into sunshine.

As my eyes adjusted to the light, I could see the tall towers that lined the central square inside the Tower of London. The bulk of the White Tower loomed in front of us as we stepped around Tower Green and then past the Bloody Tower itself.

I continued my protests as I was hustled along towards a large carriage, practically a cage on wheels, inside of which I could see the manacled forms of Joshua and Byron.

"Wait!" called a voice, and my escort ground to a halt as we turned to see a moustachioed officer march towards us. "What are you doing? We have strict instructions that these prisoners are not to be moved."

"I have new orders, sir," said Pearce, handing him a piece of paper. "Signed by the Prime Minister."

The other officer frowned at the paper, trying to find something at which he could pick fault. "This is most irregular," he concluded.

Pearce shrugged. "I agree, sir, but ours is not to question, eh? If you are satisfied that all is in order?"

The officer grunted. "As you were." He watched with a sceptical eye as I was bundled into the cage before turning to march off back towards the barracks.

"Afternoon," I said as I settled myself onto the hard wooden bench. "And how is everyone?"

"Shut your trap," snarled one of the soldiers who had joined us in our cage. I stared back at him with a half-smile on my lips, showing that I could not be cowed by him and his overbearing manner.

Pearce climbed up into the cab next to the driver and, fully laden with armed soldiers, we started off out of the gates. A half-dozen mounted soldiers gathered round to escort us, cutting off any thought we may have had of escape or rescue.

I looked over at Joshua and Byron, sharing short nods with each of them. While I could feel my strength returning, Joshua looked in a worse state than I had been when I was suffering in my cell. He still seemed drained by the exertions of our voyage through the Aether, coupled with the battle with the Warlocks. I shook my head; I had harboured a faint hope he could work some form of magic to help us break free, but it looked like we would have to either find another option or bide our time until he was strong enough to re-join the fight. In the meantime, it best served our purposes for us to stay quiet and observe.

We rounded Trinity Square and headed up Great Tower Street towards the City. The roads were as busy as ever, with costermongers lining the route and businessmen marching to and fro on whatever business it was that preoccupied them. A group of women paused their conversation to stare with barely disguised glee at the chance to glimpse some grand scandal or other, while a gaggle of children ran along the side of our cage, shouting questions and obscenities at us. The racket was enhanced by a gang of workmen standing outside a tavern, drink fuelling their confidence and repertoire of insults.

"Always a pleasure to take a turn round town," I said to the others.

"Be quiet back there," barked Pearce from up front. "I don't want a riot breaking out on your account."

I shrugged and turned my attentions to affecting an unconcerned air as though there were nothing in the world unnatural about my present condition or mode of transport. Our carriage looped round St Paul's Churchyard and down Ludgate Hill, the crowds becoming less concerned with us the further we went. I grunted as I realised that we were headed down to Whitehall; maybe Maxwell could help us.

We clattered to a halt outside the familiar bulk of 24 Whitehall, and I watched as Pearce held a hurried discussion with the guard who opened the door; it appeared as though we were not expected. Pearce waved the man aside, ordering him to stand down while we stepped from our cage.

"I will take it from here, thank you," Pearce said as the soldiers made to escort us into the building. "There are plenty of my men inside to keep them out of trouble."

"As you say, sir," said the Sergeant, stepping aside and handing Pearce a ring of keys.

We clanked our way through the front door and into the hallway, surprised to find the room empty. The front door slammed shut and Pearce darted past us. "Follow me," he said, "quickly!"

Joshua and Byron glanced at me and I shrugged. We had precious few options although I was surprised at the amount of trust Pearce had in our sense of honour, given the circumstances.

He led us to the kitchen at the rear of the building and glanced around outside. Satisfied, he beckoned me forward. "Give me your wrists."

I watched with raised eyebrow as he unlocked each of our manacles in turn. "What's going on, Captain?" I asked.

"I probably do not deserve that title any more," he said, "as I suspect I will be as wanted as you three in a short while." He opened the bag he had been carrying and tossed the runic sword to me. "You will probably need this."

I caught the weapon one-handed and bit back a sigh as its restorative energies flowed into me, expelling the remaining weaknesses that had afflicted me in the Tower. I grinned at Pearce. "Does this mean we are no longer prisoners?"

"Time for talking later," he said. "Come with me."

He led us out of the door and into the yard behind. He pulled a crate over to the rear wall before jumping up on to it. Whatever he saw over the other side satisfied him, as he nodded and then waved us forward. "Over, now."

We did not hesitate, clambering over the wall to find a carriage waiting on the other side. "Afternoon gents," grinned the coachman from under a wide brimmed hat.

"Sergeant Jones," I said with a smile. "You are mixed up in this… whatever this is… as well, then?"

"You could say that, sir," he said. "If you would oblige me in taking your seats, sirs, we need to get movin' afore them out front realise what's goin' on back 'ere. I'd rather not have to shoot my way out this alley."

We piled into the carriage and then Pearce barked a short command for Jones to get us moving. We pulled the curtains closed and sat back in a tense silence, listening to the sound of the street beyond as we made our way out of Spring Gardens and onto the main thoroughfare of Piccadilly.

I shot a questioning glance at Pearce and he shook his head. All in good time, he seemed to say as he turned his attention to the window, leaning his head to peep out of the small gap between curtain and panel.

The four of us kept our silence as the carriage bumped and jolted along the road, hardly daring to make a noise lest it betray us to those without. We pulled to a halt and held our breaths as the sound of a handful of horses clattered alongside, fearing that they were the same soldiers who had escorted us from the Tower. I looked to Pearce; he was ramrod straight and keeping a wary eye on the window, his hand on his pistol.

"You there," barked a voice, so near it made us flinch. "Where did you come from?"

"Who wants to know?" Jones replied.

"I am a Sergeant in Her Majesty's armed forces, and this is a restricted area for civilians."

"That it is," grunted Jones. "Which is why I'm not carting civilians."

I felt my heart skip a beat; had we been betrayed already?

"What do you mean?"

"I've come from the back of Horseguards," said Jones. "Ask yourself whether there are any people who might want to be coming and going from there unobserved by the masses. Then ask yourself whether you'd fancy being the one who delayed them."

We held our breaths as the other Sergeant mulled over these words. I fancied that I could hear his mount shuffle closer to our carriage, and I shrank away from the window in response.

We jumped at a shout from one of the unseen riders, a harsh "Yah!" followed by the stamp and clop of the horses being spurred into motion past us.

We exhaled as one, shaking our heads as we sank back into our seats and let the coach rock us onwards to safety.

After a few moments, Byron cleared his throat. "Gus, there is something we need to talk about."

I frowned at him, struggling to concentrate on his words in my tense state of mind.

"It appears that we were gone for longer than we thought," he continued.

"I know," I said slowly. "We never expected the delay caused by the Warlock taking Kate."

"Not quite that," he said. "When we arrived back in St Albans from the Aether, we were surprised by how quickly the government had gathered soldiers to arrest us, were we not?"

"Yes," I said. "We were only gone a few hours; even if Horseguards had found out about our trip as soon as we left, there is no way they could have mobilised in such numbers so soon. They must have been forewarned."

"Or you were gone much longer than a few hours," said Pearce.

I frowned at him, and then looked over to Byron, who nodded.

"I am afraid that is correct," he said. "Time has a tendency to travel at different speeds in different realms. Whilst from our perspective we were only in that other place for a few hours, from the point of view of this realm—Earth—we were gone for two weeks."

I opened and closed my mouth. "Are you sure?" I asked finally. "Why did you not warn me of this beforehand?"

"We did not know; it was the first time we had visited that realm."

I turned to Pearce. "And I suppose you are still not going to tell us what is going on?" I asked.

Pearce ignored me, staring out of the window.

The rest of the journey was uneventful, and we relaxed as the minutes ticked by. Pearce resisted any attempts by us to draw him into conversation, save to reassure us he was not acting as our captor any longer.

"So we're free to go?" I asked.

"You can, but I suspect you won't get very far when the word gets out that you have escaped from the Tower. Which is probably already the case."

"What's the plan, then?" asked Byron. "Where are you taking us?"

"All in good time," he said again. "The person I am taking you to meet would not be best pleased if he found out I had stolen his thunder by giving you the full story."

I mulled over whether it was likely to have been Maxwell or Andras who had orchestrated this prison break. There was precious little love lost between Pearce and Andras, not to mention that we had not seen the demon for many months. So Maxwell it was, I concluded as I sat back and readied myself for the inevitable tongue-lashing that my brother would no doubt relish delivering. He had warned us plenty of times that we should play ball with Gladstone, at least until we had no other alternative. He would have regarded our little trip as a superfluous distraction and a risk that had jeopardised what little trust the Prime Minister had in us. The annoying thing was that he was right.

I disembarked the carriage somewhat reluctantly when we pulled up in front of a long row of terraced houses. By the amount of time we had been travelling since leaving Whitehall, and in particular the lack of any bridges, I had reasoned that we were heading north towards St John's Wood and Hampstead and a quick glance around me confirmed this. At the end of the street, over to our right, I could see the greenery of Regents' Park; we were within spitting distance of the Lord's Cricket Ground, somewhere I had had precious little opportunity to visit for far too long.

"Do we have time to take in a game?" I asked. "Maybe just a couple of innings?"

The others looked at me quizzically. Apart, that is, from Pearce, who scowled. "It is best we do not linger too long out of doors. Try to look natural."

As we followed Pearce towards the nearest house I bit back a grin at the thought of a Pooka, a half-demon, a sorcerer and an army Captain looking natural in this most English of high-class residential streets on the outskirts of the city.

Pearce opened the front door without knocking and ushered us inside, glancing up and down the street before shutting it behind us. I looked around the hallway, drinking in the fine furnishings and calm serenity. Something was not quite right; there was not enough noise, mess and smell for Maxwell to be in attendance.

"Why are we here?" I asked as Pearce pushed past us. He opened a door midway along the hallway and held it open for us, gesturing that we should enter. I shrugged to the others and walked through.

We found ourselves in a large sitting room shrouded in darkness, the only illumination coming from a handful of candles and a small slit in the curtains through which the sunlight struggled to penetrate. Turning away from the curtains to greet us was a tall, thin man with a shock of greying black hair receding from a high forehead, a hangdog face framed by that famous chin-beard.

"My dear fellow, you are here at last!" he exclaimed, making his way over.

"Prime Min—" I started, then corrected myself: "Mr Disraeli."

"Please, call me Benjamin," he said, shaking my hand vigorously. "We have no more need of honorifics these days. We are all mere mortals are we not? Ah, the Pooka!" He turned to greet Byron, who accepted his hand with a bemused smile.

"It has been a long time, Benjamin," he said. "Do you remember Joshua?"

"How could I forget? Good fellow, how are you keeping?"

I smiled as I watched the former Prime Minister bounce around us like an excited puppy. Such a transformation from the last time we had met; losing office to Gladstone had hit him hard, particularly as it had been as a direct result of the demons' influence. To then be succeeded by a man who specialised in pious inertia was the final straw. He had appeared broken and bent in the aftermath, his confidence and standing destroyed in one fell swoop.

The last time we had seen him, shortly after leaving office, he had worn every one of his 60-odd years and more. However, the man before us was positively rejuvenated, his old bright-eyed intensity in full attendance along with a confident posture that spoke of his keenness for action. I felt my spirits lift as I followed him round the room: in spite of my fears, maybe all was not quite lost.

Disraeli was still fussing around us. "Please do sit down. I am afraid there are no servants here to tend for us: we had to send them away so we could be guaranteed privacy. You see, I am not supposed to be here: is that not right, Captain?"

"You are correct, sir," said Pearce, standing to the side of our chairs, as formal as ever. "To tell the truth, none of us should be."

"Quite true, quite true." Disraeli patted a hand on his knee in a miniature tattoo. "Captain Pearce told me about Miss Thatcher. Kate."

I turned to look at Pearce, my mouth opening in sudden understanding as I took in his stiff demeanour, as though it was taking an effort of will to stop himself from charging around the room in a mad panic. Of course.

"Captain," I said. "I did not realise…"

My words were cut off by the cold stare he turned on me. "Realise what, exactly?" he asked.

I looked around for support but there was precious little

being offered by the others.

"I knew you and Kate were close, but…"

"A friend of mine is stranded behind enemy lines," he said. "Alone, unarmed and probably in great danger. I will not stand by while that state of affairs continues."

"Which is exactly what I know our esteemed Prime Minister will choose to do," said Disraeli. "Stand by and wait, that is. Which is in turn why I have brought you here."

Joshua frowned. "Forgive me, but I thought we were brought here on the Prime Minister's orders?" He turned to Pearce. "You showed the guards at the Tower an order signed by the Prime Minister, didn't you?"

Disraeli coughed. "Yes, ah, that would be my doing. You see, I retained some headed notepaper when I left office. For sentimental reasons, you understand." There was a mischievous glint in his eye as he continued: "And I can mimic Mr Gladstone's hand in a rather passable manner. The man has no imagination, you see, and such things cannot be hidden from the pen."

We looked at him with a mixture of amusement and disbelief.

"Desperate times call for desperate measures, gentlemen, what?" he said, waving a long finger at us.

"But is this not criminal behaviour?" I asked. "That you would take such a risk…"

"I am the one taking the risks," said Pearce. "Mr Disraeli has no part in all of this." He walked over to a candle and held the counterfeited order over the flame, dropping it in the fireplace when it was well alight.

"As much as it may seem devious and maybe even cowardly," said Disraeli, "it serves our purposes for me to fight the good fight from within. May Allah forgive me, as I'm sure He will, for He must have a sense of humour to burden us with such a leader. Mr Gladstone is not short of enemies within Parliament, and I for one intend to encourage them."

I smiled at the glances that the others gave him at the reference to Allah, the mention of the Muslim God seemingly at odds with his status as a sometime Christian of Jewish descent. However, I knew from experience that Disraeli took great pleasure in wrong-footing people by playing with their expectations, almost relishing the accusations and rumours that painted him as an exotic Asian sorcerer.

"And the Queen?" Byron asked Disraeli.

"Especially Her Majesty," he grinned. "We still correspond on a regular basis, and Mr Gladstone seems to have not yet learnt the finer arts of keeping our dear monarch happy." He leaned forward. "I always say: everyone enjoys flattery, and when dealing with royalty, one should lay it on with a trowel." He looked around at us, savouring our attention. "The secret to my success. Mr Gladstone, alas, seeks to lecture Her Majesty, treating her more like a subservient schoolgirl. As you can imagine, this does not amuse her."

"But I always thought Mr Gladstone was a good sort?" said Joshua. "The G.O.M.—the Grand Old Man and all that?"

"Pah! Grand Old Man… God's Only Mistake more like!" Disraeli wielded the pun like a vicious weapon. "The problem with that man is that he has no redeeming defect. Never trust a man with no vices, that's what I say. Speaking of which: I see cognac over yonder. Shall we partake?"

I waved for him to remain seated as I went over to the drinks cabinet and poured us all stiff measures. "So I take it you are back in the fight?" I asked.

"With a vengeance, young man, with a vengeance," he nodded as he accepted the glass from me. "Thank you. I appreciate that I was somewhat flattened by the events following St Albans, but I have been revived and cannot sit by and watch any longer. In his floundering to do the right thing, Gladstone is achieving precisely nothing. Worse: every moment that passes is a chance for our enemies to strengthen and plot. I do not just mean the demons; the other Earthly nations are also seeking to take advantage. The French are always keen to cause mischief, as are the Prussians, to name but two."

"But the threat from Almadel is not just directed at England," I protested. "Do they not see that?"

"I am afraid not. Many do not believe the fantastical stories emanating from our country, and in a way one cannot blame them. Others do believe, but affect not to concern themselves in the hope that we will be distracted with our 'domestic' issues long enough for them to take advantage in the Asiatic countries. Our interests in India and Turkey are under threat just to start with."

I shook my head. "Such things are the least of our concerns, are they not?"

"The duty of a leader and statesman is to consider all fronts and all interests. At present, we have no interest in the Aether except as a threat. The British Empire, on the other hand, is very much our concern and remains so as long as there is still a world for us to worry about. Something that is in danger of being destroyed thanks to Gladstone's endless vacillation. The man is prevaricating on at least two fronts."

Byron cocked his head to one side as he considered this. "But surely the other countries must see that there is also a risk to them here? Not just in terms of contamination from the demon threat, but also the advantages of our being so close to the magic and the assets of other realms?"

Disraeli stabbed a bony finger at him. "And there you are also correct. It suits our enemies and erstwhile allies to isolate and distract us with temporal concerns. You will have heard the reports of people trying to flee England, the demon threat and the inevitable next invasion, but being turned away from the Continent?"

"I thought those were exaggerations," I said. "Surely English refugees are no threat to the French?"

"You would think so. But the Emperor contends that there could be demons mixed in with the innocents, infiltrating the Continent amidst a flood of refugees. The message has been skilfully deployed across our neighbours, instilling a fear of destruction and terror like that which we have suffered. So they send back our refugees, forcing us to expend our efforts in dealing with camps of desperate displaced people that grow in size by the day. One more distraction from the demon threat, and one that plays rather well to the hand-wringing preacher we have for a Prime Minister."

Byron shook his head. "If I live another thousand years, I swear I shall not understand your ways."

"In another thousand years, I would hope we had grown a bit of sense," grumbled Disraeli. "In any case, much of this has been allowed to pass as a result of a criminal dearth of communication from Gladstone. Nature abhors a vacuum and so other things rush in to fill that space: rumours, disinformation and so on. Never fear, though, old Dizzy is already mobilised: I have recommenced my correspondence with a number of contacts on the Continent."

Pearce cleared his throat. "That is not why we are here, though, is it sir?"

"Quite, quite," said Disraeli, his demeanour at once shifting to a much more sombre one. "The issue of Miss Thatcher's abduction."

"You intend to mount a rescue mission?" I said to Pearce.

He nodded. "You three will come with me." It was a statement, not a request, and while none of us would have disagreed, I bridled at the idea of being ordered around.

"We did not intend for this to happen, you know," I said.

"You returned without her," he replied coldly. "Something that we will rectify forthwith."

I bit back a retort, saving it for later. Pearce was carrying a large amount of anger, and it served no one's purposes for us to have a blazing row now of all times; especially not in front of Disraeli.

"So when do we leave?" I asked, keeping my voice level while I let my eyes convey my displeasure towards Pearce.

"As soon as possible," he said. "As soon as Joshua is strong enough to transport us."

"About that," said Joshua. "We have one small problem. I can transport us, but I don't know where to." As Disraeli and Pearce started to reply he held up a hand. "What I mean is: I know we need to go to Almadel. The only problem is that I have no idea where Almadel is. We could try to work it out but it could take years."

Disraeli and Pearce shared a smile. "We thought you would say as much," said Disraeli. "That is why you have one more stop to make before you can travel through the Aether."

Chapter Four

We watched the horizon as the grey bulk of the French shoreline drew closer, resisting the urge to dive undercover or below-decks lest we were spotted. The English white cliffs were a distant memory behind us, a relic we hoped to see again soon. Until then, we had one more mission.

"How are you feeling?" I asked Joshua as we both leaned on the rail and contemplated the English Channel's churning greyness.

"Much more revived," he said. "Do not worry, I will play my part."

"That was not quite what I meant," I said. "There has been little time to talk, what with you immersed in your studies and voyaging to the Aether. Not since…" I let the rest of the sentence linger in the air between us, unwilling to finish it and give voice to the man's loss.

He nodded. "I have been busy. It is good to keep busy."

"Byron says your powers have increased immeasurably."

A small smile played across his lips. "Yes. What I once struggled to do are but mere parlour tricks to me now."

I shuddered, remembering the mess he had made of the Fury, the terrifying creature that had killed his sister in the aftermath of the Battle of St Albans. With a few short words he had turned a huge and seemingly invulnerable demon into a screeching, flaming torch. If that was now a 'parlour trick' to him, well…

"I am glad you are on our side," I said, watching him closely.

He nodded, a sharp gesture. "You need not worry about my abilities."

"I only asked because I could see how much transporting us through the Aether drained you."

A pained look flashed across his face. "There are different magnitudes of effort required. But conducting magic solely within this realm is much easier."

"Even this far from the Fulcrum?" We were by now hundreds of miles from St Albans, the epicentre of the phenomenon where the balance between science and magic was being inexorably tipped in favour of the latter. The world was changing, but only at a gradual pace; Maxwell had calculated that the Fulcrum's impact was expanding at a rate of around one mile a month. As a result, the world beyond English shores was still the same as it had been all our lives. For the time being, at least.

"With Byron's help, a simple misdirection spell is not a problem. Magic is akin to a muscle; the more you exercise it, the easier it gets, even without the Fulcrum's help."

I tried a different tack. "I would never call into question the power of your abilities. But how are *you*?"

He blinked at me. "I do not understand."

"After what you lost, I appreciate that it must be hard…"

"Nothing is forever," he said, staring out across the sea.

"But sometimes we must accept things as they are," I said. "When Max and I lost our parents, we found it very hard to carry on. I remember often wishing that—"

"You were a child then," he said.

"Yes. And, after many years of acting out of grief, I learnt to move on with my life."

"I am happy for you." He was as implacable as the rolling waves around us.

"That is not what I meant," I sighed. "I appreciate that you

35

still miss Lexie: we all do. But—"

"You hardly knew her," he snapped.

I acknowledged this with a nod, hoping that it would presage an outflowing of emotion, or something, from Joshua. Instead he continued his rigid contemplation of the horizon.

"How is your mother coping?" I asked, readying myself for another snapped retort. Instead I received little more than a shrug in reply. "Have you spoken with her?" I persisted.

"I wrote to her," he said. "I am not in any mood to receive her blame for what happened."

"Surely she would not cast aspersions, under the circumstances," I frowned. "Or has she?"

"I do not know."

"She did not reply?"

"She did." He waved his hand in a vague gesture. "The letter is unopened somewhere."

I stared at him. "Shouldn't you…?"

I flinched as he turned from the railing. "I need to prepare the spells," he said, marching away.

I leant back against the railing, blowing a frustrated breath out from my cheeks as I watched him stomp across the deck.

*

We stood to one side of the deck, Pearce and I trying to look as inconspicuous as possible while Joshua and Byron chanted on either side of us. The deckhands bustled about their duties, occasionally glaring at the French soldiers intent on checking every inch of the vessel.

I held my breath as a soldier paused and seemed to stare straight at us, his brow furrowed as though he were trying to remember something half-forgotten. Joshua increased the intensity of his words and they acted as a push on the Frenchman's resolve; he blinked before moving away and I shared a relieved nod with Pearce.

After ten minutes, the soldiers were satisfied that the ship was not carrying anyone or anything it shouldn't and gave the signal for the crew to disembark. At a gesture from Byron we shuffled along to follow the French soldiers, still amazed that no one was paying the slightest interest in us.

We stepped off the gangplank and made our way through Calais harbour, blissfully ignored by all around us as the bustle of the port continued unabated. We picked our way past stevedores who grunted and sang as they loaded and unloaded crates. The stench of their body odour competed with that of the sea and the rotting fish for most offensive to the nose.

I heard a commotion to our left and turned to see a gaggle of people, some clearly middle class by the cut and style of their clothing, being herded into a fenced-off area.

"Look here," shouted one elderly gentleman at the soldiers. "You can see that we are no threat to any of you. I have visited France many times and—"

"France is no longer welcoming to you and your people," snapped back a soldier in heavily accented English. "We will not allow contamination by demons."

"Look at us!" bellowed the man. "Do we look like demons to you?"

"Please," begged another man, his clothes in tatters. "We have nowhere else to go. The demons have driven us out of our homes, that is why we are here…" A rifle butt hit him hard in the face and he staggered backwards, blood pouring from his ruined nose. Still he persisted, shrugging off the helping hands offered by his fellow refugees and begging the soldiers: "At least let my wife and children through…"

I shuddered as I watched. "We should do something," I muttered.

Pearce put a hand on my shoulder. "We have a bigger task ahead of us. We must focus on the mission."

"But surely…" I persisted, seeing the logic in his words but unable to tear my eyes away from the scene before us.

"England is not yet so overrun that they have nowhere to return to," said Pearce. "If nothing else, there are plenty of camps along the south coast."

"But what about if—when—the demons spread their influence?" I asked. "If there is a full-scale invasion from the portal and anyone who tries to flee meets with this treatment… Well, it would be a massacre!"

"And that is why we should focus our energies on our mission," said Pearce. "The first stage of which is to rescue Kate. Then we deal with the rest of the threat, as agreed."

I nodded slowly as I followed the others towards the dockyard gates. I was as keen as anyone to get Kate back but I wondered whether we were in danger of ignoring the bigger picture. Then again, given the alternative of submitting to Gladstone's infuriating inertia, any form of action was a veritable tonic.

The dockyard gates loomed up ahead of us and I glanced at my comrades, wondering how we could get the guards to open them for us. We stepped to one side to allow a cart to rumble past before following in its tracks, Joshua and Byron still mumbling their spells and incantations.

The soldiers spoke to the driver of the cart, checking through his papers and then inspecting the items loaded behind him for any signs of tampering, contraband or hidden refugees. All the time, they appeared oblivious to our presence.

After a few moments, the guards signalled their satisfaction and opened the gates, waving the driver through. We followed the cart at a steady pace, fighting the urge to break into a run. As the gates closed behind us we looked up to catch our first glimpses of the bustle of the town of Calais itself.

The road from the port led straight to a large square bordered on three sides by a jumble of tall and imposing buildings. Everything before us looked as though it had fallen straight out of a book of fairy tales, with regular arched windows and colourful slanting roofs all around. It was all sublimely foreign, the mundane exoticism of the scene feeling fresh in its contrasts to the dull, grimy English streets to which we were accustomed. What a difference a short stretch of water makes, I marvelled.

The next thing to assail us was the smells, more complex and nuanced than the pure fishy stench of the docks, but no less offensive for it. The ever-present odour of the sea provided a canvas for the noxious fumes from the huddled masses in and around the square. There was the food being hawked, both fresh and rotten; the stench of sweaty and unwashed bodies stirred up by their exertions; and of course, the faeces and urine liberally distributed by stallholders and customers alike. I wrinkled my nose as an old man dropped his breeches in plain view and defecated against a wall; at least back in England he would have had the decency to go around a corner and out of sight.

Pearce glanced behind us. "I think we are safe now," he said to Joshua and Byron, who ceased their chanting and relaxed. A nearby boy jolted to a startled halt as he suddenly noticed us, the magical cloak that had hitherto obscured us having been lifted.

"You rest here," Pearce continued. "Gus and I will find us some transportation. We need to make it to Paris as soon as we can."

I followed him, mentally running through my French words in preparation. "I am still not convinced this is a good idea," I said.

"If you have a better one, I am more than happy to listen," he replied. "Unfortunately, there is no choice; he is the only person who can take us where we need to go."

"Assuming we can trust him to not double-cross us when we get there," I pointed out.

Pearce nodded. "If he tries to do that he will soon learn that he is not the only one who can inflict pain beyond imagining."

*

It was an unassuming house in a grand if quiet and nondescript Parisian street. I knocked once more on the door and waited as the sound echoed its way into oblivion around us.

"Are we sure this is the right place?" I asked.

"Positive," sighed Pearce. He turned to Joshua. "You said your spell pointed here as well?"

The young man nodded. "Yes, there is no doubt."

"He could be out shopping or taking in the sights," said Byron. "Paris can be very pleasant at this time of year. We could take a stroll along the Left Bank…" He winked at me.

"I have a better idea," said Pearce, ushering me aside and then bending over the lock. After a few moments the door opened with a barely perceptible click.

"Captain Pearce," I said with mock indignation. "Do my eyes deceive me or did you just pick that lock?"

"I learnt a few tricks of the trade from Kate," he said, gesturing for us to enter. "I suspected that they would come in handy one day."

Joshua hesitated on the threshold. "Should we…? I mean, this is technically illegal, is it not?"

I put an arm around his shoulders, drawing him into the building with me. "My dear fellow, we are breaking and entering. It is not merely technically illegal, but also *actually* illegal. But needs must when the devil drives."

"Literally, in our case," said Byron. "Come. I suspect that our unwitting host has constructed defences that will require our particular talents to disarm."

Ten minutes later, Joshua, Byron and I were seated in a lavish sitting room, debating our next move while Pearce paced the room like a caged tiger.

"Something is not right," he muttered. "Can't you cast another one of your divining spells and find out where he is?"

"My spells all point to here," said Joshua simply.

"Which means if he is not actually here, then he has gone to some lengths to disguise his true location," added Byron. "We are powerful, but not as powerful as him."

"So we sit here and wait," Pearce spat.

I picked up a whisky glass and nudged its fellow towards him. "There are ways we can while away the time," I pointed out.

He stabbed a finger at me. "How can you think of drinking at a time like this? I thought you cared more for Kate."

My glass froze less than an inch from my lips. I hardened my glare at him as I slowly and deliberately took a long sip before setting it firmly back on the table.

"Do not think you can judge me, Captain Pearce," I said. "I am as close to Kate as anyone, and care as much for her as—"

"Then why did you let her be taken? Surely the famed Augustus Potts with his magic sword could fend off *one* demon…"

"The creature was holding her close," said Byron. "It was a—"

"He can talk for himself," snapped Pearce, "without needing you to defend him all the time."

I flicked an imagined piece of dust from my trouser leg, fighting to keep my voice calm. "You are out of order, Captain. Even if you had been there—"

"If I had known about your foolish trip, I would not have let you leave in the first place. That is what is truly at stake here: your inability to follow even the simplest of orders!"

"Orders are for soldiers," I shot back. "By the by, how is the whole rigmarole of following orders going for you right now?"

He clenched his fists. "I have given up my life and career to fix your mess—"

"Enough," I raised my voice, pushing myself to my feet. "I will not—"

"Erm, Gus…" said Byron.

I held up a hand in his direction, not wanting to divert my red-hot rage away from Pearce's puritanical righteousness. "If you care to settle this with our fists, I would be happy to oblige," I said to Pearce, stepping towards him.

Pearce laughed, moving forwards as well. "My pleasure."

"Gus! Albert!" shouted Byron, barging between us and pointing at the window. We turned to see Andras stood there, arms folded across his chest. He was dressed in the height of fashion, grinning that implausibly wide grin from beneath a tall top hat, while the rest of him was clothed in a fine Italian evening suit of exquisite tailoring.

The demon clapped in a slow, almost mocking manner. "Please, do not stop on my account. That was most diverting; do we get an encore? I could open a book on any fight you two use to settle this. Byron, you like a flutter: will you join me in a wager?"

Andras appeared completely unchanged since we had last laid eyes on him, which was shortly after the Battle of St Albans where he had helped us to drive back the Almadites led by Gaap. While the Pooka's help had been welcomed and rewarded, our memories of the pain and suffering Andras had caused in the past was still far too fresh to bear. After all, Andras had been the one who had first tried to subject our world to the creatures from beyond the Aether at the Battle of Greenwich, some four years earlier. We had defeated and turned him into his more benign N'yotsu alter ego, only for the amoral demon side to resurface thanks to the machinations of Gaap, an evil Almadite demon who was an aide to the fabled Four Kings. Many lives had been lost thanks to Andras' past actions, and him fighting with us for once was not enough to assuage those memories.

"Shut up," said Pearce, diverting his anger from me to Andras. "You will come with us."

Andras tutted. "Is that how you speak to the host when you're a house guest?"

"We are not your guests—"

"Ah yes, that's right: because *I did not invite you.*" He glared at us. "How did you find me?"

"Your friend Disraeli told us where you were," I said.

He frowned. "I told him to only share that information if there was an emergency."

"Well, there is," said Joshua. "Kate has gone missing."

Andras shrugged. "As entertaining as she is, I do not think her disappearance alone warrants ending my self-imposed exile, do you? I have other important work to attend to."

"She was taken by a Warlock," I said. "To Almadel. That's why we need you." I shook my head. "And what 'other important work' do you mean?"

Andras ignored my question. "A Warlock, eh? When was this?"

"Two days ago," said Pearce.

"Where were you when this happened?"

"We were on a scouting mission beyond the Aether, in another realm," said Byron. "We're not sure which one."

Joshua took up the tale. "I had sensed Almadite presence in that realm, and so we went to investigate. We foiled their plans but then Kate was seized by a Warlock that pulled her through another portal. They disappeared before we could follow."

"And while your powers are growing all the time, you cannot navigate to a realm that you do not know the location of, correct?" grinned Andras.

"I could," pouted Joshua, "but it would take too long for me to find it. You, on the other hand, know exactly where it is."

"Maybe," said Andras, throwing himself into a chair and draping his legs theatrically over an armrest. "But then again, maybe not."

"Don't play games with us, demon," snarled Pearce, "or I'll—"

"You'll what?" asked Andras. "You cannot compel me to act against my will, whereas I could play you like a puppet if I so wished. For all you know, I could have been doing that already, bringing you here as a part of my grand designs. Why do you think I let Prime Minister Disraeli know of my whereabouts?"

"He is no longer Prime Minister," I said.

Andras tutted. "Of course, I forgot: it's now that stuffed suit Gladpole, isn't it?"

"Gladstone," I corrected.

"Whatever," Andras waved a hand. "It is so hard to keep track; it's not enough that you have the lifespan of over-elaborate mayflies, but then you keep chopping and changing your leaders all the time."

Pearce shook his head at the frustrating irrelevance of this line of conversation. "Will you help us or not?"

Andras picked at one of his claws. "It so happens that our purposes may be intersecting. What did you say the Almadites were doing in this other realm of yours?"

"I didn't say what they were doing," said Joshua, glancing at the rest of us. "Not yet."

"Oh, don't look at them," said Andras. "They are much less intelligent that you and I. Not to mention nowhere near as devilishly handsome. Pun intended. So, tell Uncle Andras what the naughty demons are up to."

I shrugged and then nodded. "Go on, tell him."

Joshua stood and walked over to the bag that he had lugged with him on our journey to this apartment. "They appeared to be attempting to activate a device. At first I thought they were trying to create a portal through to our world."

"But…" prompted Andras, waving his hand in a circular motion to encourage him to continue.

"But," said Joshua, "it lacks the utility to achieve such a task. It is not an active device; indeed, all the runes and incantations upon it point to it having very much a passive purpose."

"Such as…?" prompted Andras again.

"As though it were created to find something." He pulled the main part of the Warlocks' device from his bag, a cone-like metallic object inlaid with red and black symbols that hurt the eyes to look at. He took it over to Andras and turned it round to show him the full extent of the inscriptions. "But what they intended for this to find, I do not know. My first thought was another entry point akin to the Fulcrum on our world, but that does not accord. These symbols here are so unusual…"

Andras held out a hand. "May I?" Without waiting for a response, he snatched it and took it over to the window, holding it up to the light. "Very clever," he muttered. "Well, they have two already, so it would be a simple extrapolation to work out what properties they shared…" He turned back to face us. "Who was in this little scouting party of yours? The four of you?"

Pearce shook his head. "I was not there. It was these three, plus Kate." He glared at us.

"Ah, sore point, eh? Upset you weren't invited to their little party?" Andras' grin stretched wider. "No, that's not it, is it? What was that ditty? 'Heaven has no rage like love to hatred turned…'"

"…'Nor hell a fury like a woman scorned'," I completed for him. "Which brings us back to the point of Kate being missing and imprisoned on Almadel. Would you be willing to risk *her* fury if she knew you were dilly-dallying in this way?"

"Well played that man," said Andras, nodding at me before turning back to Joshua. "I am curious, did the Warlocks' device react in any way to your presence?"

"We attacked them before they could activate it," said Joshua.

"And you have all the components here?"

"Yes, but…"

"Good." Andras tossed the object over his shoulder and Joshua dived forwards to catch it. "Take good care of that thing," the demon said. "It is very important. Well, gentlemen," he grinned at us. "It looks like we are a team once again!"

"Why do I sense we are doing you a favour, rather than the other way round?" I asked.

"Oh, don't take it personally," said Andras. "That is the way food always feels when confronted by a predator. Now, something is concerning me: by the way you are dressed and the smells you are giving off, I would surmise that you travelled here by sea?"

"Yes," said Pearce.

"But I thought time was of the essence? Kate in mortal danger and so on?"

"How else do you suggest we should have got here?" I asked. "France is hardly welcoming of foreigners, and an airship would have drawn far too much attention."

"Why did young Joshua not create a portal? Do you not think that would have been a lot simpler and quicker?"

We all gaped at him. "You can do that?" I asked Joshua.

"To the Aether, yes," said Joshua. "But that is all."

Andras tutted at Byron. "You are causing me to downgrade my opinion of Pooka tutors. And that *is* saying something."

"I agree that it is theoretically possible to travel by portal within realms," said Byron, "but only when they are much more soaked in magic than this one. The Fulcrum still only reaches so far…"

"But it still *exists* in this realm," said Andras. "Use that as your focal point and then do what you would normally do. Much easier than punching through to the Aether."

Joshua shook his head. "I have tried before, but to no avail. I am not powerful enough."

"Balderdash," said Andras. He looked around the room as though he were sizing up our relative locations. "Try again now."

I glared at him. "What are you plotting?"

"Come on, Gus," said Andras. "We're all on the same side here."

"Are we?" I asked.

"Yes." For once the grin slipped and he looked almost human as he stared back at me. "I fought alongside you at St Albans. If I had wanted to destroy you, I could have done so many times over by now. But I haven't. Even the Pooka believe in my bona fides. Why can't you?"

"Greenwich," I said. "The Aether. Yorkshire. Killing my parents. Trying to steal my soul. Trapping us in the Aether. Taking N'yotsu from us. Need I go on?"

He waved a hand. "In the past."

"For you, maybe." I stood and stomped over to the far side of the room, struggling to regain my composure.

Joshua frowned and then shrugged. "I suppose there is no harm in trying," he said, flexing his shoulders.

"That's the spirit," said Andras. "Augustus, be a dear and

bring that bag over here, would you?"

I glared at him but complied, picking up the heavy bag and dumping it next to Byron, all the time ignoring Andras' hungry look as he watched me.

As Joshua started his chanting the air became charged with a tension like that preceding an electrical storm. Once more the runic sword at my back reacted to the magical energies, humming in unison with Joshua's words as though it were trying to help by echoing and magnifying his incantations.

I looked up as a breeze touched my skin. A vortex swirled into existence in front of us, increasing in extent until it was the size of a large window. We peered through it to see grass, trees and a grey sky beyond.

"Is that…?" I asked.

"St Albans," said Andras. "Best to get through there before the soldiers realise what's happening, don't you think?"

We dived through the opening, taking the sack containing the Warlocks' device with us. I landed heavily onto the hard ground and looked around; thankfully this time we were just under a mile away from the main camp that housed the soldiers guarding the Fulcrum.

Chapter Five

While the journey from France had taken mere moments, the 30 or so miles west to Hughenden Manor at the southern edge of the Chilterns seemed to take an eternity.

We approached the squat red brick building with caution, keeping an eye out for soldiers or the police. Everything, though, was quiet as we worked our way through the trees lining the approach to the manor house. I strained my eyes for anything out of the ordinary, my unease growing the longer that everything remained quiet and unremarkable.

"Why do you people insist on creeping around all the time?" tutted Andras.

"You forget that we are fugitives," I hissed, "who have escaped from the Tower of London, probably making us the most wanted people in the country!"

"Someone seems to have delusions of grandeur," he sniffed.

"Our crimes were no doubt compounded by bringing you back into the country," I added. "Something I regret with each minute that passes."

Andras ignored me, turning instead to Pearce. "You say you went to great lengths to make sure that no one could connect Disraeli to your actions?" he asked him.

"I did."

"And I am guessing the last place that any sane escapees would go to is the home of the Prime Minister?"

"*Former* Prime Minister," I reminded him again.

Andras waved away my words. "Given all of that, why are we skulking about here? This is very undignified, you know."

Annoyingly, the demon proved to be correct when we were admitted into a house empty of anyone bar a handful of servants, Disraeli and my brother.

"Max," I greeted him with a warm smile. "So good to see you."

"And I you," he said, nodding a greeting from his wheelchair. "You have caused quite a fuss with all of your actions over the past few weeks. What on Earth possessed you?"

"Please, Max," I said, holding up a hand. "This has all been done to death without you adding your tuppence worth. I know it was a stupid thing to have done, but I am determined to make it right."

"If you occasionally listened to me, maybe you wouldn't need to run around cleaning up all the messes you created."

"Max," I said, softly but firmly, "This is neither the time nor place for you and I to fight."

He frowned. "Maybe not. Although…" He shook his head. "Very well. But your actions have taken their toll on all of us, you know."

"You have been questioned?" asked Pearce.

"Of course. And I was under surveillance as well. Probably still am."

We stared at him in disbelief but Disraeli chuckled. "Do not worry. We still have some friends in London. I arranged for Mr Potts to be secreted here from his laboratory; in the meantime, those purportedly caring for him are continuing with their routines as usual, creating an illusion of occupation for the time being."

"As you know, I do not often venture from my laboratory," said Maxwell. "It would not be considered out of place if I am not seen for a few days. Although the risk that our ruse will be discovered increases with every day that I am absent."

"Then we should press on," said Pearce. "I presume Mr Disraeli has briefed you on what we need?"

"Weaponry and transport," nodded Maxwell. "Fortunately for you, I have had plenty of time to ponder such matters. I have just the items." He spun his wheelchair round and led us into an adjoining room that he had commandeered in his own imitable fashion, with every available item of furniture stacked high with a profusion of gadgets, tubes, cogs and assorted bric-à-brac.

Maxwell propelled himself to a long table that had once served as a sideboard but was now a makeshift workstation. He cleared aside the looser items gathered on it with a few judicious sweeps of his arm to reveal a dozen weapons—two LeMat pistols, two Lancaster pistols and two Snider–Enfield rifles—resting on top of mismatched wooden boxes.

"These have been adapted along the lines of our previous occult weapons, with the bore in the barrels specifically tailored to generate the particular spin and harmonics that inflict the maximum amount of damage on demons and their kind."

"Fatal damage?" asked Andras with a glint in his eye.

I picked up a Lancaster pistol, feeling its weight in my hand as I glared at Andras. "Shall we test it?" I asked.

"That will not be necessary," said Maxwell quickly. "I can assure you that they work perfectly well."

Pearce inspected one of the rifles, testing the balance and looking down the barrel. He opened one of the boxes and ran his fingers through the bullets contained within. "This should suffice," he said with a nod.

"I was slightly concerned that I had overdone the munitions," said Maxwell.

"Not at all brother. I suspect that where we're going, you cannot have too many weapons."

"How right you are," muttered Andras, staring at the guns as though he suspected they would jump up to attack him at any moment. Then he frowned. "There is something else you have not included here. What about the Compound?"

I shuddered as I remembered that hideous man-made mist, one of Maxwell's creations originally intended to cure me of my demonic predisposition. However, the Compound turned out to attack all living creatures indiscriminately, both human and demon, and N'yotsu and I had barely escaped with our lives when Maxwell had tested the mist on me. In the process, it had conjured up hideous visions—not unlike those I had witnessed when the Warlock had attacked me in the Aether— and attempted to dissolve me from the inside-out. At the Battle of St Albans Maxwell had used the threat of the Compound to force the demon leader Gaap and his minions into retreat, and we had always assumed that that was the ultimate threat still keeping them at bay.

"That would certainly cause trouble," continued Andras, a glint in his eye, "if we were to release it into the middle of the Citadel in the centre of Almadel. I would love to watch that."

"We could not wait around long enough to witness the results," Byron pointed out. "Not without rotting to pieces ourselves."

"In any case," Maxwell said as he glanced at Disraeli, "the Compound is no longer available for use."

"Why not?" asked Andras. "If ever there was a time to use it, now would be perfect, surely?"

"I am afraid that the small quantities of the Compound that I have produced to date have become increasingly unstable," said Maxwell. "I believe it has been impacted by the growing influence of the Fulcrum. I have not been able to—"

"It is not a viable weapon," snapped Disraeli. "To wield it would kill us as well as the Almadites, and I have seen nothing to indicate that it can be controlled in any way. I have ordered its destruction, have I not?"

Maxwell looked down. "Indeed you have."

I shrugged, hefting my chosen pistol, a solid Lancaster, in my hand. "I think we have enough here."

"We do," said Pearce.

"You are actually going to do this?" Maxwell asked, looking up at us.

"We have to get Kate," said Pearce as he checked the mechanisms of each of the weapons. "We have no choice."

"Then I shall come with you," said Maxwell, glaring back in defiance as we protested as one. "I am as concerned as the rest of you for Kate's welfare; of all of us, I probably know her the best."

We had to concede the point. Since the Battle of Greenwich where Andras had crippled Maxwell, he had relied on Kate for his care at all times of the day and night. As a result, they had forged the sort of close bond that naturally comes from such a relationship.

"The place to which we are going," said Andras, "is not very conducive to a person with your mobility issues, if you understand me."

"That was almost tactful," I said. "Not to mention brave, given that it is your fault he is in that wheelchair in the first place."

"Nevertheless," said Pearce, "the demon has a point. Maxwell, we cannot afford the risk."

"I would also not put it past the Almadites to be planning something to take advantage of Kate's kidnapping," said Byron. "While the Fulcrum remains a source of much instability, your scientific methods are still effective in this world. When we pass through the Aether and to the realms beyond, those things may be completely useless."

It was Maxwell's turn to concede the point. "I have been brushing up on my occult knowledge…"

"But with all due respect," said Joshua, "Byron and I are much stronger and more practised in those matters than you are."

"And me," said Andras, waving a hand in the air.

"And back here on Earth," continued Byron, ignoring the other demon, "you can still do plenty of good with your inventions and scientific knowledge, especially if the Almadites try to invade again."

"I will need company here in this world, in any case," said Disraeli.

"Actually Benjamin, I need you to do something," said Andras. "I suspect that everyone is correct as to the Almadites' intentions, and I have taken the time over the past few months to prepare the ground."

"For what?" I asked. "What exactly have you been up to during those months since you left us after St Albans?"

"While you have been gallivanting around losing people in the Aether, I have been busy maintaining my networks and building new ones. In particular with some people in the French, Prussian, Russian and Austrian courts: Emperors and the like. I believe you are also acquainted with those people, Benjamin?"

Disraeli nodded slowly. "I am. But given how touchy our Continental cousins are when it comes to anything even remotely demonic, I am surprised that you were able to obtain an audience with them."

Andras tapped a clawed finger against the side of his nose. "They say the devil has all the best tunes. He also has the best book of contacts. It is usually those in power—or those who desire it most—who are most receptive to what I have to offer."

I felt a cold chill run down my spine as I remembered my own experiences of what Andras offered; I had once bargained away my soul to him in return for the fleeting joys of fulfilling my dreams of literary success and recognition. I could still feel the empty hole deep inside me which was created when Andras had started to exact his price, before Maxwell entered into the bargain that had doomed our whole world to the on-going conflict with the creatures from beyond the Aether.

I looked up to see Andras watching me as though he was reading my thoughts. He shrugged and continued: "You are correct that there is much hostility to my... or even our..." he nodded to Byron, "kind, but I have been dealing with such people for thousands of years. Whether you approve of my methods or not, I do have a unique insight into the minds of your people—in particular those in positions of power."

We glared at him in a silence that would have unnerved any normal person, but which did not seem to faze the demon in the slightest.

Disraeli cleared his throat. "Well, erm, indeed. But you said you needed me to do something. I would have you know that I will not be party to any of your machinations, nor anything immoral or against God or the Queen."

"Besides aiding and abetting two known demons and a pair of fugitives to act against the express commands of your country's appointed leader?" Andras said.

Disraeli cocked an eyebrow at him. "Everything is relative, as I am sure you know."

Andras cackled. "That's the spirit. Don't worry: I am not asking you to do anything you would not wish to do. I have been laying the groundwork for this world's defences, and I need you to go on a tour of a few countries to ensure that they are sufficiently rallied to our cause." He handed Disraeli a folded piece of paper. "This should help to persuade any naysayers."

Disraeli glanced at the contents and grunted in surprise. "Indeed it should."

I looked around the room, conscious that everyone seemed to have forgotten something rather important. "This is all well and good," I said, "and no doubt highly useful, but what about the small matter of our transportation through the Aether?"

Maxwell grinned. "Now that I know you will appreciate. It is waiting for you at King's Cross."

*

"I am not sure that this will work," I said as we made our way through the station, attempting to look inconspicuous in our dull brown overalls.

"I know it's hard, but just try to look like you know what you're doing," said Andras, prancing along next to me without a care in the world.

"You are actually enjoying this, aren't you?"

"But of course," he grinned that wide grin of his. "I am finally going home!"

I gave him a long, hard stare. The Aether had been the source of many of my worst nightmares ever since I had become aware of the place. Now, not only were we willingly heading back there, but we were planning to use it as a bridge to the source of my other nightmares: Almadel, the home of the demons that had plagued us for so long.

"I thought you were an exile," I said. "Surely you should be as nervous as the rest of us."

He waved a hand dismissively. "You are confusing me with a creature that is naturally burdened with such improvident emotions."

"Look lively now," muttered Pearce. "There she is."

We had rounded a corner and before us stood a train that put all others to shame: a brilliant flower in the midst of a field of parched grass. There was the Juggernaut in all her shining glory. I had last laid eyes on her when she had been but a shadow of her former self, lying battered and broken at the side of the tracks between Sheffield and Nottingham after we had successfully fought off a horde of demons. We had had to abandon her then, but she had been salvaged afterwards and restored under Maxwell's guidance, a process that was still evidently underway but which looked very far advanced. The engine was as sleek as ever, a metallic stallion with a nose that pointed intensely forwards from a body that was as beautiful as it was impregnable. The metal bodywork, which had been dented, battered and scratched during the battle with the demons, had been hammered back into shape and repainted, now gleaming brilliantly in the sooty sunlight.

"Still takes the breath away," I said proudly, as I had had no small input to its construction, for once overruling Maxwell's pedestrian utilitarianism with some design flourishes that stirred the soul as befitted an engine as fast and powerful as this one.

"Remember our roles," said Pearce. "And keep the two demons out of sight as much as possible."

Byron and Andras nodded slightly, pulling flat caps further down over their faces as they muttered incantations to make the human eye want to do nothing more than skim over them. I blinked as the spells took effect: even though I knew they were there, my brain wanted to look around and past rather than at them.

A soldier barred our way as we approached the platform, a rifle casually slung over his shoulder. I felt a small wave of relief; we had feared that security would be tight around the engine, but the sight of just this one guard and his negligent manner gave me hope.

Pearce waved some papers at him. "Inspection," he said. "We need to put it through its paces, make sure it's still working all right. You'll have been told to expect us?"

The soldier nodded and stepped aside. "You're early."

"Aye, well, the sooner we get this done, the sooner we can get to the pub, eh?"

"Lucky you," he grumbled. "I'm nursemaiding this contraption all bleeding day."

"Well, we'll try to put on a show for you," I said. "Keep things interesting."

He flashed me a bored smile as he waved us past, not bothering to look at our papers. I checked my pocket watch. "We have 30 minutes before the real inspectors arrive," I muttered to the others.

Pearce nodded, then sprinted to the cabin and jumped aboard while Joshua ducked underneath to check the wheels and sandpipes. I noted with relief that the track was free of any carriages or other engines and that the Juggernaut was not coupled to anything that might slow us down. This was a mixed blessing as, while the engine's cabin was bigger than most, it would still be a squeeze to accommodate all five of us. However, that was a problem for later, assuming we were able to get the thing moving at all.

"Gus, the water gauges," called Pearce, gesturing for me to jump up onto the footplate. I did so and ran through the checks that Maxwell had forced me to rehearse over and over again. At the time, I had thought he was simply being far too petty in his usual way, but now I was standing there on the side of the train I was grateful for having been schooled so thoroughly. Once I was satisfied that both water gauge glasses were working, I nodded to Pearce and pulled down the levers that turned on the injectors, watching closely as the gauges filled with water.

Pearce had already ensured that the various brakes were engaged and we were in gear, while Byron and Andras busied themselves with loading kindling and then coal into the grate. I was pleasantly surprised to note that Andras had submitted to the task, for he had grumbled through our rehearsals at the indignity of everything—even more so than I.

I looked around for the coal shovel, cursing as I stood on it and caused it to slam against the side of the cab. "Careful," hissed Pearce, waving to the soldier to show that everything was fine.

"I did not realise it was there," I snapped as I righted the shovel and pulled a rag from the pocket of my overalls. "What sort of place was that to store it?" I asked as I placed the rag on the shovel's broad blade.

"I put it there," said Pearce. "I thought I would save time and be helpful."

"Well… thank you," I snapped, attempting to show exasperation as well as graciousness. From another pocket, I removed a vial of paraffin and poured it over the rag, being careful not to spill any onto the floor.

I patted my pockets and then swore. "Who has the matchbook?"

The others stared at me askance. "I thought you had it," said Pearce.

"Yes, well clearly I don't. Do none of us have any matches?" I leaned out of the side. "Josh," I called. "Do you have the matchbook?"

"I thought you had it," he replied.

I ducked back in and swore again. "Ask the soldier?" suggested Byron.

I rubbed a hand over my brow. "If there was anything to make him suspicious, a train fireman turning up without something to light a fire is bound to do it." However, I could think of no other option in the circumstances.

Andras cleared his throat. "You know, if you ask me nicely…"

I glared at him. "I did."

"No. You asked if I had a matchbook. To which the answer is still 'no.' However, that is not the real question, is it?"

"This is no time to play games, demon," hissed Pearce.

Andras held up his hands. "Fair enough." He turned back to shovelling coal.

Byron glared at him and sighed. "Andras, can you set fire to that rag? Please?"

"There you go," said Andras, turning back to the paraffin-soaked rag with a grin. He clicked his fingers and a small flame appeared just above his hand. He dabbed the flame to either end of the rag and then straightened up as it smoked and then caught fire.

"Couldn't you have offered to do that straight away?" I asked. "Without making us go through that rigmarole?"

"And miss out on an opportunity for you to learn something?" Andras replied, theatrically blowing out the flame that had been hovering above his hand. "What if I had just popped up and lit stuff for you all those years ago when your ancestors were living in caves? How would you have ever evolved into the shaved monkeys that you are today, eh? Then again," he frowned, "maybe that was my mistake…"

I shook my head and turned my attention back to the rag. Once I was happy that it was flaming nicely, I picked up the shovel and deposited it into the middle of the coal and kindling pile before standing back as Byron slammed the firebox doors shut.

"Now comes the painful part," said Pearce. We made a show of doing various checks while we waited for the fire to take hold of the coals, resisting the temptation to open the firebox to check.

Joshua had been for a walk along the platform to see if there were any obstructions further along the track. As he returned, he pulled a face at us while making a show of being nonchalant as he walked back as quickly as he dared. We held a huddled conference in the cab under the increasingly interested eye of the soldier.

"We have a problem," said Joshua. "The track's locked in the wrong position."

"What do you mean?" I asked.

"I mean, it's pointing in a different direction to the one we want to go in," he said.

"So? Change it," offered Andras.

Joshua stared at him. "They're operated from a cabin up there," he said, pointing to a signal box partway along the track. "But anyone in there is bound to ask why we want to move the tracks, especially when the engine is not supposed to be going anywhere."

Andras shrugged. "Then kill them and do it yourself." We stared at him. "Oh, that's right; we are supposed to be on the side of good and light. I keep forgetting. This is all so confusing. Oh well: leave it with me." He climbed down to the platform.

"Where are you going?" I asked.

"To sort out this mess for you," he said. He started to walk towards the signal box and then stopped. "Which things do you need changing?"

"You see those tracks there?" asked Joshua, pointing. "They need to be aligned in the opposite way to how they are at present."

"Very good. And this magical control cabin?"

"It's a signal box—there," pointed Joshua again. "Maybe one of the other of us should—"

"No, no," said Andras. "It will give me something to do. And you're sure I can't kill anyone? Not even a little bit?"

"No," I said. "And no stealing of souls either."

He glared at me in mock exasperation. "So much easier doing it my way," he muttered as he stalked off.

I turned to ask the others whether this was such a good idea after all, when I noticed the soldier wandering towards us.

"All fine up there?" he called.

"Absolutely," I replied. "Just a few more checks and then we'll be done. Our friend there just needed a bit of a walk." I flinched as the words left my lips.

The soldier frowned. "Can I have another look at your papers?"

"Of course," said Pearce. "Ah. One moment. We just need to… gentlemen, I need a hand?"

The soldier shifted uneasily. "What's going on here?"

"A critical moment," shouted Pearce. "If we don't release the pressure, it could blow. Give me one second."

We all huddled round him in the cabin. "We need to move now or he'll call for reinforcements and we are finished," he said.

I nodded, checking my pocket watch. "This is about to become moot: the real inspection team will be here at any moment."

"Then it's decided," said Pearce, gesturing for us to take up our positions.

"What if the engine is not ready to move?" asked Joshua.

"It has to be," said Pearce grimly.

Joshua and Byron shovelled coal into the firebox while I kept an eye on the steam pressure levels. At first there was nothing, and I began to fear that we had started this phase too soon. "Keep going," said Pearce. "I'll see if I can keep that man occupied."

I watched as he jumped down and ran over to the soldier,

pulling the forged papers from a pocket in his overalls and waving them at him. From my elevated position, I could see a group of men dressed in a similar fashion to us making their way across the station towards our platform. I turned back to the gauges, willing them to show some movement.

"Wait," Joshua said to Byron. "If we put any more coal on we might smother it."

Byron frowned as he nodded. "We're running out of time. Maybe Andras should have set fire to all the coals while he was here."

"Was that an option?" I asked incredulously.

"Well if he could set fire to that rag, then I suppose…"

I threw my hands in the air, disgusted at my stupidity as much as the demons' irritating lack of practicality. "What is wrong with us?"

"We are under pressure and panicking," said Byron. "Those things never lend themselves well to clarity of thought or deed."

"Stop being so annoyingly rational," I said, my voice trailing off as I peered at the gauge. "I think the pressure is starting to rise."

"Really?" Joshua pressed his head next to mine to look.

"I can feel it," said Byron. "And not a moment too soon."

While we had been speaking the engine had slowly, imperceptibly, woken up. After a few more seconds there was no mistaking the feeling of a beast straining at the leash, desperate to sprint away. The brakes were holding her still, but I was not sure how much longer that would be the case.

Not that we wanted the Juggernaut to remain stationary, for the men in overalls were almost upon us, breaking into a run and shouting as they realised that the engine was in operation. I opened my mouth to warn Pearce but he had already noticed, drawing his pistol and disarming the soldier before forcing the engineers to come to a jumbled halt.

"Can you remember how to move this thing?" I asked the others.

"I thought Maxwell told you," Byron said. "I was in charge of coal."

"My job was the pressure gauges," I said, gesturing at them. "Pearce is the one who knew all of that other stuff."

Joshua pushed us aside. "How did you two manage to save the world? Defeated by a train!"

"My brother's the technical one," I protested.

Joshua ignored me as he considered each of the levers in turn, his brow furrowed in concentration. "I am pretty sure that this one will release the main brakes. Do we have enough pressure?"

"I think so," I replied. "There's only one way to find out."

"Get moving!" Pearce shouted from below, backing up towards the engine while keeping his pistol trained on the soldier and engineers, who were now lying prone on the ground with their hands on their heads. "Get the train moving now!"

"A good plan. Why did we not think of it?" I muttered sarcastically as Joshua released the brake.

Pearce jumped aboard as the vehicle jolted forward, handing me his pistol and taking over the controls. I leaned out the cabin to see that the soldier and engineers had got to their feet and were running along the platform. "Ah, Pearce, they're coming after us," I called over the increasing noise of the engine.

"Then deter them," he called back. "Fire some warning shots."

"Do you remember how bad a shot I am?" I asked.

"Then aim right at them," he replied. "That should ensure you miss them comfortably!"

I bit back a retort and fired above their heads, wincing as I did so and then breathing a sigh of relief when none of them fell down wounded. My shots did have the desired effect in checking their advance, sending two of them running back towards the station building, no doubt to call for reinforcements.

I returned to my gauges and noted with relief that everything still seemed stable. We were starting to get up a good head of steam, and would soon be beyond the reach of any pursuers. Assuming, of course, that the rails pointed us in the right direction and remained free of obstructions.

A dark blur shot from the side of the tracks and landed lightly on the cabin roof. A few seconds later, Andras dropped down to join us. "I have saved the day. Again," he grinned with a bow.

Chapter Six

The track to St Albans was clear of any vehicles or other obstacles. We quizzed Andras on what he had done at the signal box, but aside from assuring us that he had not harmed anyone, he was suspiciously reluctant to divulge any details.

We gave up asking as we drew closer to St Albans, moving aside to allow Joshua the space for him to make the arrangements for his spell. While Andras and Byron helped him, Pearce and I occupied ourselves by dividing our attention between the Juggernaut's machinery and the outside world, making sure we remained free of any pursuers.

After a few minutes, Joshua stood back.

"All set?" I shouted over the noise of the engine and the wind.

"I think so," he called back. "I've never done this when moving before, and the timing will need to be spot on, so…" He shrugged.

I peered through the front window. "How far to the Fulcrum?" I asked Pearce.

"A couple of minutes, I think," he replied. "That last turn put us on the branch to Smallford, so we're literally on the right track now."

Andras dangled a pendant on a thin silver chain in front of me. "While I remember, you will need to wear these," he said, handing similar ones to Joshua and Pearce.

I examined it with a suspicious eye. The stone was an almost perfect rectangle, around the size of my thumb, and glowed a deep red from within. "What is it?" I asked.

"It is a charm that will protect your senses from the worst of the Aether and Almadel. It will save you from being driven insane as a result of the things you will experience out there."

"But we have travelled through the Aether and never needed one of these before," said Joshua.

"Correction. You have travelled in a purpose-built device, which has shielded you from the particular experiences of the Aether. The Juggernaut has not been designed to provide any such protection. Gus ventured into the Aether without such a device once, but had the remnants of his brother's house to offer familiar surroundings to comfort his senses."

I shuddered as I remembered that time when we were transported to the Aether as a part of Maxwell's doomed attempt to foil Andras' plans all those years ago. The device that spirited us there had indeed also taken half his house with us, but we had still been very much aware of the creatures shambling around the vast black void beyond. I remembered the hungry, anguished noises they made as they scrabbled to gain entry and get to us…

"But I have been to other realms and not—" Joshua persisted.

"You have been lucky," snapped Andras. "Some realms are more familiar than others. But trust me—Almadel is way beyond your limited comprehension. You are of more use to me sane and alive, but if you choose to ignore me…" He held out a hand for us to return the pendants.

Byron cleared his throat. "For what it's worth, this is one of the few times I agree with Andras. Don't worry: the charms are benign."

With a deep breath and a glance at the others I donned the pendant, relieved to note that I felt no different once it was around my neck.

"Here we are," called Pearce, gesturing ahead. He and Joshua put on their own charms and then turned back to their tasks. The familiar thick vibration ran through the sword strapped to my back as Joshua started his incantations, the intensity increasing as we approached the centre of the Fulcrum and the power source that would punch us from our reality and into the Aether.

Then there was a blinding white flash of light…

*

Travel through a portal to the Aether has always been an unusual experience, jumping into a void that grabs and pulls you at speed before jolting you to land upside down a second later. This time was no different, except that the Juggernaut in its entirety was suddenly and bizarrely deposited inside a wood-lined train carriage. I looked round: plush velvet seating lined the walls, filled with slumbering old men and women. The inside of the carriage was lit with a golden yellow light thanks to ornate lamps placed at regular intervals along the walls, with a brazier crackling away on the far side. Glasses chinked together inside a nearby cabinet, a high-pitched syncopation that marked the motion of our steady progress.

I looked out of the nearest window to see an unending inhospitable desert, with skeleton-white sands lying beneath a jet-black sky. There was no sign of anything, living or dead, in that wasteland.

"Where are we?" I asked.

"The Aether," said Andras, staring intently out of the window.

"Is it just me, or are we still in a train?" I asked.

Byron nodded.

"We are travelling through the Aether," said Joshua. "I suppose this is the closest allegory our minds can conjure up. It is interesting that we all have the same perception of our surroundings: Maxwell would no doubt want us to compare notes on what we experience."

I smiled. "Who are these others?" I asked, indicating the

torpid passengers in their seats.

Andras looked at them with something approaching a sad gaze. "They are the residents of the Aether. The poor souls trapped here in an endless cycle of nothingness. Don't worry: as long as we stay within the protections afforded by the Juggernaut and my charms then they cannot sense us."

My breath quickened as I looked around, remembering the glimpses I had had of these creatures in the past when I had experienced the Aether in all its glory. The wasted bodies and deep-set, hungry eyes; the grasping claws that sought to pull us down to them…

The people sat around us seemed so ordinary and, when I said as much, Andras laughed. "They were once normal people like you. Why should you not perceive them as such?"

"And you?" I asked him. "You're not wearing one of these charmed pendants. What do you see?"

He looked at the nearest one dismissively. "I see nothing worth worrying about." He turned back to the window.

I glanced questioningly at Byron but he shook his head. "Best you don't know," he said. He had also forgone the need for a pendant, having been more than accustomed to the various other realms in his time. As a result, he did not share the same reassuring illusions as Pearce, Joshua and I, although the more I thought about it the more that I wondered how much of a boon our ameliorated perceptions really were. I itched to remove my pendant and see what was really before us, the true faces of the creatures and places we were passing by, even though I knew that the sights would no doubt drive me out of my mind.

Andras snapped me out of my reverie. "Ah, here we are," he said, looking through the nearest window.

We followed his gaze towards a vast tunnel looming up in front of the train and swallowing it, carriage by carriage, into its dark maw. Then everything went black.

Chapter Seven

The Juggernaut was standing at an empty train platform. We jumped down to find that the ground was firm and paved, whilst the tracks themselves looked like ordinary train rails; that is if one discounted the fact that they dissolved into thin air a hundred yards or so in the distance.

"This way," said Andras, leading us towards a doorway, through which I could see a stone archway and then a street.

"This looks just like Euston Station," I said.

"I'm sure it does," said Andras. "I can buy you a guidebook if you fancy." He kept walking without looking back.

I exchanged a glance with Byron, sharing his unease in being at Andras' mercy in his home world. As though he had sensed our thoughts, Andras turned and glared at us. "Look, I'm not the most welcome person here either, you know. After they deposed and banished me, the Four Kings would tear me to pieces if they knew I was here. Just try to blend in. Pretend that you are still in London; if you walk around as though you own the place, everyone will assume you belong. Now, please, do come on."

I looked at the others and nodded. I felt my heart beat in my chest as we walked, fearing the scrutiny of the Almadites and knowing what they would do if they realised we were there. Andras had reassured us that the pendants round our necks had a dual purpose: placing a veil over not only our own perceptions but also those of everyone we met. As a result, the Almadites saw whatever they expected to see, as opposed to what we truly were. Regardless of this, we knew that we should not do anything to draw attention to ourselves, as the charms would not work under close scrutiny.

Passing through the archway and down the street, I had to keep reminding myself that I was in another world rather than our own London. Grey and brown stone buildings crowded around the muddy streets, filled with the shouts and bustle of hucksters, street urchins and harassed adults. At first glance I thought we were back in Seven Dials, but then the scene shifted to Fleet Street and then Whitehall. I felt dizzy with the constant movement and changes: every time I focused on a feature or landmark it was snatched away. My head whirled and my stomach churned as I dashed back inside the station so I could lean against a wall for support.

I became aware of the others gathered around me. "Are you all right?" asked Byron.

"Everything keeps changing," I said. "Just as soon as I think I recognise where I am, everything changes and we're somewhere else. I'll be fine; just feeling a little nauseous."

Andras tutted. "You're over-analysing, trying too hard to hold onto the world you know and impose it on here. The point of that charm around your neck is to help you see comforting familiarity, not the exact same things as back home. Stop fighting it and just accept everything as different. Although if you really are feeling weak, you should probably let me take your sword. Just in case, you know?"

"No." I screwed my eyes shut and tried to let the sense of his words penetrate my mind. *I am not in London*, I thought. *This is just a country overseas, one I have not visited before.* I opened my eyes and took a deep breath. At least everything had stopped spinning around me.

The buildings seemed to be the same as back home, but that

similarity was only skin-deep. They stretched up beyond two, four or even ten storeys in height until they twisted and merged into a single mass high in the distant sky. The road beneath our feet was covered, not in mud or faeces, but in a springy brown, almost leathery substance. *Like skin*, a remote and sadistic part of me suggested. The people bustling around before us were dressed in normal clothing but their bodies and faces were unmistakeably Almadite: all harsh angles, searing red eyes and elongated teeth.

"Better?" asked Andras.

"I think so," I replied. I turned to Joshua and Pearce. "How are you two?"

"I'm fine," said Joshua. "I've been through it a few times." He glared defiantly at Andras as he said this.

Pearce smiled at me. "Looks like none of us are as sensitive as you."

I glared at him. "You didn't feel a thing? Not even slightly discombobulated?"

"Nope. Thing is, you're hankering after home. I've not thought of London as home for a long time. The benefit and burden of being a soldier."

*

The first test of our resolve was stepping out into the press of demons wandering the streets. We tried to act as though we were just another group of denizens, at home and going about our business. I held my breath as we did so, every sinew tensed and ready to fight or flee. I felt exposed amongst those strange creatures and had a sudden flash of a recurring nightmare from my youth of finding myself in the streets stark naked with everyone looking and pointing at me.

Except that no one so much as glanced in our direction. We were loitering in the middle of the thoroughfare, and as a result a few demons jostled us and muttered curses at us, but that was no different to what would have happened back in London.

"Told you so," grinned Andras as he led us off to the left.

We passed demons standing behind tables and with a jolt I realised that they were costermongers selling their wares. The first one we walked past had great slabs of meat on display, anonymous fillets interspersed with heads, limbs and other less recognisable cuts of flesh. Another was hawking items that I took for the equivalent of fruit and vegetables, although one plant on his grocer's stall followed my passage with an unblinking yellow eye, its trunk twisting to keep me in view.

I shuddered and turned to see a row of street entertainers. A demon was weaving fantastical shapes out of fire, much to the delight of a group of infant creatures clustered around him. Another gave a loud shout before winking out of existence, only to reappear a few seconds later, floating in the air above his audience's heads.

"Parlour tricks for the ignorant masses," sniffed Andras.

I grinned, turning to see a demon in long, flowing robes shouting to his throng. As we drew nearer I could make out some of the words:

"...where a new land of plenty awaits, a fresh source of energy and hardworking slaves. Our valiant warriors even now are amassing..."

"He's talking about our home, isn't he?" I said to Pearce. He nodded grimly as we continued on our way.

Andras pulled us to the side and made a show of examining some wares for sale, gesturing for us to do likewise. When I shot him a questioning glance he muttered: "Warlocks approaching. They must not see us; keep your heads down."

Out of the corner of my eye I saw them—tall figures clad in dark robes, they seemed to glide through the streets whilst the crowd deferentially parted before them. I bent over a small box and pretended to listen as the stallholder described his contraption's properties and benefits. I could feel the Warlocks passing in a cold wave as the salesman cracked open the box to reveal a small imp inside, the creature that powered the device's actions.

Andras straightened up and nodded to us to indicate that the threat had passed, turning to lead us back on our way through that bizarre place.

After a while I stopped trying to consciously match landmarks and revelled in the pure other-worldly nature of the place in which we found ourselves. Everything was at the same time familiar and yet fantastical. The buildings were the most perfect mix of reality and dreams I could have ever conceived, merging shapes and directions in ways that defied all the laws of physics. On one corner, a building not unlike London's Royal Exchange drew up from a familiar onion-domed roof into a point that continued skywards for miles before taking a sharp right turn and then returning to ground to form another structure that reminded me of Tower Bridge in its outline, although it was larger and brasher than anything found in my corporeal realm.

The sky was a hot red, the fires of Hell brought to life in the heavens and casting an angry light on us. I looked around for any form of sun and found three, one high above us while the others sat on opposite horizons. They were fainter and redder than our own back home, and a dozen small moons obscured portions of the lower ones so they appeared to have had pieces bitten out of them.

I looked round and then stopped, causing someone to bump into me from behind and curse me for not watching where I was going. I did not care, transfixed by the impossible beauty before us.

"What are you doing?" hissed Andras, grabbing my arm and trying to pull me along. "I told you to not draw attention to us."

"What is that?" I asked, pointing.

It were as though all the clouds in the world had been gathered together and twisted into a rope that stretched across the sky from one horizon to the other, sprinkled with the lights from a billion distant stars. As I stared it came into focus and I saw that, rather than one entity, it was a band of millions and millions of tiny near-translucent objects, like dust all pulled together in one place.

"Beautiful," Joshua muttered.

"The rings," Andras said with a dismissive wave. "It's just flotsam and jetsam."

"It is the remnants from a thousand civilisations," said Byron coldly, "chewed up and spat out by the ravenous monsters that feed and power this world."

"Not quite," snapped Andras. He turned and looked around. "This is hopeless. If we're going to get anywhere without you idiots pulling us up every few minutes, we need to find transportation."

Even the conveyances that the Almadites used were perversely identifiable. Some demons rode mounts with six thick legs, trunk-like bodies and the heads of wolves. Others were transported in carriages that were moved by some form of gaseous propulsion piped out from within: not unlike a steam engine but also completely unlike one, for these vehicles travelled through the air as well as on land. The sky above us was thick with them, all travelling in different directions with little sign of logic or coordination between them as they circled and criss-crossed, tipping their hats to each other as they passed.

It was one of these carriages that Andras hailed, raising his hand and yelling into the air. He pulled us to the side of the thoroughfare and a few moments later a black metallic object glided to the ground, landing beside us in a cloud of sulphuric orange smoke.

Andras bundled us inside as he barked orders to the driver seated on the roof. I looked around the small vehicle, which was fitted with a pair of velvet-lined benches. The walls were covered in intricate carvings that I at first took for random patterns until I looked closer to see likenesses of faces, twisted into varied degrees of agony and despair.

"Nice," I muttered. "Very homely."

"They give one something to look at," Andras said. "And act

as useful handholds. Speaking of which, I'd brace yourselves if I were you."

We had no sooner sat down and shut the door than the carriage lurched sickeningly upwards, pressing us back into our seats. We tried not to shout out in alarm lest we alert the driver, but terror was writ large on our faces. Was this Andras' betrayal? Had he entrapped us?

The carriage froze, hanging above the city. I chanced a look out of the window and saw that we were level with the higher reaches of the taller buildings we had seen from the ground, with other carriages whistling past us. From this fresh vantage point I could see that the buildings had an almost organic look to them, and what I had assumed to be brickwork or plaster was in fact a continuous flesh-like membrane. Windows were picked out at regular intervals and I could see Almadites within, working and performing other duties too bizarre for my comprehension. I blinked and then through another window I saw a room full of clerks bent over desks made of tree trunks, writing on long scrolls in the light generated by floating globes.

We were jerked back into our seats by the carriage pulling forwards and braced ourselves for yet more violent commotion, but this time the ride was much smoother.

"You can relax now," said Andras. "It is the process of taking to the skies that is the most jarring."

"What about going back down to land?" Joshua asked.

Andras grinned and I shook my head. "You had to ask, didn't you?" I muttered.

I distracted myself from thoughts of sudden impacts by looking back at the ribbon of sparkling dust cutting across the sky, trying to distract myself from a sudden bout of vertigo. "What did you mean earlier?" I asked Byron. "About that being the remnants from all those civilisations?"

"Almadel owes its continued existence to on-going harvests from other realms," he said, ignoring Andras' glare. "This realm should have died many millennia ago but they have instead prolonged its life by feeding on the energy from other worlds, the ones they conquer. Just like the steam emitted from an engine, such processes have by-products and that is what you see."

"It is not quite that straightforward," said Andras.

"You deny it?" Byron snapped.

"No, not at all. But what you see is not just the by-products of the energy harvested from other realms. It is also the souls we have gathered and cast off, the death agonies of millions of creatures given physical form." He shrugged as we stared at him. "I promised to tell you the truth; I didn't tell you that it would be palatable."

Joshua shook his head. "Just when I thought I had seen enough barbarity…"

"It is not barbarism," said Andras. "Do you know how much skill goes into properly harvesting a soul, extracting the useful elements and then twisting what remains into something that is still aesthetically pleasing?" He gestured to the sparkling ribbon and I shuddered, reappraising my views of it.

"What do you do with them? The 'useful elements', as you put it?" Joshua asked.

Andras gestured around us. "They are an expedient form of energy, powering everything from lights to transportation."

I felt sick and lightheaded. "You mean that this carriage is being propelled thanks to the suffering of some poor creature?"

"Everything is."

"I want to get out of this thing. Now."

Andras shook his head and sneered at me. "This is no time for squeamishness. Everything comes at a price, even in your own so-called perfect world. Are you so naive as to think that you are any more superior? Do you really think that the resources you consume in your world are untainted by the suffering of others in far-off places? It is the natural way of things, regardless of which realm you are in."

"Not in my world," I said.

He barked a short laugh. "The meat on your table: do you

think the animal that it came from gave up its flesh willingly and without suffering? Or the coal that powers your engines of industry: do you think that the children down the mines do not suffer as they toil to extract it from the guts of the Earth? What about the clothes on your back, stitched together by women forced to work for a pittance? Or if we're talking of real slavery, what about the cotton used to weave your fabrics or the sugar you use to sweeten your food? I have seen the plantations, as I know you have. I did not see too many happy volunteers there— did you? So spare me your petty carping and base hypocrisy."

I shook my head as I tried to think of a response, but nothing instantly came to mind.

"He's got a point," muttered Pearce.

We rode in silence for a while, looking down on streets that twisted and turned without any form of logic, a network of living worms writhing in, around, over and under each other.

We approached a wide river and I stared open-mouthed, marvelling at how it perfectly reflected the roiling red sky. After a few moments I realised that it was no reflection; the river was a flowing mass of flame and molten lava. Bridges bisected it, unaffected by the swirling heat that we could feel even from our great height.

Andras pointed at a building looming up on the horizon ahead of us. "That is the Citadel," he said. We followed his finger to a large, castle-like structure with crenelated walls surrounding a tall white tower that my mind wanted to liken to the Tower of London, except that this one stretched upwards until it disappeared into the diaphanous clouds, its sides dotted with thousands of dark, forbidding windows.

"Looks lovely," I said drily.

"That," said Andras, "is where the Warlocks live and work. I suppose 'preside over Almadel' would be the right phrase." He pointed over the river. "That is the Consul building, where the Leaders of Almadel reside."

"The Four Kings?" I asked, taking a perverse pleasure from

the pent-up anger in Andras' nod.

The Consul building was just as large as the Citadel, but adorned with gothic arches and turrets instead of the mediaeval brutality of its cousin on the other bank. Both buildings were linked by a long, thick branch-like bridge looking like two stout arms shaking hands across the river's fiery torrents. The buildings still seemed a couple of miles away, but even at that distance they seemed to dwarf everything else around them.

Byron shuddered. "Are we heading over there? I would rather be as far away from that place as possible."

"What's so bad about these Warlocks?" asked Pearce.

"They are immensely powerful beings," said Byron, "and utterly ruthless. They are sorcerers, for want of a better word, masters of magic who have dedicated their lives to learning how to do whatever they wish for the furtherance of their own twisted ends." He turned to Andras. "Does that about cover it?"

"I suppose it's an economical digest, given the circumstances. Maybe less of the moral turpitude next time and don't skimp on the hubris," he said. "Actually, they are technically inferior to the Leaders' caste, which is headed by the Four Kings at present. Despite that, they are the true power in Almadel. The Leaders, you see, of which I was one, are immensely powerful in our own right. We can do things that you humans may consider magical, but which are mere parlour tricks to the Warlocks. Our skills lie in strategic cunning and manipulation, while the Warlocks are the ones with the blunt power. The Leaders cannot rule without the Warlocks' consent, you see."

"Why don't the Warlocks just take over and rule without the Leaders?" I asked.

"Because there are many aspects of leading and ruling in which they are not in the least bit interested. They prefer to content themselves with their studies and experimentation and let the Leaders get on with the business of ruling, gaining power, raping and pillaging and all that good stuff. As long as the Leaders leave them alone and undisturbed, of course."

"So it is a form of uneasy truce?" I said.

"Yes. As long as everyone sticks to their own roles, all is fine. The Leaders lead, the Warlocks do their sorcery, the Warriors fight, the Workers work and the Slaves… well, they do what they do."

"Like suffer and die," said Byron coldly.

"In a sense. But sometimes useful stuff before that. I don't know, it is the Workers who deal with the Slaves; I never really had any cause to engage with them. The point is, our society is strictly organised and finely balanced, and it works perfectly well as long as everyone sticks to their appointed roles."

I frowned. "Where do the Mages fit into all of this?"

Andras shuddered. "The Mages are a creation of the Warlocks, the product of one of their past experiments, along with the Berserkers and certain other creatures."

"Wait, the Berserkers, those things we keep fighting all the time?" asked Pearce. "Big aggressive demons? Aren't they the Warriors you just spoke of?"

"No. The Warriors are trueborn Almadites and form the leadership and specialised areas of our armies: analogous to your own officers, ruling elite and the like. The Berserkers are the expendable foot soldiers that we send ahead of the Warriors to soften up the enemy. The Mages are similarly unfortunate."

"And they're created by the Warlocks?"

"Yes. I had the misfortune to witness their Birthing Chambers once; an experience I have not been in a hurry to repeat. The Warlocks see the Mages as their supreme creations, a way of bestowing great honour on conquered creatures. They take other races and then turn them into—"

"So you don't bestow this 'great honour' on your own people?" I asked with a raised eyebrow.

"No. Not even the Warlocks are that twisted. At least, not as far as I know. You see, they take someone—usually it's either a Slave or a prisoner—and they set about deconstructing that creature. A complex set of rituals is undertaken to ensure that the subject is not killed in the process. Then a Wraith is sent into the creature, via the eyes, to scorch their essence from the inside-out."

"Their essence?" I felt sick, almost as though I were witnessing something vile but which I could not help but keep watching in spite of my innate revulsion.

"Yes. Memories, personality, values, belief—all that kind of thing. It all combines to give them their own free will. That's the main prize, you see: stripping away the free will so they are totally and unquestioningly subservient to their masters. The best ones are those with the most to lose, the ones who care the most about family, friends, community, ties. The ones with all of that good stuff usually have it exposed and on the surface so it can be scraped easily away."

"Those who don't?" I asked. "Who don't care and don't have 'good stuff exposed on the surface,' as you say?"

"Most of them are driven mad," he said. "They become the Berserkers: intent on doing nothing except fighting and killing, taking revenge for all the pain they've felt at the hands of their Wraith."

"They feel everything?" Joshua asked.

"Oh yes: right up to the point when they finally give in and the Wraith steals their soul. Then they're a Mage."

"Sounds truly delightful, the volunteers must come flocking in droves," I muttered. We lapsed into an uneasy silence, staring down at the landscape that passed beneath us and trying not to think too hard about the twin edifices looming up ahead.

"But what about the rest?" I asked, turning back to Andras. "You said that most victims are driven mad; what happens to those who aren't?"

"Oh, there are always exceptions to a rule. Some people have a natural propensity to fight the particular pain that the Wraiths inflict. People who are used to locking away their feelings: those that experienced a tough childhood, traumatic upbringing, unimaginable horror and so on. It's difficult to tear someone apart with their feelings and memories if they've spent a lifetime doing that sort of thing to themselves. Those ones… well, it's interesting: I asked the exact same question of the Head Warlock once and clearly hit a raw nerve. From what I could understand, they usually are able to spot them; the Wraith's influence affects the host's body as well as their insides, and most people can't put up a show of pretending not to react to such a shock when they first see what they've become."

I nodded, remembering the Mage I had encountered a few months ago, the one that Andras had killed at the Battle of St Albans. It had seemed almost skeletal and spectral. "So the host takes on the appearance of the parasite?" I asked. "The Wraith?"

"Correct. If the host, as you put it, doesn't fully surrender to the Wraith, then they are mortally shocked by what they find themselves turned into. The Warlocks then pick up on that reaction and…" He ran a finger across his throat.

"This is all very fascinating in a hideously terrifying sort of way," said Byron, gesturing toward the huge bulks of the Citadel and Consul buildings, which now filled almost the whole vista outside our windows. "But is there a reason why we are approaching those buildings?"

"Yes there is," said Andras. "If Kate was taken anywhere, it would be here. And I know someone who might help us." He banged on the roof of the carriage.

Landing was not quite as terrifying as taking to the air, although I suspected that part of that was because we were braced for something much worse than the lurch to the surface we in fact endured. We stepped down to the ground and headed away from the Citadel building, something I noted with relief.

As we walked we seemed to turn back on ourselves so many times that we should have arrived where we started, but we never did. It was as though the fabric of the world itself was playing with us, a living organism that was shifting and moving beneath and around us. I had a sudden memory from childhood of playing with a money spider that had found its way onto my palm, moving it from hand to hand and finger to finger and watching as it scuttled along, unaware that it was no further forwards than when it had landed on me. My head spun as I wondered if that was what was happening to us.

We paused on a bridge, peering round gargoyles shaped from things beyond our worst nightmares as we looked down on the scene below. A mass of beings shuffled to and fro in a large square, subserviently following upright Almadites or being shouted at or beaten by them for their ineptitude.

Andras darted down the steps at the side of the bridge and we ran to keep up with him. When we were among the creatures he stopped and looked around, then moved towards the centre of the square. Those surrounding us were little less than cattle, their eyes devoid of any curiosity or intelligence. They shuffled to the side to let us pass, their eyes downcast and shoulders slumped. Unlike the other areas of the city we had seen, where the Almadites were identifiably from the same race, each one of these here was different, as though this was a zoo encapsulating the dregs of every civilisation that had ever existed.

"What is this?" I asked.

"A slave market," said Byron. He shot desperate eyes around as we walked.

Andras came to a halt in front of a tall creature, not unlike an Almadite but with the same dull eyes and downcast demeanour of her fellows around her. He held her shoulders and glared at her. When she refused to meet his gaze he gripped her face in his hands and turned it this way and that, clearly looking for something in her features and eyes.

"Hey," came a shout. "You want to buy?"

Andras ignored him, peering at the poor creature, forcing her to raise her head.

"You want to buy?" The burly Almadite slave master was now standing next to Andras. When there was no reply he put a hand on his shoulder.

Andras turned and snarled before releasing the slave and

marching away. We left the market with backward glances and plenty of relief.

We walked in silence for a while, each locked in our own thoughts of what we had seen, what could have happened to those creatures to make them so devoid of any spark of sentience. What fears I had had of being in the centre of Almadel were intensified; if we were captured, surely we would join the ranks of those poor creatures? Furthermore, if the Almadites did finally manage to invade Earth, then I had a horrible feeling that we had just glimpsed the fate of all humanity: reduced to cowed, shuffling husks.

Chapter Eight

Half an hour later we sat in a corner of a tavern, trying not to look at the gold coin that Andras had placed on the far corner of our table. He had been in a filthy mood ever since the incident in the market and his demeanour grew worse the longer we sat there, his arms folded and refusing to speak to us. He had wanted to visit this taproom on his own but we would not let him out of our sight. He had—not very graciously—given in after some heated debate.

I looked round the tavern over the rim of my mug of ale. It was a dark and sparsely furnished place, with a long table at the far side serving as a bar. Demons were scattered around the room, as well as a few other creatures that I did not recognise. "You know, this is not too bad," I muttered, swallowing another mouthful of ale.

"You really should not be drinking that," said Byron. "For all we know, Almadite drinks could be poisonous to humans."

"I'm half-demon," I said, "and I feel fine." I took another swig to spite him.

A server came over to collect our glasses and we looked down, avoiding eye contact just as we had been ordered. When she had gone, we looked up to see a scrap of paper wedged under the coin. Andras casually placed his mug on top of paper and coin and swept both towards him, depositing them in his lap. Pearce, Joshua and I leaned forwards in mock discussion, obscuring Andras and Byron from the rest of the room while they examined the paper.

"What is it?" I asked eventually.

"Instructions," said Andras. "We'll stay here for another hour or so and then we go for a walk."

"And then what?" asked Pearce.

"They'll come and find us."

*

We approached the run-down building separately so as not to raise any suspicions. I had insisted on staying with Andras, much to his inexhaustible disgust, and we reached the door within seconds of each other. He tried to slam it in my face as he entered but I grabbed it before it could swing shut. "Good way to stay inconspicuous," I muttered.

"Shut up," he growled back.

We were faced with a steep and rickety set of stairs that led up to a mezzanine level overlooking a main warehouse floor. I did not like the look of the building; there were too many places for demons to hide and too many avenues for attackers to come at us from. We were sitting ducks up on that over-sized balcony.

"Where are they?" I asked, looking around the empty, echoing space.

"Maybe this is another one of their convoluted tasks," Andras said with barely disguised contempt. We had spent the past couple of hours following clues from one building to another, only to be met with yet more notes and further instructions. We had hoped that we had finally reached the end of the road, our optimism buoyed up by the name of this latest supposed rendezvous point.

"Is this really called Cato Street, or is that just my altered perceptions playing with me?" I asked.

"We demons do love a nice bit of irony," said Andras. "But maybe you are just imagining me saying that as well."

I glared at him. "I only ask because the Cato Street Conspiracy hardly ended well for the plotters. As omens go this isn't the best, even if my brain is just mistranslating whatever the real word is in your language."

Almost half a century earlier, a group of men had gathered in a house in Cato Street in London to plot the assassination of the Prime Minister and his entire Cabinet. However, the authorities had been tipped off and the house was raided by the police, the conspirators being arrested and either hanged or transported to Australia. I did not fancy the opportunity to learn the Almadite versions of those punishments.

Any further discussion was halted by the others joining us. "Another empty building," muttered Pearce. "They're selling us a dog, aren't they?"

Andras held up a hand. "They are understandably nervous about whether we genuinely are on their side. We will have been watched every step of the way. If the Leaders and the Warlocks knew about the people we are trying to meet… well, not even the worst torture from your most hideous daydreams comes close to what they would do."

We milled around the room, checking for anything that might offer a clue to our next move. Byron and I kept wary eyes on the exits, while Joshua was a study of quiet contemplation: we had asked him to keep himself ready to create a portal home at any moment, just in case.

"There you are," said Andras after a moment, making us jump. We turned to see him addressing a shadow in the far corner.

"Who are you?" asked a female voice from the shadows. It had a sing-song quality to it that gave her old-sounding voice a youthful cadence. I strained to see the speaker but could discern little more than a dark, huddled form.

"I think you know by now," said Andras.

"I wish to hear it from your own mouths."

Andras looked round at us and I could see the indecision writ large across his face. If she were a Warlock then to speak our names could give her power over us, but our situation was desperate enough to warrant such risks: every minute that ticked by was a minute that Kate was in the demons' hands.

"I am the Leader who was banished by the Four Kings many moons ago," Andras said. "These people are travellers from a world that the Four Kings seek to enslave."

"They are humans, and a Pooka." There was a tinge of amusement to the voice. "I have not seen their like in a long time. They are very far from home indeed." The shadowed form shifted and I fancied I could see her head turning and a finger pointing at Andras. "But I will have your names."

Andras clenched his fists at his sides. "I am Andras, Sire of Var," he said through clenched teeth.

The figure nodded. "Good. Why are you here, Andras, Sire of Var?"

"We seek to help you, and to acquire your help in return."

"You could help us? With what?"

"To rise against the Warlocks and the Leaders and overthrow the Four Kings."

"These are treasonous words you speak, Andras, Sire of Var. Why do you believe we wish such a thing?"

"I have been speaking with your comrades: Workers and Slaves who managed to escape and make their way to the humans' realm, a place in which I have been trapped for more years than I care to remember. They told me that things have changed much in my absence, that those of you in the lower orders are becoming more and more dissatisfied with your lot."

"No," she said, the word making my heart sink. "In your arrogance, you have misunderstood."

I looked at Joshua, willing him with my eyes to be ready to open a portal. He nodded and started mouthing words soundlessly.

The figure continued. "Things have not changed at all. We

have *always* been 'dissatisfied with our lot', as you put it. During your rule, and those of your forebears, stretching back to when we were first cast into the Hell you all built for us, were you always so arrogant as to believe that we would meekly surrender to our stations in mind as well as body? I ask again: why are you here?"

"We wish to help you; to help you to be free."

"What is freedom? What would we do with such a thing, that which many of us have never known? You may as well offer us the stars. I ask again: why are you here?"

"We offer our assistance in the overthrow of your current masters. We could distract them, split their forces—"

"We have not said that that is what we want, so why would you offer it? *Tell me: why are you here?*"

I sighed: the conversation was becoming circular. "A friend of ours has been captured by Warlocks and we have come to save her," I said. "We seek your help to free her, and in return we will do whatever you wish us to do to help you."

"Good," there was a hint of amused satisfaction to the voice. "That explains the humans. What about the Pooka?"

"The person he speaks of is a friend of mine as well," said Byron. "She is a brave soul who has done much to stop the Almadites invading their home realm."

"And presumably you have taken refuge in their realm and do not wish to suffer yet another invasion?"

"That is correct," said Byron. "My world was taken from me, my family enslaved. I will not lose yet more."

The figure nodded and then turned back to Andras. "Then the question remains: why are *you* here, Sire of Var?"

"I have spent a long time in the humans' realm," said Andras. "It has changed me. The girl who is being held is an ally in the fight to save their realm. I do not want to see that place fall to the Four Kings."

"No. Try again."

Andras frowned. "I have experienced much. I have lived

among them as a human for considerable time, experienced their emotions, been… contaminated by them. I feel guilt for some of the things I have done. I am no longer—"

"No. Try again."

"I wish to help, to atone for what I have done—"

"*No.* Try again."

Andras hissed in frustration and then exploded in rage. "I was usurped by the upstart Gaap and his simpering masters. I spent millennia trapped in the Aether, clinging onto my hatred of Gaap and the Four Kings. That rage was the only thing that kept me from turning into just another one of the ghouls that dwell there. I plotted what I would do when I finally returned, and when I did manage to escape the Aether I was instead trapped in the human realm, a primitive place where my magic was subservient to *science*, of all things.

"I tried damned hard to retain who I was, but too much has happened: I don't even think I'd recognise myself from back then if we were to meet face-to-face. Do you want me to tell you I'm good or evil now? There's no such thing. I am me."

He stepped closer towards the shadow and the figure, to her credit, did not appear to show any signs of wanting to back away as he continued. "What I want is my birthright. I want to see Gaap and the Four Kings suffer the way I have suffered and I want to see every plan of theirs torn to pieces and pissed on. They will have a reason for taking the girl, and so taking her back will frustrate whatever plans they have. I want to take back Almadel from them and I don't care how I do it, as long as they suffer."

We stared at him in silence as he subsided, breathing heavily and glaring at the dark form.

"Good," she said at last. "We finally get to the truth of the matter. But if we replace the Four Kings with you, what then? When you get your 'birthright' back, what are your plans for the rest of us? Leave us alone? Let us live our lives in peace while you preside over… what?"

Andras stared back at her and she laughed, clapping her hands together. "Amazing!" she said. "You have spent so long hating that you have lost sight of what it means to achieve your desires! You are like a child who lusts after a shiny object in a shop window just because it's there, but with no concept of what you'll do with it when and if you finally get your greasy hands on it."

Andras snarled and spun away, marching to the other side of the room.

The figure addressed the rest of us. "Why do you ally yourselves with this flawed creature? You know all that it has done; why help it?"

"We find ourselves in an impossible place," I said. "We need help, whatever form it might take. We have a saying in our realm: better the devil you know."

She grunted. "I like that, very apt. So your aim is save your friend?"

"Yes. Can you help us?"

"For a price, yes."

"What is your price?" asked Pearce, his voice tight as he glared at the creature wreathed in shadows. I sympathised with him, as this exchange was like trying to draw blood from a stone.

"You help us to defeat the Four Kings. Once and for all."

"Can such a thing be done?" asked Byron.

"It has not been done for a very, very long time."

"But it has been done? It is possible?"

"When they were less developed, before the Warlocks created the Mages. You see, how can you fight an enemy that can stop you *wanting* to fight them?"

"But it can be done?" asked Pearce again.

"I like your persistence. In theory, yes: if you are stronger than them and the Mages are kept away from battle."

"With your help it could be possible," mused Pearce. "If you have allies then we could both attack them at the same time and split their forces—"

"And they slaughter my people so that yours can succeed?"

"Or vice versa," piped up Byron. When I looked at him questioningly he shrugged. "I'm just saying: the converse could just as easily happen." He turned back to the figure. "My people, the Pooka, have nothing left to lose. I would wager that the same applies to you and your people. The humans still have a world to fight for, a world lusted over by the Almadites. I wonder, what sort of army is more likely to fight hard: one with nothing to lose and everything to gain, with their backs against the wall, fighting for all they know and love? Or an army with everything already but which merely wants more and more just because they can?"

We held our breaths while the figure considered this. She nodded. "Your people have always been wiser than you at first appear."

"Thank you," said Byron, "I think."

"But we still have the question of Andras," she said, "the creature that no one trusts. What is your place in this grand scheme?"

Andras turned and shrugged. "You talk of creatures with nothing left to lose. What do you think I am? What do you think happened when I was banished to the Aether? What do you think I left behind? I had a family as well. You know what they did to them?"

"I do," said the figure softly. A silence stretched between them, an agonising lack of information.

"What?" I asked after a moment.

"My Sire was a Leader and his before him," said Andras. "My family was one of the most exalted in Almadel. Removing me would not have been nearly enough. Before I was banished, I was forced to witness the worst possible punishment. Even by my standards."

I thought back to the slave market, the way he had darted around and grabbed at that Slave, trying to discern something in her face. Such creatures should have been beneath his notice unless he was trying to find people who could fight with us—

but there was surely no one in that place capable of such an act? Unless…

"They turned them into Slaves, didn't they?" I said.

Andras nodded. "So you ask what my place is, why I am here. I do not come just to conquer: I come to devastate. All of them, all of those who destroyed me and mine. Is that enough for you? Am I making myself clear now?"

The figure regarded him in silence for a few more moments and then nodded. "Thank you for the gift of your truth. I will help you." She stepped forwards into the light to reveal a hunched old woman, albeit with the same angular features as Andras.

He nodded. "It is good to see that the rumours of your demise are as false as I had suspected, Mama."

I gaped at him. "She is your…?"

He laughed. "No. That is her title. Or at least it was, before…"

"Before you turned me into a Slave," she said. "But now I am useful to you once again it seems."

"Yes," said Andras. He turned to us. "You see, she serves in the Citadel."

"So you can get us in there?" I asked.

"I can," she said. "Whether you should want to go in there is another matter."

I took Andras to one side. "Can we trust her?" I asked.

He shrugged. "About as much as you can trust me."

"That little?" said Pearce.

Andras gasped in mock outrage. "Captain Pearce, you wound me. But seriously: beggars, choosers and all that. She is the only option we have, short of wandering over and knocking on the door or trying to fight our way in: neither of which will end well for us. Her way," he gestured to Mama, "has a slightly higher chance of success."

"Slightly higher?" I queried.

"We *might* not die," he said.

Chapter Nine

The damp, cramped tunnel stretched on forever in front of us as we progressed at an agonisingly slow pace, the only illumination being the spluttering torches in our hands. Mama was leading us and as such we were forced to walk at her speed; while she was much nimbler than her hunched form suggested, the speed she kept was still slower than we preferred.

"Will we ever see the end of this place?" I whispered.

"In time," said Andras. "Bear in mind that we are approaching from beneath: there is a lot of tunnelling to be done to get under the Citadel's walls."

"Are you sure that this is a safe way in?" asked Pearce. "Should we expect guards?"

"No," said Mama. "This is just an outlet. They would never believe that anyone would be stupid enough to attempt to come in through here."

"An outlet?" asked Byron. "For what?"

"For the Warlocks' magical energy," she said. "All of that power has to go somewhere, you know."

"And we're wading through it?" asked Joshua, looking around, his voice rising in panic.

"Don't worry: they're usually resting at this time."

"Usually," I repeated.

"I make no guarantees," she said. "You're more than welcome to turn and go back, but this is the only way you'll get in without them noticing."

"Maybe we should go a little faster," said Joshua.

"Young man, you will go as fast as I wish," Mama snapped.

Andras chuckled. "I'm actually growing to quite like her."

I glared at him and then turned my attention back to picking my way through the darkness, my imagination painting all manner of strange beasts just beyond the dancing shadows cast by our torches. I tried to focus my attention on the way ahead, straining for any sign of an end to this interminable darkness.

After a while Mama stopped and held up a hand. We held our breath as we waited, trying to perceive what she had sensed. She edged forwards and then disappeared.

I looked at the others. Was this a trap? Had she abandoned us, having delivered us right into the Warlocks' hands? Even Andras appeared on edge as we waited, tensed and ready for an attack. Then a shuffling sound came from ahead and she reappeared, thankfully alone. I realised that she had just gone round a bend in the tunnel, the lack of light having lent the illusion of her sudden disappearance. "All is clear," she said. "It was just one of my comrades, cleaning out the entrance to the outlet. I have sent him away, so we are free to proceed."

"What did you tell him?" Andras asked.

"Why, the truth of course."

"Very funny," he replied, then frowned at her. "You're not joking, are you? You actually told him that you are bringing intruders into the Citadel and then sent him away! What makes you think that he won't just alert his masters?"

"Because I know him. And besides, even if he did alert the Warlocks, what difference would it make? Do you really believe you will spend more than a few minutes inside the Citadel without being detected anyway? Speed will be your friend in either case."

Andras grunted and then turned to the rest of us. "Best make yourselves ready." He turned to me. "It might be a good idea if you were to turn into your superior form now, rather than wasting time later."

"My superior form?" I asked.

"You know, the better looking one," he said. "Less human, more demon? The fewer of us who are constrained by human weaknesses, the better." He held up a hand to quieten any arguments. "You can all protest at my insults later, if we survive. From now on, time is of the essence. Now, if you don't mind?"

I frowned and then drew the runic sword from the scabbard at my back, allowing the power to course through me and change me into that other thing. There was once a time I had feared and resented the changes that the sword's magic wrought on me, but I had learnt to embrace them as a part of me, something that enhanced rather than corrupted. After all, whilst I might be a demon, I had chosen to be a demon on the side of humanity.

My senses sharpened as I transmogrified, the tunnel lightening around me such that I could pick out the rough-hewn walls as they curved around us and just in front. I could sense the power emanating from the building into which we were about to enter; raw, hideous power that made me want to tear at my skin to be rid of it. I took a deep breath to calm myself and then nodded at Andras.

"Good," he said. "Let's go."

Round the corner we came to an arched gateway, a large grille swinging open at its entrance. Beyond was a dull half-light. We stepped through into what first appeared to be a cellar but upon further inspection revealed itself to be a trench-like construction at the base of the Citadel.

I looked up at the building. At first glance it seemed completely ordinary, a stone structure like so many others in our own realm. Just another castle. But then the reality of the scene shifted sickeningly and I reeled as the never-ending height of the creation stretched up and up to the clouds and beyond. I had the strangest feeling of vertigo whilst standing at ground level.

"You're over-thinking again," noted Andras, wagging a finger at me before turning to walk towards the building.

In front of us was another stone archway with a black placard situated dead centre above the open entrance. White text twisted and curled malevolently on the sign. "What does it say?" I asked Andras.

"You really don't want to know."

We walked through the archway, surprised to emerge at the other side unchallenged. The path led over a bridge guarded by stone monsters to either side.

"I would resist the temptation to look over the side of the bridge," Andras said.

"Why?"

"Because I want to get inside the building in one piece. Now, come on."

We passed through another archway to find ourselves in a corridor bordered on all sides by monolithic stone blocks that stretched up into darkness. I had not been aware of us entering a building and yet we clearly had done so. We passed a window and I looked out, gasping to see that the city was now hundreds of feet below us.

"Oh, yes," said Andras. "You should be aware that anything pertaining to the so-called laws of nature, in any realm, doesn't apply here. It can be disconcerting if you allow yourself to think about it. My advice is to keep going forwards and don't get distracted."

The corridor stretched on before us, uniform stone walls interspersed at regular intervals by rectangular windows. Our footsteps echoed around us as we walked. "Be on your guard," warned Andras. "This building may feel empty, but I can assure you it is not."

We followed Mama round a corner that I could have sworn had not existed mere moments before, and then through another archway to a junction where four passages led off in different directions. Out of the corner of my eye I sensed another handful of passages that surely couldn't be there. I spun round to look and my head reeled as it attempted to comprehend an endless number of passageways running off in an infinite number of directions.

Byron caught me before I fell. "Are you all right?" he asked.

I nodded as Andras reminded me: "Do not try to think about anything here, or spot things you would normally expect to find. Simply accept it and keep going, otherwise you will be driven insane."

I focused on the floor as I followed the others, fighting my natural urge to scrutinise everything around me. A few more deep breaths and I felt my equilibrium return enough to look up, surprised to see how ordinary everything was. The stone-lined corridor could have been in any other building back on Earth, were it not for the fact that it stretched off into infinity.

"How much further?" I asked.

"Not far," Mama said, gesturing ahead and to the right. "Just over that way."

Andras stopped. "Are you sure?"

Mama turned and glared at him. "Of course I am," she snapped. "I was here when she was brought in, and in any case there is nowhere else she will be."

Andras rubbed at his forehead. "But… that is…" He looked back at the rest us. "Change of plan. Kate is lost, so we need to go to the Council Chamber."

"What? What do you mean 'lost'?" I asked, as Pearce shook his head.

"No," Pearce said. "We are not giving up on her."

"You do not understand," said Andras. "She is either dead or as good as dead. In any case, it is pointless and suicidal to continue this way."

Pearce pushed him aside. "I will not believe it until I see it for myself." He glared at Mama. "You can take us to her?"

"I can," she said, her voice carrying a touch of amusement. "Are you sure you want to, though? He seems pretty adamant," she nodded at Andras.

"It would appear that the rest of us are made of sterner stuff than the demon," said Pearce quietly. "Lead on."

Mama continued on her way and we followed, leaving Andras standing alone in the corridor, pacing to and fro as he glanced up at us. After a few moments he muttered what I assumed were curses and then ran to catch up.

"This was not the arrangement," he said. "The deal was you take us to the girl."

"And that is what I am doing," Mama replied.

"You know as well as I do that whatever is now in there is absolutely, categorically no longer the same creature that went in."

"Wait," said Joshua. "What do you mean?"

"She is taking us to the Birthing Chambers," Andras said.

I frowned, searching my memory for a link. "The...?" I asked.

Andras turned to look at me, and for the first time I saw genuine fear in his eyes. "The Birthing Chamber. Where they transform prisoners into Mages."

I looked over to Pearce, walking straight and tall in front of me, and perceived a stiffening of his back. "How long does it take?" I asked. "How long before she is turned into a Mage?"

"What does it matter? As soon as she entered the Chamber and was infected by the Wraith, she was no longer the same person you once knew. You need to accept that Kate is gone."

Chapter Ten

We stood and pondered the door that Mama had indicated we should enter, which led into the complex that ultimately housed the Birthing Chamber. Andras was keeping as much distance from it as possible, now almost beseeching us to desist.

"You have no idea of the risks you will take just by opening that door," he said. "The things they do in there…"

Byron peered at him. "You are actually scared, aren't you?" He shook his head. "I never thought I'd see the day."

I felt the blood pumping fast in my head as I contemplated this. For something to scare Andras, well…

I looked up to see Pearce's eyes on me. "Gus?" he asked.

I took a deep breath and then nodded, in spite of every one of my baser instincts. "If there is anything of Kate still in there, then we owe it to her to help her," I said, trying to keep my voice as firm as possible. "Whatever the cost."

He nodded, and I felt as though I had passed some form of test. He then turned to Joshua, who nodded as well.

"I'm not leaving without her," he said simply. "And besides, the opportunity to study such a place should not be passed up."

Byron chuckled mirthlessly. "You are as insane as any humans I have ever met." He hefted the axe he carried as a weapon.

"What the Hell, this is as good a day to die as any other."

Andras shrank under our combined gazes. "You do not understand," he said again. "What lies beyond there… you will beg for something as welcoming as death, you have never—"

"We're going in there," said Pearce. "And you're coming with us, so stop your bleating."

Andras' eyes darted from one face to the other of us, finally settling on me and the runic sword. He took a deep breath. "Very well. But when you die, I'm having that sword," he told me.

"I'm not planning on dying," I shot back.

*

I had half expected to find a screaming pit of hellfire when the door opened, or at least some form of hideous torture chamber, and was mildly disappointed to find yet another nondescript corridor.

"Are you sure that this is the right door?" I asked Mama, peering inside. "It doesn't look much like a Birthing Chamber to me."

"This is the set of corridors and antechambers that lead to where you need to go. There is still a little way more before you reach the Birthing Chamber," she said. "This is the next line of defences. Just step through and you will see. But be warned that there are consequences."

I frowned at her and then stepped forward, my sword raised and ready to fend off any attackers.

As soon as I passed over the threshold I felt it, a huge oppressive weight that threatened to crush me. It was the torment of a million souls, all their pain and terror and loss turned into an atmosphere soaked in a suffering that made me want to run and hide.

Pearce looked at me as he followed. "Are you all right?" he asked.

"Can you not feel it?"

Pearce frowned as he cocked his head, straining to comprehend what was as clear to me as a sledgehammer to my head. He shrugged. "I am not quite sure…"

"You are wasting your time with him," said Andras, wincing as he stepped through the door. "Humans do not have the capabilities to sense the torment that has made this place."

Joshua sniffed the air, seemingly the only person keen to be there for its own purpose rather than out of necessity. "There is a distinct sense of the Aetheric in here," he said with mounting enthusiasm. "Almost akin to that which accompanies a summoning."

"I suspect that comparison is pretty apt," said Byron, glancing round warily.

"Indeed," said Andras. "I told you that the Warlocks use Wraiths and other demons as a part of their experiments. Such things always leave behind… residue."

"Like the pained souls wrenched away from those poor creatures unfortunate enough to be forced here against their will?" asked Byron with an acid tinge to his voice. He realised too late the meaning of his words and shook his head. "I am sorry," he said to the rest of us. "I did not mean—"

"Regardless," said Pearce, "the fact remains that the more we tarry here, the longer Kate is in their hands. So if you do not mind?" He gestured to Andras and Mama to lead us on.

I felt increasingly light-headed as we made our way along the corridor, the sensation making it harder and harder to concentrate on the task at hand. A few steps further and I could no longer recall exactly why we were in that place, or even where we were.

I turned at a humming sound to my right to see a familiar figure melt out of the shadows. She looked just as I remembered her, the same warm smile playing across her lips. My heart leapt to look upon her once more. "'Ello, Gus," she said.

"Rachel," I breathed. "How…? But you were—"

"Gone?" she shook her head. "I never left you; I've always

been here."

"But you died," I said. "I saw it, I held your body."

"Funny thing about death," she said. "It's not as permanent as it used to be." She stepped forwards and I saw that her clothing was riddled with scores of slashes, the blood still seeping thickly from the mortal wounds that had been inflicted by her oldest friend, the boy who had been so jealous of her attentions towards me.

"I am sorry," I said. "I never—"

"Meant to kill me?" she asked. "Maybe not, but you still did, didn't you?"

I shook my head, partly in denial but also to try to free my mind from this hellish encounter. "That's not it," I persisted feebly.

The memory was still painfully fresh: finding her in that darkened alleyway when we had finally been so close to escaping that wretched life together, only to have it snatched away from us. I still remembered the words of her murderer as he had stood over her battered body, tears running down his cheeks: *If I can't have her, no one will.* I looked at my hands, seeing them as raw and bloodied as they had been that night when I had gained my brutal revenge for what he had done.

The memory conjured up another ghoul to confront me, Rachel's murderer following her out of the shadows. "No," he rasped. "But he did for me, didn't he?"

I frowned, the spell broken. This was all too convenient, too contrite, too familiar. Over the past few years I had had my deepest and darkest fears and memories pulled out of me and exposed like a raw nerve. One malicious spirit had even worn my mother's voice as it had compelled me to commit suicide, using my pent-up feelings over her death and the mess I had made of my life to twist my feelings in a near-fatal manner.

But what animosity could Rachel possibly feel towards me? I had tried to save her, and I had done so much more since then.

I was Augustus Merriwether Potts, damn it! Sometime

demon and fulltime saviour of mankind. I had nothing left to feel guilty for.

The realisation thrust me back into the corridor with a jolt and I looked around, shamefaced, fearing that my weakness had cost us all precious time.

I realised that I had not been alone in being afflicted by visions. The others cowered or ranted around me, oblivious to all save whatever torments were playing out in their minds' eyes.

Byron was nearest to me, bending down and pleading with someone only he could see. "Please," he whispered. "You must remember who I am."

I grabbed him by the shoulders and shook him roughly in the hope of jarring him from his twisted reverie, but to no avail. I turned and looked around, shaking my head as I did so; I could feel the sickly tug of the monstrous visions at the edge of my consciousness, still trying to pull me back under. I now knew them for what they were, however, and as such was able to find the strength to resist them.

Partway along the corridor Andras ranted and raved at shadows while Mama cowered in a corner. Pearce had his back to us all, but Joshua was closer at hand and waving his arms around erratically. Given the potential for accidental—and no doubt fatal—magical discharge, I turned to Joshua first, approaching him with caution.

Tears ran down the young man's cheeks as he shook his head. "I did everything I could," he whined. Then, cocking his head as though listening to someone: "She didn't—"

He bowed his head under an onslaught I could neither see nor hear. "I tried, but she should not have been with us in the first place…" He flinched. "I did not mean… I just…" His voice choked into a fit of sobbing.

I risked bending closer to discern the nature of the visions that were afflicting him, in the hope that I could help him force his way back to reality.

"Mother, please…" he whispered.

So that was it: he was being tortured with the thought of telling his mother about Lexie's death at the hands of the demons. As he had told me on the ship to France, he had resisted meeting her in person, instead choosing to write to her about the dreadful news. The response when it arrived had left him very shaken and upset. That was not much of a surprise: I had only met their mother once, but had been struck by the lady's strong-willed nature. The blame that she clearly had attached to Joshua for her daughter's death was very unfair though, for her son had been opposed to Lexie joining us on our adventures in the first place; it was mainly the stubborn insistence of their mother that had set his sister on the path towards her untimely death.

Be that as it may, as someone who had also suffered at the hands of an overbearing mother, I sympathised with him. However, my more immediate concern was the damage that Joshua's magical powers could do to us in his current agitated state. Already I could see sparks and flashes of energy flare and strobe around him as he continued to play out his imagined conversation.

I grabbed him by his shoulders and shook him as roughly as I dared. I may as well have plucked on his sleeve for all the success it had in distracting him. I attempted everything save for hitting him across the face but failed to elicit any form of response. I took a moment to pause and consider my options and, as I did so, the pull of my own visions within my mind tried to reassert themselves anew. I shook my head; I would not allow myself to be dragged back, as I was at that moment my friends' only hope.

I drew in a deep breath and allowed it to escape as a sigh. Throughout all of this, I was painfully aware that Kate was still imprisoned. Should I abandon my friends? Maybe freeing Kate would, as a side effect, also free them? I looked around in desperation and noticed that Mama was watching me intently.

I walked over to the corner where she huddled and peered at her. "You are not affected by all of this?" I asked as I noticed her eyes focus on me.

She took a deep breath. "I am, just not in the same manner as the rest of you."

"Explain," I said.

She spoke as though she were trying to use as little of her body as possible, in the manner of one attempting to remain motionless to avoid the attentions of a stalking predator. "The spells prey on your worst fears, paralysing you. That way they ensure that any intruders are stopped, without the need to post guards."

"But you are not experiencing the same visions that the rest of us are?"

"I work here," she said. "It would not serve if I were incapacitated by the simplest of defences. My fears only assert themselves when I venture somewhere I should not be, at a time when I should not be there."

"Such as here," I said.

She nodded, shivering. "But they are not as intense as yours; merely enough to deter me from going any further."

"Why did you not warn us that this would happen?"

"I told you that there were consequences to entering here. I assumed that the Almadite had warned you of exactly what to expect."

I looked over to Andras, still ranting and raving on the other side of the corridor. "Yes, well, I got the impression he was not too keen on us proceeding this far, didn't you?"

"With good reason," she said. "I knew you non-Almadites would be able to free yourselves though."

I grunted. "Only me so far. How do I liberate the rest of them?"

"How did you break yourself from the fugue?" she asked.

"They pushed the wrong levers," I said. "I have already paid the debts with which they tried to bait me. In any case, I have been taunted before by spirits much more spiteful than these."

"Then there is your answer," she said. "You need to help them realise that what they are experiencing is just a mirage."

"I have tried," I said. "But they do not respond."

She shook her head ever so slightly. "They are oblivious to anything in the physical world; you can only reach them by going where they are right now."

I frowned at her, her habit of talking in riddles grating on my patience. "What exactly do you mean?"

"You need to go into their visions."

I laughed and shook my head. "I may look like a demon but my powers are some way short…"

"And yet you alone managed to break free of the Warlocks' spells."

"Yes, but—"

"You feel it even now, do you not? The pull of the visions, trying to lure you back under?"

I ran my fingers through my hair as I allowed my senses to probe inwards with a tentative touch, enough to feel what was there but not enough to allow myself to be ensnared. The tug of the visions was as strong as it had been since I escaped them. "But if I go back in there, surely I would be lost once more?"

"You now know the visions for what they are," she said. "So you can use them to your own ends. It is one spell that afflicts all of you, therefore your visions are all interlinked. As long as you retain your sense of reality, your sense of self, you will be able to ensure that the grip of the spell is not so strong as to ensnare you, and thus can interact with your friends. Have you had any experience of navigating through visions?"

I was about to answer in the negative when I remembered a couple of Christmases ago when I was drugged and imprisoned in the slums of St Giles. I had experienced a series of visions that I had at first attributed to the effects of laudanum, but which had taken me to places I could not possibly have known about: Kate's past and into N'yotsu's mind, to mention but two. My interactions with them since that time had proven to me that the visions had been anything but inventions of my fevered mind. Maybe I could do it, although surely my powers were so much more rooted in the physical world than the magical.

"I am not sure that I am experienced enough to do this," I said. "Can you not…?"

She shook her head. "As I said, the spells that afflict me are different to those currently holding your friends prisoner. I am of no use to you. But I will say this: the Warlocks will be aware that you are here. Every moment that you delay makes it more likely that they will be here to capture you. So hurry."

Chapter Eleven

I took a deep breath as I closed my eyes, lowering my mental defences and allowing the magic to encroach on me once more. Given that I knew what was coming, it took a great effort of will to relax as I felt the tide approach. I forced my mind to welcome it, allowing the malevolent wave to engulf me.

I stood in the hallway of my old apartment, listening to the insistent ring of a bell from the sitting room. I felt a strong compulsion to investigate the sound, pulling me as though I were attached to its source by a rope. I opened the door and there, on a table, was the squat box-like device that Maxwell had christened his Aetheric Sound Conduit: a creation that used the Aether to allow people to communicate over great distances.

The box continued its call, demanding that I answer it. Something tugged at my mind as I approached it and reached out to pick up the speaking and listening trumpets. Had I been here before?

"Augustus," croaked a familiar voice from the other side.

"Mother," I replied, my throat dry. I opened my mouth to say more but then the shock of memory overwhelmed me. I knew what would happen next: this voice, this spirit from the Aether that spoke in my dead mother's voice, would try to compel me to open a vein, fashion a noose, leap to my death. N'yotsu would then rescue me and we would continue on the mad adventure that eventually led to our saving the world, but not before Andras nearly stole my soul—and actually stole my humanity.

My head cleared as I remembered where I really was and my purpose. Mama had been right: it was so much easier to free myself of the spell's influence now I knew the nature of the visions. However, I did not want to be completely released; not yet.

I dropped the twin trumpets that allowed communication through the device and addressed the empty room. "A much better effort," I said. "But still not good enough." Resisting the urge to push all of the way back to consciousness, I looked around and saw four doors lined up along the far wall, a wall that in reality should have contained little more than an inglenook and a fireplace. Nothing was inscribed upon them but by looking I could sense that each was a gateway to another vision and another mind: Pearce, Byron, Joshua and Andras.

Which to free first? My initial instincts had been Joshua or Byron, if only for the magical powers they could bring to bear, but I hesitated to do so given how agitated they had both been. I was conscious that I had a steep learning curve ahead of me and would probably benefit from a simpler, more stoic character to test my powers of persuasion upon. That absolutely ruled out Andras on so many levels and I therefore stepped towards the one remaining door—leading to Pearce's visions.

As I passed through I found myself standing in a meadow on a balmy English summer afternoon. My initial instinct to bask in the warmth was cut short when I noticed that everything was still: too still. Birds and insects hung in the air as though painted on canvas, a disconcerting effect as I walked under and around them. Just before me gathered a group of young men and women making merry around a picnic blanket. One of them was a younger Captain Albert Pearce, standing stiffly in an Ensign's uniform.

As I ran over I could make out two of the other men poking

fun at him. "…the brains of the outfit, were you Albie?" laughed one. "Not even close!"

"But then I suppose you do not need brains to beat people up, eh?" added the other. Both of the taunters bore a strong resemblance to Pearce and with a shock I realised that they must be his older brothers.

"I will make my own way," Pearce muttered.

"As have we," said one of the brothers. "And we are happy to offer our charity to our less talented and much poorer younger brother. And the other spoils to boot." He put his hand round the backside of a girl standing next to him and squeezed. She responded with a squeal and a giggle, trying to wrench herself free in a playful fashion.

Pearce's brother responded by pulling her closer. "Don't be a tease," he said. Even from a distance I could smell the alcohol on his breath. "You have tasted our hospitality, now let us taste yours."

I found myself at Pearce's side, unable to move, sensing the maelstrom of emotions whirling through his head. Knowing he should side with these cads—that blood was thicker than water and they were responsible for paying his way in the army and giving him the funds he needed to buy his commission. Without their continued patronage, he could be trapped as an Ensign forever. Worse, he would be forced to leave and join the scores of other ex-soldiers struggling to make their way in a civilian world that was no longer theirs.

But could he stand by and watch an innocent person be abused by these beasts, even if they were his kin?

There was a shout and a screech and the brother reeled away from the girl, his hand to his cheek, blood running between his fingers from the scratch she had gouged there. "You bitch," he muttered, stepping towards her.

In a flash, the girl's face shifted to that of Kate's, staring back with that amused defiance that she wore so well. Then Pearce was upon his brother, pulling him away, the merry gathering descending into noise and confusion around us as I fought to regain my senses. I had allowed myself to be pulled into his vision: I needed to retain my perspective.

"Pearce," I said, my voice sounding reedy and hollow. "Albert."

The scene shifted sickeningly fast around us, grass turning to mud and stone, blue skies to black, a girl in front of us, pounding the streets, her cheeks stained with tears as she ran from some unseen horror. A slightly older soldier—a Lieutenant now—stopped and comforted her. My breath caught in my throat as I saw that it was a young Kate, warily accepting charity from the concerned Lieutenant Pearce. Deep down I had known that they were acquainted before my own path had crossed with Pearce's for the first time in Windsor, when Andras had attempted to conjure Hell on Earth. But I had always assumed that Pearce's knowledge of Kate had been as a client of her services when she had walked the streets. This suggested something more proper, more intimate almost. I stepped around them, straining to hear what was being said to better understand the relationship they had.

With a jolt, I realised that I was again being lured by a vision that was not my own, a clever trick-within-a-trick that the Warlocks had weaved to keep us ensnared. I shook my head and stepped between them, facing Pearce.

"Pearce," I said, then louder: "Captain Pearce! Focus on me!"

He frowned, at first looking through me but then starting to pay attention, like recalling a half-remembered dream.

"That's it," I said. As soon as the words had passed my lips he seemed to slip away and I felt a rising panic. I had no idea how much time I had already wasted; at any moment the Warlocks could be upon our bodies while they rested insensate in the Citadel and all would be lost.

I punched him, hard, across his jaw.

Even though I knew that none of this was real, my hand still hurt like Hell. Pearce looked at me with a look of surprised rage and the scene melted away from around us. "What…?" he asked.

"None of this is real," I said. "You are trapped in a vision created by Warlocks. You need to wake up: now." He glared back at me in confusion and so I hit him again. "Wake up!"

He opened his mouth and then popped out of existence. The world started to suck itself into oblivion around me, the parasitic vision no longer having anything to feed on. I did not know what would happen if I stayed there while everything disappeared, and had no desire to find out. I saw a door in front of me and dived through it.

I landed in Hell.

The world around me was wrong, twisted, corrupted. Even though I had never before seen that place I knew it was a foul shadow of whatever it had once been. Byron had described it to me once: *Tir na nÓg*, the home of the Pooka. His face had had a wondrous radiance to it as he had spoken of its fantastical spires and luscious fields and golden sunsets—all of which had been burned and plundered by the Almadites.

I knew which vision was plaguing Byron and had no desire to witness the pain that had scarred my friend so badly. But I knew I had no choice.

I ran down a hill made of shattered rocks and bones. My foot caught on something and a child's rag doll went flying through the air. *None of this is real*, I told myself as I ploughed on towards the group of people milling around listlessly before me. In their midst was a familiar figure, bent over and pleading with a small creature before him.

"It's me," Byron said, trying to smile reassuringly but still projecting nothing but pain. "Please say you recognise me."

The child in front of him stared back blankly while her fellows wandered about like little more than cattle, devoid of purpose or any form of sentience.

I squatted down beside my friend. "Byron," I said softly. "You need to wake up; none of this is real, my friend."

He turned to look at me through eyes filled with tears. "I

know," he said. "But I cannot help but try once more. A part of me hopes that maybe..." He shrugged, turning back to the child and giving her cheek one last stroke before standing up. Released from her interrogation, the girl wandered away aimlessly.

"So now you see it with your own eyes," he said. "What Andras did to my people. What his kind do when they conquer a world." He looked around and said, softly: "They were my family once."

"Byron..." I said again.

"I know." With one final breath, it was as though he no longer chose to see the painful picture around us. "This is some form of illusion created by the Warlocks, I presume?"

"It is. We have each been trapped in our own form of Hell. I managed to break free and so..."

"Augustus Potts to the rescue once more, eh?" he said. "Forgive me for tarrying, but it has been so long since I last saw them. Even though a part of me knew this for what it is, I could not bear to tear myself away."

"I suspect that that is a part of the spell they wove to ensnare you," I said. "Now, you should awaken while I go to Joshua."

He shook his head. "I should come with you. Joshua has a number of... surprising powers. He may be more than a match for you alone in his current condition."

I opened my mouth to argue but shrugged as I saw the sense in his words. Maybe two of us would be able to awaken him even quicker. I turned to see a door hanging in the air before us. "Let us get this over with then."

The sensation was not unlike being incredibly drunk. The world spun around us every which way it cared, shifting speed and direction without concern for our senses or stomachs. In the rare, precious moments that the motion slowed I could make out snippets of a life from Joshua's perspective, some scenes I recognised but many more I of course did not.

In the centre of this madness stood Joshua, in front of a high-backed chair in which sat his mother. I did not need to listen in to understand what was being said or the emotions running between the two of them.

I stumbled as I tried to make my way forward, saved from falling headlong by Byron. "Good grief," I managed.

"Indeed," Byron said. "It would appear that our young friend is in rather a desperate state."

We made our way towards him, leaning into each other for support as we were reduced to little more than two drunks in the midst of that swirling landscape. "Joshua!" I shouted as we approached.

A harsh admonishment from his mother elicited a mournful sob from our friend, which in turn found physical form in a gale that blasted us from our feet. I struggled upright and looked round to see that Byron had been thrown a dozen yards away. He gestured for me to continue as he started forwards and so I pressed on to Joshua. I reached out to put a hand on his shoulder and was swatted aside by an unseen hand, landing with a force that expelled the breath from my body.

I lay there, winded, a part of me wondering at how I could experience such things even though my body was nowhere near this place. No sooner had I started to consider this than my mind wandered over the possibility that maybe the physical symptoms I was experiencing were a direct result of some actions in the real world. Maybe the Warlocks had found us and at that very moment were dragging us off to some dungeon, or simply choking the life from our bodies.

The thought gave me renewed impetus and I pulled myself upright, only to be faced with a figure that made me shout in shock and fear. Lexie's cadaverous face grinned at me, blood seeping from the gaping wound in her torso from which her life had flowed. I tried to step around her but she kept pace with me, always there two steps in front.

"Joshua!" Byron called out, and I looked past Lexie to see him approaching our friend. Then the dead sister's face filled my vision once more.

"Lexie," I said to the figure. "I am so sorry, but we need to help your brother right now." She cocked her head to one side as I continued: "Your brother is in danger. I wish that we could help you, but… I know you are not really here. This is all Joshua's vision." The words solidified into an idea that made me feel light-headed. "I am talking to you right now Joshua, am I not? This is all you, all of this. Listen to me: we are in great danger. You need to wake up now or…"

"I will join Lexie?" Joshua's voice came from Lexie's lips. "Maybe that is what I want. After all, what is left for me in my world?"

"We are," I heard Byron say, addressing the other avatar of Joshua. "Your friends. Your mother."

Both Joshua and Lexie shook their heads in unison. "Not enough." Then Lexie's eyes in front of me lost their focus, as though she were seeing something between us, before she winked out of existence.

"Interesting," breathed Joshua, and then the world pitched and threw itself headlong into the abyss.

I found myself lying down on a hard floor. "Are we…?" I asked, looking around and seeing everyone gathered around me: Byron, Pearce, Mama and Joshua.

"Free of the visions?" asked Byron. "No, not quite. We are in a fresh one, aren't we Joshua?"

"Not fresh," he replied. "Old. Very, very old." He turned and gestured to the shadows, where I could just make out the form of Andras.

The demon was chained up, held aloft and spread-eagled, his limbs stretched to the four winds. He was indistinct and distorted, as though we were viewing him through a heat haze that ebbed and blossomed as we watched. His face and body contorted in impossibly fast jerking motions, as if electricity was passing through him.

"Why am I here?" asked Pearce. "I thought I had awoken."

"You had," said Joshua. "But it is only fair that you witness this."

I looked at Mama. "I did not think that you could join our visions," I remarked. "You said that the Warlocks' spells did not affect you in the same way as us."

"That is correct," she said. "I should not be here."

"I wanted you to tell us the truth," said Joshua.

"We do not have time for this folly," she snapped. "Every moment that we delay here the Warlocks get that little bit closer. Do you wish to die?"

Joshua laughed, a cold and mirthless sound that echoed around us. "Ask my friends here and they will tell you that such an outcome does not hold quite as much fear for me as it might for others."

"Joshua, please," I said. "We need—"

"We need to hear the truth," he interrupted, turning back to Mama. "Tell them. You knew this would happen to us—you planned it."

She glared at him and then shrugged. "What of it? It has served its purpose: the Almadite is ensnared." She gestured at Andras. "All of this also serves a wider purpose: the Warlocks will be distracted. My people will be able to do what needs to be done."

"Which is what?" asked Byron.

"The first steps to our freedom," Mama replied. "The overthrow of the Four Kings."

"That's great," I replied. "We want the same thing. But we need to free our friend first."

Mama shook her head. "Andras was right: she is lost."

"But you said—" Pearce said, storming forward.

"I spoke the truth, all of the way through," she glared at us defiantly. "I did not contradict Andras when he spoke the truth, that she was lost as soon as she entered this place. You were the ones who decided to press on regardless."

"He knew," I said, watching Andras' writhing form. "He tried to warn us."

"No," said Joshua. "He only wanted to save his own skin, as always. This is still the way to find Kate, but it is more than that, is it not?"

Mama frowned at him. "I have no idea what you mean."

"Yes you do," said Joshua. "You know what state our friend will be in when we find her, and you also know how we can cure her." When she stared at him in open astonishment he grinned and tapped his head. "I saw everything while I was being afflicted by the Warlocks' spell, all of your visions. But I was also able to span the divide to your head, Mama. I know your thoughts too, and what you intend, how we can all help each other."

"That is not possible," she muttered, holding her hands up.

"Problem is," said Byron, "that the extent of young Joshua's powers never cease to amaze me."

"And so you know what we need, and what I am going to do," Joshua continued, staring levelly at Mama. "And you know why we need Andras."

Mama's mouth opened and closed a few times before she nodded her head with a steely glint in her eyes. "It could work even better, a much broader distraction. Very well."

"Good," said Joshua. "I was hoping you wouldn't make me threaten to trap you here with Andras if you didn't help." He gestured towards the writhing demon. "Shall we?"

Mama nodded and they both turned and walked to where Andras was being held. A sibilant chanting filled our ears before the world exploded in a painful flash of light.

We found ourselves back in the corridor, blinking and rubbing our heads.

"Are we awake now?" I asked.

"Very much so," said Joshua. He nodded to Mama. "You know what needs to be done. Take them there; I will be back." Before we could react, he mouthed a series of words and I felt my runic sword hum in unison with the spell that transported him from that place.

We stared at the empty space where he had just been standing.

"He can do that?" I asked. "Why didn't he just pop open a portal right where we needed to go, rather than us having to do all of this the time-consuming way?"

"Because," said Andras, "that is akin to blowing a very loud horn announcing our existence to every creature with magical powers in this building. And there are a lot of them. We need to move quickly. Now."

Chapter Twelve

I felt the oppressive atmosphere close in on me the further we ran, finding myself jumping at shadows as I imagined them stocked full of demons and revenants waiting for us to drop our guard so they could devour us. There had been no time to question where Joshua had gone or formulate some kind of plan; the only option we could see was to keep moving lest we be ensnared once more.

The corridor looped around impossibly again and again until we finally came upon the entrance to a large antechamber. In point of fact, 'large' was a term completely unsuited to describing the cavernous space that we now found ourselves at the threshold of, for sounds did not bounce and echo around as much as stretch away into infinity, as though we were at the top of the tallest mountain. Walls and ceiling were lost to us in the distance, and yet they were also close enough that I felt we could cross the space in a matter of minutes. I blinked and shook my head; if I had a lifetime in that place I would still not be able to comprehend the physics that held sway there.

"Where now?" asked Pearce.

Mama pointed with shaking fingers to our right. "Over there," she said.

Andras nodded. "The Birthing Chamber, where the subjects

for conversion are stored and observed."

I looked around. "Am I the only one slightly unnerved that there is no one here?" I asked. "Given that by now they must know of our presence, should there not be at least a few guards milling around and getting in our way?"

"You misunderstand the nature of the Warlocks," said Andras. "They do not see the need for physical security when they have such an impressive amount of magical tools at their disposal."

I shrugged. "But we broke through them, didn't we?"

"We did, and that is hopefully something they did not foresee, which should hopefully buy us some time so we can rescue Kate and then get out of here. Hopefully."

"There are a few too many 'hopefullys' in there for my liking," I muttered.

"It is what it is," snapped Pearce. "Let's go." He darted out of our meagre cover in the direction that Mama had indicated. Wordlessly, we followed.

It was a peculiar sensation, making our way through that cavernous space. The lack of perspective or any landmarks meant that it was nigh on impossible to gauge our progress and I had the unsettling sensation that I was running through a dream. Eventually the structure hove into view, and a short time later we came to a halt in front of it.

It was a rectangular, cabin-like construction with a windowed wall facing us, interrupted only by a large door inlaid with symbols and a large cog mechanism attached to a lever. Through the glazing we could see three figures strapped to the walls, each of them wearing a long, shapeless white robe. Around them spun and shifted what I at first took to be Aetheric mist but on closer inspection I could make out shrieking skulls and malefic eyes within the swirling forms. I took an involuntary step backwards as I realised that these were the Wraiths that created the Mages from innocent flesh.

"There," said Pearce, nodding at the figure on the left. I gasped as I made out the form of Kate, her face pale and drawn, lips pulled back in a silent scream as she struggled against whatever battles were being fought within her mind and body.

"The Wraiths," I pointed out to him. "They are outside, not inside their host bodies. Maybe we're not too late?"

He grunted. "In any case we should move quickly before we are discovered."

"Too late," said Andras from behind us.

We turned to see the Warlocks starting to materialise. At first there was just one, on its own a sight to chill the blood. It solidified into existence to the side of the Birthing Chamber, malevolent eyes glaring at us from a round face. In spite of the situation I found myself surprised by the creature's condition; I had become accustomed to fighting demons and the ones we had always encountered were battle-hardened, muscular and toned. This creature, by contrast, showed all the signs of a softer life, much less used to exercise. Its arms were grotesque in their size and shape, reaching out from a body that quivered with roll upon roll of fat. The Warlock regarded us hungrily as others shimmered into existence around us, a crowd of Almadites beginning to fill the room.

"Andras," boomed a voice. "Do not be a fool. You of all people should know the risks involved in breaching the Chamber before the appointed time." A familiar figure stepped forwards through the throng of Warlocks.

"My dear old friend Gaap," replied Andras, his voice dripping with malice. "I had hoped that you had perished after our last meeting, possibly executed for gross incompetence. But then again, that never seems to happen, does it? I wonder why."

"We achieved our objective," Gaap said, stepping from the ranks of Warlocks. "Do not forget: we always play the long game."

"As do I," said Andras.

We glared at Gaap, the demon that had once impersonated Maxwell's doctor to kidnap my brother. He had then compounded this crime by using a Mage to force my brother to create the portal through which the Almadites had attempted to invade our world. Gaap was the lackey of the Four Kings, their right-hand and a manipulative schemer who had turned our friend and ally N'yotsu back into the demon Andras, and then used his Mage to almost kill us all. Worse: he had commanded the creature that had killed Lexie.

I nodded to Pearce and he put his hand on the lever set in the door.

"Don't!" barked Gaap.

I looked round and noted that he and the other Almadites had taken a step backward. "They are scared," I breathed.

"With good reason," said Mama, appearing at my side. "You see those Wraiths in there? They are hungry for living flesh to inhabit. If the door is opened without the proper precautions, they will swarm out here, and…" She paused, and then shrugged.

I looked at the creatures inside the Chamber. They were milling around behind the glass and pressing against the door, clearly sensing that something was about to happen and keen to take quick advantage when it did. I shuddered, remembering what I had seen such creatures do to people back in my own world, the devastation they could wreak on living flesh. And yet…

"The Wraiths I previously encountered always made short work of their victims," I said. "They ripped away their souls and sucked the flesh from their bones in seconds. And yet Kate and those others in there seem still whole."

"That is because *these* Wraiths have been bound to act as parasites, not predators," she said. "But such an action is against their nature and so they are very *very* upset, to say the least." She looked back to Gaap and the Warlocks. "That is why they are afraid."

Gaap laughed, a mite uneasily to my ears. "You underestimate us, Slave. I would remind you that you are a lot closer to the Chamber than we are. If you were to open the door then you would be the first to be attacked. Surrender yourselves now and the Four Kings may choose to be lenient."

Andras pulled out a pocket watch and examined it. "Tempting, but no," he said, snapping it shut and then licking a finger and holding it in the air as though testing the direction of the wind. "I think you are the ones running out of time. Captain Pearce, get ready to open the door on my command."

"But the Wraiths?" asked Pearce, his eyes flicking over the glass.

Mama stepped over to Andras. "Do you remember our deal?" she asked.

He nodded. "I do."

"Swear a blood oath. Now."

He sighed. "Really, do you think that this is the time?"

"I do not trust you, Almadite."

Andras laughed. "Trust? You were the one who betrayed me just a few moments ago!"

"Then we are even." She glared at him and he relented with a resigned shake of his head. He ran one of the clawed fingers from his right hand across his left wrist, causing a line of black blood to bead on his skin. He glanced nervously at the Chamber as the Wraiths grew more agitated at the sight and muttered a series of phrases that I could not comprehend. Mama held out her own left wrist and Andras deftly—almost gently—scored a cut there also. After muttering a further series of phrases of her own she pressed her wound to Andras' so that their blood flowed together. I felt that I was witnessing something profoundly intimate, which was over as soon as it had begun.

Mama stepped away and nodded at Andras, blood dripping from her wound. "Then it is done. I believe it is about time, don't you?"

Andras looked at her for a moment and I thought that I could perceive something that approached sorrow in his eyes. Then it was gone, as he cocked his head and pulled out the pocket watch once more.

"Captain Pearce," he barked, "you will open the door on the

count of three."

"No," hissed Gaap. "You fools. You will all be killed. The Four Kings will—"

Andras held up a finger to quieten the Almadite and glanced back at Mama. "One condition: you leave Gaap for me. I have need of him."

"Agreed," she said in a firm voice completely at odds with her shaking body. "I am ready now. Do not delay any further please."

"Of course," Andras said, holding his pocket watch up to the light. "Captain Pearce: three, two…"

I felt my sword tremble with the familiar warm energy of a magical spell in the offing. But not just any spell: this was the same vibration I felt whenever Joshua summoned a portal.

"One!" shouted Andras, throwing himself at Gaap.

Pearce pulled down on the lever and the mechanism of cogs and wheels that it was connected to started to whir and turn; an unstoppable dance had been put into motion that would no doubt end in our deaths. Pearce threw himself to the side around the corner of the Chamber.

I felt a tug on my sword arm and allowed myself to be pulled out of harm's way by Byron.

Mama was now standing alone in front of the door to the Chamber, her arms held aloft as dark, slick blood dripped to the floor. The door swung violently open and the Wraiths screamed out, a curtain of malevolent fog that streamed towards her.

I opened my mouth to shout a warning to her, but the shrieks of terror instead came from the Warlocks. I looked around to see some of them starting to weave magical spells in the air and my sword's agitation grew as a result. A few of them looked at their hands in wonder, as though they were achieving much more than they had expected.

Andras grabbed Gaap and pulled him aside, mere seconds before the Juggernaut popped into existence, sliding across the hall from left to right and carving a bloody path through the ranks of those Warlocks unfortunate enough to be standing in its way.

I let out a whoop of victory as I saw Joshua at the helm, his face set in a determined grimace. Then I remembered the Chamber, the Wraiths, Kate.

Mama stood rigid in front of us, her arms stretched to either side as the Wraiths swarmed in and around her, drawn to the fresh blood and open wound. As I watched, a couple of strands twisted away, tempted by the carnage that the Juggernaut had created. A nearby wounded Warlock saw this and screamed, dragging himself backwards across the ground as the Wraith reached for him.

A flicker of movement at the Chamber entrance caught my attention. Pearce ran inside and pulled at the bindings that held Kate in place against the wall. I sprinted to help him, using the point of my sword to slice through the rope at her ankles and waist. Pearce released her final wrist restraints and she slid limply on top of him.

He hoisted her onto his shoulder and started out of the Chamber. I followed, wondering if we should do something to assist the other two poor creatures. They were both pale and emaciated demons, not unlike the Slaves we had seen in the market earlier. One of them opened an eye and what I saw in there made me back away in shock, for they were pits of despair and loathing, greedily seeking me out. I quickly decided that the other victims were lost and hurried after Pearce, hoping that Kate was not as far gone as they clearly were.

We ran around Mama, who was locked in a horrifying battle against the Wraiths that besieged her ravaged body. I wanted to help but I knew that, however powerful it was, my sword was little more than a toy to those creatures.

"There's no time," said Byron, pulling me onwards. "She has made her choice; let's not waste the chance she's buying us. Come on!"

With one last glance back, I ran after my friends and leapt up into the cab of the Juggernaut. Andras was pinning a struggling Gaap against the far corner, while Joshua was already starting the incantations that set my sword pulsating anew. Pearce was lowering Kate's motionless form gently to the vehicle's floor.

A clang like the chiming of a thousand bells rang out, heralding the appearance of four vast shapes at the far end of the room, silhouetted in the light from the now-open doorway. Gaap laughed hysterically as they approached us, four huge demons mounted on dragon-like beasts. "Now you're done for!" crowed Gaap. "The Four Kings are upon us!"

Andras punched Gaap in the face as I gaped at the creatures making their unhurried way across the vast space. The Four Kings: Asmoday, Abaddon, Bileth and Belial—names that had haunted entire species since the dawn of civilisation. The evil and capricious rulers of Almadel, and Andras' mortal enemies.

"It's about time," Andras shouted to them. "I was beginning to think you'd never get here." He turned to Joshua. "That should give you the extra energy you need: can you feel it?"

"I can," he said, his face lit up with a fiery energy. "I have never felt so much power. But how…?"

"There will be time to explain later," said Andras. "Just take us there before that lot try to disembowel us!"

Joshua bent over and recommenced his chanting. My sword vibrated so much in response to the incantations that I feared it was trying to shake itself loose of my grasp. Gaap let out a low moan as the world melted away from around us.

The darkness of the Aether folded into existence on all sides of the Juggernaut, but before we could settle into the accustomed terrifying inertia of that space, everything jerked and whirled around us. My breath was pummelled from my body by a gale that beat at every fibre of my being, pushing me out and through the very fabric of reality.

The runic sword was a blur in my hands as it reacted to this fresh, strong magic, a frantic motion that made my wrists and forearm ache with a red-hot pain. I dared not release it, though, in case it spun off into the void to be lost forever.

I had the sensation of being undone. I realised that I knew where I had felt that feeling before: when Andras had started to tear my soul from my body all those years ago. What trickery was this? Had Joshua not been able to spirit us away in time before the Four Kings reached us? Or was this the work of the Wraiths that we had released from the Chamber?

Then, after both mere seconds and a whole eternity of that unbearable sensation, it was over. We collapsed, dazed, to the reassuringly solid floor of the Juggernaut.

"Where are we?" I gasped. "Is this the Aether?"

"No," said Andras. "We are beyond the Aether. Way beyond it." His voice sounded thin and shrill in the emptiness.

Gaap tried to fight his way past Andras, staring wide-eyed around us. As Andras struggled to pin him back to the side of the cabin, Gaap managed to gasp: "The Druj! You fool, you have doomed us all."

Andras finally managed to subdue the demon, silencing him by pressing his hand firm against Gaap's throat before turning to shake his head at us.

Joshua rose to his feet as I looked questioningly at them both.

"We've made it," said Joshua with a broad, triumphant grin on his face. "This is the afterlife."

Chapter Thirteen

For a moment, we stared at him in mute disbelief.

"You mean the afterlife as in the spirit world?" asked Pearce. "As in the Aether?"

"No," said Joshua. "At one point, Maxwell hypothesised that the Aether was the spirit world, but that is not quite accurate. Some unfortunate spirits get trapped in the Aether, but that is not the same as the spirit world itself." He swept an arm around us. "No. This is the actual afterlife, where all our mortal souls will find their final resting place."

"What?" Byron, Pearce and I shouted together.

I straightened up and peered out of the Juggernaut. We were perched in the middle of a grey wasteland, a featureless expanse that stretched all around us. A sickly wind plucked at my skin, carrying with it a faint odour of decay. I looked up at what first seemed to be a night sky, but the longer I gazed at it the stronger the feeling grew that I was in fact staring into a void. However, this was more than the blackness of space that we were accustomed to seeing in our own night sky. Instead it was an all-pervading emptiness: devoid of clouds, stars or any form of celestial bodies. It was even more than the blankness of the Aether, for that was populated with the mist and the creatures that dwelt there and bounded by the various realms, of which ours was just one. My mind swirled as I looked up into a blankness beyond human comprehension, for I instinctively wanted to populate it and build walls in and around that emptiness. It was not just that I could not see anything above us: *there was simply nothing there to see, ever.* I couldn't tell if it ended 10 feet above my head or stretched on to the far reaches of outer space.

I shivered as I tore my eyes from the darkness above and the desert around us, back to the comparative warmth of the Juggernaut's small cabin.

"How did you even manage to do this?" Byron asked, looking around. "Are you sure? You do not have the power to be able to achieve such a thing. No one does."

"I always thought so too," grinned Joshua. "But Andras showed me…"

I rounded on Andras. "You," I snarled. "I knew your pretence at being on our side was too good to be true. What fiendish scheme is this?"

Andras held up one hand, the other still engaged in pinning Gaap's neck firmly against the side of the Juggernaut's footwell. "I mean no ill feeling. Please do not doubt my bona fides," he said.

"We need to go back to Earth right now," said Pearce, a steely edge in his voice that I fancied could cut through stone. "Kate needs urgent medical attention."

I was still glaring at Andras. "You have not changed, have you?" I said, the anger rising in me. "All this time you have been cultivating Joshua, moulding him to your own ends."

Andras shook his head. "You wanted to save Kate. Taking her straight back to your realm would just doom her, and all of you for that matter."

"Explain."

"She has been infected," said Andras in a low voice. "There is a Wraith in her, slowly turning her inside out. If it is allowed to continue unchecked then… well, there would not be a Kate to rescue. Instead, you would have a Mage on your hands, and you really don't want that."

I looked at Kate's inert form lying cradled in Pearce's arms. I shuddered involuntarily as I remembered the Mage we met all those months ago and how it had wormed its way into my head, at first commanding me to kill my friend and then, once that was done, to kill myself. I could still feel the cold firmness of its touch inside my mind as it took control over every aspect of me, forcing my body to do the one thing that is most alien to any living body: to shut down completely.

"But surely Kate would not…" I attempted.

Andras shook his head. "Once the Wraith finishes its work, there won't be anything left of the person you once knew, or even anything human at all. I am assuming, of course, that there is still enough of Kate remaining in that body to rescue."

We glared at him, the silence broken only by a strangled cackle from Gaap as he wriggled to gain a degree of release from Andras' grip on his neck. "You fools," he crowed in a choked voice. "We will all die here in the Druj; you will kill us all…"

Andras shook his head and, in an almost offhand manner, pulled Gaap up before slamming the demon's head hard against the metal interior of the Juggernaut. He released his grip, allowing Gaap's unconscious body to slide to the floor as the sound of the impact echoed around us.

I could not help but nod my relief at Gaap's incapacitation, although Andras' keenness to silence him raised my suspicious. "He mentioned that word when we first arrived: the Druj. What does that mean?"

Andras straightened up and wiped his hands, as though he had just completed a messy piece of housework. "He is mistaken. The Druj is the Almadite equivalent of what you would term limbo, somewhere beyond even the afterlife. It is where gods go to die. Somewhere you would never wish to venture."

"So not here then?" I asked.

"Definitely not here," said Andras. "It would require much greater power than even Joshua has at his disposal right now."

I frowned at him. He seemed to be keeping too many things far too close to his chest for my liking.

"How do we cure Kate, then?" asked Pearce, bringing the subject back to the matter at hand before I could ask any more questions.

"That is if you really are telling us the truth," I commented tartly.

"Oh come now, Gus," snapped Andras. "I appreciate that I have not been the most reliable ally in the world, but it is time for you to stop this self-indulgent whining." He held up a hand to prevent my outraged response. "We need to act before this here," he gestured at Kate, "becomes a Mage. You of all people will know how disastrously that turn of events will work out for us all." I struggled to find a suitable retort, settling for fixing my steeliest glare on him.

"The process of creating a Mage is commonly believed to be irreversible," continued Andras, "however, Mama did tell me of one way that a cure can be achieved; or at least, how we can expel the Wraith from her body."

"And that is why we are here," said Joshua.

"How did you get involved in Andras' plans?" Byron asked him. "I do not recall you two having any conferences."

"The vision in the Citadel," Joshua replied. "At the end, as you all were making your way back to reality, Mama, Andras and I were together. They told me what I needed to do—to get the Juggernaut and bring us all to the afterlife."

"And this is where your cure is?" Pearce asked Andras.

"Once a Wraith has taken residence, no mortal means can be used to expel it," said Andras. "Therefore, we needed to come somewhere decidedly not mortal. Mama told us of a resident here who has the power to be able to expel the demon."

"Take us there," said Pearce. "Now."

"Of course," said Andras. "First of all, we need to make sure that our friend Gaap here does not cause any mischief." He rummaged in an inner pocket of his coat and pulled out a length of chain and a hank of rope.

I frowned in surprise. "Where did all of that come from?" I asked.

He blinked at me. "My pockets. Why: what do you keep in yours?" He bent over Gaap and proceeded to truss the demon up, securing his arms to his body but leaving his legs free. I winced as I watched Andras pull the bindings so tight that it seemed to verge on the tortuous. I would have felt sorry for the prisoner, were it not for the fact of who he was and what he represented. As a final flourish, Andras wound a rope around the demon's mouth to form a gag, leaving a length dangling free to serve as a leash.

"Are we safe with that fiend?" asked Byron.

Andras laughed. "We are not safe here, with or without Gaap. In any case, all of this is merely a precaution. Gaap cannot escape here without us and he would not want to risk being trapped in this place."

"Why did you bring him anyway?" asked Byron.

"You know what they say: keep your friends close and your enemies closer."

"Then what does that make us?"

Andras grinned and tapped a clawed finger to his nose. "Now, a few ground rules. You are all still wearing the trinkets I gave you prior to entering Almadel, yes? Good. They are even more important here: the sights in this realm would not just drive you insane. If you were to glimpse this place in all of its glory then the shock would kill you. Literally. On the spot."

I opened my mouth and, in answer to my unasked question, Andras held out a similar amulet that was now around his own neck. "There are sights here that no living creature should ever bear witness to," he said, "no matter how powerful they are." He examined his pocket watch. "There is a limit to the amount of time that we can safely spend here: too long and no amounts of magic would be able to spirit us back home. Or at least, not without consequences."

"How long?" asked Pearce.

"Time as you know it is without meaning here. Suffice to say that we should make haste." He gave Gaap a swift clout across the side of his head and the demon's eyes flashed open, muffled grunts emanating from behind his makeshift gag as he struggled against his bindings. Andras pulled on the rope leash, forcing Gaap to his feet. "You have a choice," Andras said to him. "Come along with us, do not cause any trouble, and you stand a chance of getting back to the land of the living at some point. Otherwise, we will just leave you here."

Gaap glared pure venom back at him.

"Good boy," grinned Andras, turning and stepping down to the ground, landing on the dirt with a muffled thud. Yanked along by his leash, Gaap was pulled out of the vehicle after him, landing in a heap on the floor. Andras did not bother to hide the pleasure on his face as he watched him writhe his way back upright. "Oh, and one last thing," said Andras, addressing us once again. "Probably the most important: do not under any circumstances eat or drink anything from here. Do not accept food or liquids, no matter how much you may think you need it or how tempting it looks."

"What happens if we do?" I asked, suddenly developing a thirst.

"You will be trapped here forever," he said simply. "Otherwise known as dying in a very irreversible way." He started off towards the featureless horizon without checking whether we were following.

*

It took a great effort of will to follow Andras and Gaap away from the sanctuary of the Juggernaut but, emboldened by each other's presence, we proceeded cautiously. I could not shake off an intense feeling of dread and despair, as though every breath spent in that place was drawing me closer to my grave.

Everything around us was muffled, and as a result I wondered if I was losing the use of my faculties.

My mental state was further impaired by the looming vast nothingness above our heads; I had never before realised how much I had been reassured by the existence of something above me, even just a cloud, the colours in the sky or even a distant star. The void in this place pressed down on me, making me question the point of anything and everything. Worse than that: it seemed hungry, sucking the energy, life and hope out of anything and everything beneath it.

I tried to distract myself by focusing my attention on what passed for the land around us. At first I had despaired at the futility of our trek as I regarded that unending bleakness: surely it would take us forever to reach any form of civilisation—or whatever passed for such a concept in that godforsaken place.

We had, though, been walking for only a few moments when the landscape shifted to reveal features and objects around us, as though they were rising out of a thick fog. From the blank desolation my fevered mind perceived a graveyard melting into existence, row after row of old, lichen-covered slabs.

Once again I found my focus drawn up to the sky, a blank expanse that oppressed us and made everything seem utterly pointless, ready to suck us all into oblivion.

No. Focus on the gravestones. Never had such a sight seemed so welcoming to me. I noticed that the scene stretched out to the horizon, punctuated by the occasional mausoleum. There was no church in that godless place, for to accept the existence of God was to accept the existence of hope.

I remarked on the environment to Byron, who grunted. "The effects of the amulet on your senses, no doubt: acclimatising to everything around us and painting a picture for you to comprehend whilst remaining sane."

"Interesting," I breathed, forcing my curiosity to overcome the barely-contained panic caused by the unasked question that my mind screamed at me: What about the sky??

I shook my head to clear my thoughts. "So we each have different experiences here, then. What do you see?"

Byron shook his head. "Best we do not confuse ourselves with each other's perceptions. If I tell you I can see a thing at odds with your own vision, it could make you question your own senses and as a result the amulet might stop working. Just accept what you see, for the sake of your sanity if nothing else."

I nodded, reluctantly. "But I see gravestones and a mausoleum around us."

Byron shrugged, as though every word was a struggle in that place.

"If we are in the afterlife, the place where dead souls go, then why do I see gravestones?"

"Just as in Almadel, all that you experience here is a direct result of your own perceptions, combined with the powers of the pendant around your neck. If you see a graveyard then that must be how you expect the afterlife to appear, maybe?"

I frowned. "I know I'm not the best Christian—" in response to Byron's knowing sideways glance, I added: "Or any form of Christian whatsoever, but I would have hoped that at least my imagination would have conjured up somewhere a mite more… heavenly than this."

Byron snorted weakly. "Expecting to go to Heaven, are we?"

I gestured around us. "Even Hell is surely more interesting and less barren than this place?"

I looked over at Pearce who was carrying Kate over his shoulder, eyes fixed firmly on Andras' back as though he were expecting or even hoping that the demon would betray us at any moment.

"How about I carry her for a while?" I asked, moving over to him. "Give you a rest."

"No," he said. "I am fine. She is no burden." His steely tone of voice did not welcome any further offer.

Instead, I turned to Joshua. He was more alert and—dare I say it?—more cheerful than I had seen him in a long time.

"How are you feeling?" I asked. "Quite a feat, as I understand it, managing to bring us here."

"Indeed it is," he said with a smile. "The final frontier. I never really believed that I could reach this place."

"No," said Byron, an edge to his voice. "You should not have been able to."

"And yet here we are." He turned to me, his eyes glinting. "It is such a shame that Maxwell cannot be here with us: he would relish the opportunity to explore this strange place."

"I believe you are right," I said, imagining him setting up experiment after experiment, heedless of the need to hurry or leave. I felt a shock of amusement tinged with fear at the thought. In my mind's eye I could see the arguments we would have, the near-misses as we rushed to escape before we were trapped there forever.

While I had been thinking my eyes had once more been drawn to the blankness overhead. I cursed. Why did the amulet not allow me to imagine something comforting up there, like a sunset or even storm clouds? Anything but that void.

I tore my eyes back to Joshua's eager face. "You seem rather… invigorated," I noted. "Given the circumstances but also… aren't you normally drained after working your magic?"

He raised an eyebrow, a smile playing on his lips as though he had not even considered such a thing until that moment. "Usually I am, yes. Although since I rescued you all in the Juggernaut I have felt almost like I have untapped an unfathomable well of energy available to me." He shrugged. "I suppose it must be the adrenaline of the situation."

"No," said Byron. "That's not quite it, is it Andras?"

The other demon turned and smiled, effecting a show of innocence. "Whatever do you mean?"

"Bringing us here is something that should not be possible, no matter how strong Joshua has become. Only the old gods had the power to perform such a feat, and steps were taken many millennia ago to ensure that such abilities were kept beyond the reach of anyone."

Andras held up a hand and pointed. "We wait there," he said, pointing to a squat building just ahead of us. "There will be time to talk later."

We followed him towards what appeared to be (to my eyes at least) a mausoleum, a rectangular stone structure cornered by thick round Greco-Roman-style pillars. The building had the appearance of being weathered by wind and rain in spite of there being a distinct lack of anything approximating the elements in that place. A large statue of a mournful-looking angel mounted the front of the building, casting sorrowful eyes over a pair of imposing doors carved into the face of the stonework.

"Does anyone else think it strange that we have not encountered anyone here yet?" I asked. "If this is the afterlife, should it not be teeming with the souls of the departed?"

Andras clicked his fingers and pointed at me. "Excellent point. For once you have been paying attention, Mr Potts." He tied Gaap's leash to a steel hoop inlaid in the base of the mausoleum. "The reason we have not seen anyone else, or indeed anything, yet is because they are still sizing us up, trying to determine whether we are a threat or a snack."

I shivered. "What now?" I asked.

He pointed to the roof of the mausoleum. "We wait up there."

"And do what?" asked Pearce.

"Wait for them to come out."

"Why would they do that?"

Andras jabbed a thumb over his shoulder at Gaap. "Because we have brought along bait."

*

At first there was nothing, and I could tell that my exasperation was shared by the others. I glanced over at Kate's body. Most of the time she appeared to be sleeping, but every once in a while she would jerk and twist, the outward signs of whatever hideous battle was being waged within. We knew that every minute was precious, and yet we had no choice but to sit and wait out whatever scheme Andras had in mind.

Every time one of us attempted to glean more information from him, or to hurry things along, we were shushed into silence. I could tell that Pearce in particular was becoming more and more agitated, the man of action not suited to such a frustrating waiting game.

At first, Gaap had thrashed and moaned at us as best he could through his gag and bindings, but after a while he had subsided into sullen silence. Indeed, he looked as bored as the rest of us.

Joshua put a hand on my arm and pointed out into the distance. "Listen," he hissed.

I strained my senses, just about making out a faint whispering and shuffling, like a pair of light curtains being stirred by a gentle breeze in another room. Then a flurry of activity below me caught my attention: Gaap was scrabbling back towards the wall of the mausoleum as though he were trying to force himself into the cracks in the mortar.

"Good," muttered Andras.

I blinked and suddenly the mausoleum was surrounded by countless bodies, all stood motionless as they stared intently at Gaap, who was now in the throes of panic, making pained grunts and shrieks through his gag.

"Are we going to let them kill him?" Byron asked.

"Unfortunately not," said Andras, rising to his feet. "I have need of him yet. But he has got their attention." He clapped his hands three times, the noise making me jump with its harshness compared to the muted atmosphere that I had become accustomed to in that place. Cupping his hands to his mouth, Andras bellowed three strangulated words, the form and meaning of which escaped me as soon as they touched my ears.

At first the noise had no effect on the shuffling masses around us. I looked up at Andras and noted that he was supremely unconcerned by this fact, humming to himself as he surveyed the scene around us. He nodded and grinned at something and I turned to see the bodies in front of the mausoleum parting to reveal a dark, hunched figure that hobbled towards us. From our elevated position the creature appeared to be comprised solely of black frayed rags that had the appearance of feathers, such that I almost fancied it was the spirit of a large crow.

Andras stepped off the side of the roof and landed soundlessly in front of the figure.

"Who dares to call us?" asked the crow creature in a croaking whisper like a rusty gate being forced open.

"I bring one who has been tainted by a Wraith, inflicted on her by the Almadite Warlocks," said Andras, his tone of voice unusual in that it almost seemed to be showing respect.

"By your own people," noted the figure. When Andras refused to answer, it beckoned. "Show me."

Andras turned and signalled that we should bring Kate down to him. I glanced at Pearce, sharing his disquiet at exposing her to risk in her vulnerable state; but if Andras was correct about the looming—and decidedly lethal—deadline we faced, then we had little choice. I jumped down to the ground, warily glancing at the soundless creatures gathered around us. I held my hands out to collect Kate as she was lowered down to me, nodding to Pearce to confirm that he could release her. I held her close, surprised by how light and limp she was, as though the Wraith was eating her very essence from within. I looked down at a face which seemed to have been carved from porcelain. Only the faintest flicker of breath puckering her nostrils gave any sign that there was still life within her body. As I looked at her I realised that this was the closest I had been to her since the rescue, for Pearce had jealously guarded her up to that point.

I turned and stepped towards Andras and the dark figure, cradling Kate gently in my arms as I kept a wary eye on the motionless forms all around me. Pearce and the others hastened to accompany me and I was grateful for their presence, although the sheer numbers of the creatures present meant that we stood little chance if they did choose to attack us.

As we neared the dark figure I realised that it was in fact a hunched and bent old woman, smothered in long black feather-like coat. Her face was partly hidden by its cowl but what I could see reminded me of the withered old crone from the Grimm brothers' fairy tales, with a long, hook-like nose poking out from between two dark eyes.

She shuffled forwards and Andras nodded at me, his eyes urging me to stand firm. She peered at Kate, poking her cheek and using stick-like fingers to prise open her left eye. After a few moments of this examination the crone grunted. "I can release the Wraith from this body, but there will be a price."

"Do it," said Pearce.

"Wait," I said, mindful of the one-sided deals that otherworldly creatures tended to strike with unsuspecting mortals. "What is the price?"

"She will have been changed by the Wraith," croaked the old woman. "I cannot guarantee that she will be the same person you once knew. Separating a Wraith from its host is no simple task, and there is no telling what the creature will do when it is free. That is the risk you choose to take, and a burden that you will have to carry."

"That is a challenge we will face when and if we need to," said Byron. "But you mentioned a price for what you will do. What do you want?"

The crone nodded, a thin and hungry smile on her lips. "What we want is something you will never give us: release from this place and passage back to your realms. No, I will not waste time in demanding the impossible. All we ask is one thing. Our price is that you give us a vessel through which we can experience your realm."

"A vessel?" asked Joshua. "You have in mind some form of device or charm?"

"No," said Andras. "That is not what you are thinking at all, is it? You want a life. You seek a permanent possession of one of us."

The crone shrugged. "A life for a life: is that not a fair trade? I do this incredibly difficult and perilous task for you, and in return one of you will allow us to experience that which we cannot. You would still be resident in your own body, but you would share it with us." She swept her hand around at the silent multitude. "You could indeed think of it as akin to a possession. You would give us a new lease of life, literally."

"I will do it," said Pearce.

"Wait," said Byron. "You do not know what you are agreeing to."

"A chance to get Kate back, but in return I sacrifice my own life? That is a bargain I would strike in a heartbeat."

"It is not as simple as that," Byron persisted. "It could be a living Hell for you. We have no idea of their intentions when they get access to your realm through you."

Pearce turned to the crone. "You described it as a possession, correct?"

She nodded with a slowness that did not disguise her eagerness. "That would be the general form of it, yes."

"Would the process impede my faculties?"

"We will ensure that you are perfectly sane; it would be of no use to us if you wind up helpless or held in an asylum as a result."

"So you would be simple passengers and observers?"

"Not quite. We need to… influence events. Not all of the time, but we will not be an entirely passive participant."

I turned my head to mutter to Pearce as privately as was possible. "I do not like this," I said.

"I do not see that we have any alternative if we are to save Kate. In any case, possessions are not necessarily fatal in our world, are they?" He raised an eyebrow at me and our eyes met. In a flash I understood his thinking: there were priests who were known for expelling unwanted demonic possessions, and no doubt Joshua, Byron, Maxwell and Andras would also have methods of containing such a curse. But even so…

"You should not be the one to make this sacrifice," I said, uncertain of the words as they tumbled out of my mouth. "She is my friend as well, and I was there when she was taken. It is partly my fault that the Warlocks took her."

Pearce put a hand on my shoulder. "I admit that I felt that way too, that I was trying to blame you for what had happened. Truth be told, I do still feel some anger towards you."

"I can tell," I could not resist noting with a wry smile.

He nodded, the ghost of a smile playing across his own lips. "I apologise, but you need to understand that I care a great deal about her."

"As do we all."

He shook his head. "Not like me. Which is why I should be the one to do this."

My head spun at this acknowledgment. "Are you two…?"

He shook his head again. "She does not know how I feel, and will never know."

I straightened my stance to stare at him over Kate's inert form. "Well, I also have strong feelings that she does not know about. What makes you think that you should be the one to make the noble sacrifice?"

"You are more important to the wider struggle than I am, what with your sword and your powers," he said.

"He's right," chipped in Andras, pointedly tapping his foot on the ground.

"In any case," continued Pearce. "I have lost enough in my life already. You still have your brother to worry about you. I have nothing. And above all else, I am a soldier: noble sacrifice is in our nature."

"The risk though…" I muttered, shaking my head.

"It is not your decision to make," Pearce said. He turned to the crone. "The deal is done; I accept your terms. Now do what you need to do to help her."

"But what if the Wraith has already taken Kate from us?" I asked him by way of one final, desperate gamble. "What if they are not able to save her?"

He turned his steely eyes on me. "Then I would not wish to live."

*

The crone led us onwards, the hordes parting in a shuffling silence to form a path for us. After a while I worked up the courage to look straight at them, trying to discern individual features and understand whether they were the souls of dead people that I might recognise. I wondered whether they were departed souls from my own past or figures whose physical appearance may provide some clues as to the era—or even the world—in which they had lived and died.

The harder I tried, though, the more indistinct they became, such that it was not unlike trying to divine the blurred features in a photographic image; indeed, it was almost as though there were nothing to see, save for a general impression.

"Do not waste your energies," said Andras, catching up with me and dragging Gaap in his wake. "The amulet will let you see what you can safely see without turning you into a gibbering wreck. For all of your many faults, you are more use to us sane."

I glanced at him, tearing my attention from the shapes around us. "You knew that this would happen, that she would force a bargain on us," I accused.

He conceded the point with a half-nod. "I knew that there would be a price; there always is. But I had no way of knowing what form that price would take."

I frowned at him and he held his hands out in mock surrender. "I have never before ventured to this place; very few of my people have. The ways of the dead are unknowable."

"But it would be not beyond your wit to guess that they would demand some form of access to our world?"

Andras shrugged and I realised—not for the first time—that there was precious little hope of getting an answer or apology

142

from him. Biting back my frustration, I tried a different tack.

"Why did you not tell us that we had to come here?" I asked.

"I did not know myself until Mama told me."

"But when she did, you still decided to keep that information from us."

He sighed. "We needed to move fast; I could not afford to have an endless debate about the rights and wrongs of everything. We were in the Citadel and under attack from the Warlocks, remember? You wanted to get Kate back, in one piece." He gestured down at the figure I still carried in my arms.

"Even so," I persisted. "The afterlife…"

"Let's just say that I had told all of you that we needed to come here. There would have been endless discussions, not least because young Joshua would have been overexcited at finally getting his chance to try to resurrect his deceased little sister, and you all would have very sensibly wanted to stop him."

I looked round at Joshua, who was still carrying himself with the air of an excited child, staring around with wide eyes. "Surely he would not consider…" I started, my head starting to reel with the possibilities.

Andras laughed. "Poor little Gus. You really do not think things through properly, do you? Of course he is going to want to try to find Lexie. If I had given him the knowledge beforehand, and you all did your endless moralising and pontificating, then there is every chance that he would have taken matters into his own hands and run over here unaccompanied, leaving us trapped in Almadel and at the mercy of the Warlocks and the Four Kings."

"He would never leave us," I protested. "We are his friends."

"Never underestimate the human capacity to undertake acts of gross stupidity when emotions are involved. Especially emotions as strong as guilt, grief and hope. I am a veritable connoisseur of such things. But to return to your original question, there is a very important reason why I keep you all in the dark: if you don't know things, then you cannot betray them. I am a closed book to these creatures, while you are not."

I frowned at him. "You mean there is more that you are not telling us?"

"Always," he replied in a patronising tone. "Ah, it looks like we have arrived."

I looked in front of us to see another mausoleum filling my view. In design it was not unlike the one we had just left, although it was considerably larger. The crone rapped on the doors and the sound of her knocking echoed around us before the doors opened without a sound.

Inside was a deep blackness that my imagination populated with all manner of hideous creatures. The crone turned and pointed to Pearce. "You will bring her. The rest of you can wait outside."

Pearce took Kate from me and made to follow the crone into the black interior of the mausoleum. "Wait," I said. "Someone should go with them."

"No," said the crone as she walked away from us, her voice already echoing round the inside of the building. "It is forbidden."

Andras shrugged while Pearce glanced back at us as he followed the old woman into the building.

"I suppose Captain Pearce can look after himself," Byron said, an uncertain tone to his voice.

We nodded, trying to convince ourselves as the figures disappeared into the blackness. The mausoleum doors remained open, but our ever-present honour guard of the dead were a looming reminder of the crone's orders for us not to consider venturing into that place.

"They will be a while," said Andras, pulling out his pocket watch. "In the meantime, how about we make ourselves useful?"

He started to walk away from the mausoleum. "Where are you going?" I asked.

"There's one other thing we need to do," he said. "Joshua, I need you to come with us."

"To do what?" he asked.

"We need to find something if we are going to be able to get home. Specifically, the rune that will give you the power to transport us away from here."

"I was powerful enough to get us here," said Joshua. "I can surely get us back. I feel so energised…"

Andras shook his head and rounded on him. "Please do not get delusions of grandeur. Byron, did you teach this child nothing?"

Joshua looked stung while Byron frowned at him. "I taught him plenty, including not to listen to scheming demons. It would appear that some of my lessons went unheeded."

Andras spat on the ground. "Spare me the cheap shots." He turned to Joshua. "Where do you think your powers come from? When you cast a spell or open a portal, does that power come from within you?"

"Well, no…"

"Of course not; the human body can only store so much. You can do what you do because you have some spark of power that is different to other humans, but also because you have a particular sensitivity to the energies needed to fuel your spells."

"Of course I knew that," muttered Joshua, his arms folded across his chest.

"So when you achieved the impossible by bringing us here, where do you think that energy came from?"

Joshua looked from Andras to Gaap and back again. "The Almadite Citadel," he said slowly. "The runes held there. The source of the Warlocks' powers."

Andras nodded. "Specific objects—runes—exist that provide the power for Warlocks to successfully conduct their spells. At the beginning of time they were all held by one entity, giving him power over all creation. When he was defeated, the runes were scattered across other realms so that no one race or creature could ever again have such all-encompassing and potentially ruinous powers."

"I remember the stories," said Byron. "My people had one of those runes."

Andras glanced at Gaap. "As do the Almadites and the humans. The remainder—"

"It was the purpose of your invasion of my home realm, I believe," Byron continued, glaring at Andras, "to get the rune for yourself. That was your overriding aim, as I recall?"

"Well, yes, but…"

"Please, *do* give us your excuses for the genocide of my people."

"Some of you survived," noted Andras. "Many others we enslaved. Technically that's not genocide."

I held up a hand between them. "Is this really the time to discuss semantics?" I asked.

"It is not," said Byron. "But his motivations are very relevant."

Andras shrugged. "Joshua punched a portal through to here thanks in part to the powers from the runes held at the Citadel."

"I feel it still," Joshua noted. "Presumably the runic power lingers for a time?"

"Yes, I suppose," blinked Andras. "But the point is that the doorway to the afterlife has never been intended as a two-way one. Entering is easy: anyone can do it just by dying, after all. Leaving, on the other hand, requires a much larger and more powerful source of energy."

"Which must be somewhere around here," I said. "You, of all creatures, would not have brought us here without a way out."

"Give that dog a bone," said Andras, clicking a finger at me. "As I was saying, there were a number of runes—"

"Five in total," said Byron.

"Correct. And they were scattered so that they could not be reunited in one creature's hands: to Almadel, Tir na nÓg, Earth, the Aether and the afterlife. If we can get hold of the one that is here, then Joshua can use its power to take us back home."

"So the power I felt in Almadel," said Joshua, "that was due to those runes? And that was the power I drew on to bring us here?

146

But if that was so, why haven't the Warlocks followed us here?"

"Because it needed more than just two runes," said Andras.

"I have felt such power in smaller quantities when I have performed spells before," said Joshua. "Not always, but… the Fulcrum: is that another rune? Or is one buried somewhere in St Albans? That would explain…"

"No," said Andras. "You need to look a lot closer to home."

I felt a chill run down my spine as I drew the runic sword, examining the strange symbols etched into it. "It is this, isn't it?" I asked. "My sword."

Andras nodded, a broad grin splitting his face. "Masterful, was it not? The way I ensured that the rune was kept safe, and it turned you into the perfect warrior to protect it."

"You used me," I said quietly, glaring at him.

Andras stifled a yawn. "Please, we have been over this plenty of times; I have been using you your whole life. I thought you had grown accustomed to the idea."

"It changed me, it turned me into…"

"And you wondered why I don't share things with you lot: without this endless debate and tedious naval gazing we could have the rune in our hands by now!" Andras turned and started to march off around the side of the mausoleum, consulting his pocket watch again. Joshua followed him, a little too eagerly for my liking.

Byron and I glanced at each other, torn. "We cannot let Andras get hold of that rune," Byron said. "We need to make sure that it stays out of his control."

"If he wanted to snatch it from us, it would take all of us combined, including Joshua, to resist him," I noted. "And even then…"

Byron nodded. "And I am not really sure that we can rely on Joshua to make rational decisions at the moment."

I looked back at the open doors. "But what about Kate and Pearce?"

Byron rubbed his chin. "There is nothing we can do for them

until they emerge from that place. I suspect that, if we tried to enter, those creatures would do their best to stop us."

I shuddered as I looked around at the silent masses of the dead, imagining their pale hands pulling us back. "So we go with Andras?"

"I don't like it, but I'm not going to leave Joshua and the rune to his mercy. Come on."

We ran to catch up with the others. "Here's a question," I said as we drew alongside them. "If there is something powerful enough here to allow a portal to be created, then why have the creatures around us not used it already?"

"What makes you think that they have not?" asked Andras. "In any case, remember that it takes more than one rune to generate the power required. Your magic sword is the missing ingredient."

"If the creatures here realise that they have another rune in their grasp," said Byron suddenly, "then they wouldn't need us to escape from here, would they?"

Andras shot him a scared glance. "Which is why we need to hurry."

"But how do you know that it is still here?" I asked.

"Oh, I know," he waved his pocket watch at me. "I can sense it. And besides: what do you think gives that old crone back there her powers?"

I felt a slow sinking feeling that I could see mirrored in Byron's incredulous expression. "You are going to take the source of her power? Do you not think she will mind?"

"I think she will mind a great deal, which is why we need to move quickly while she is distracted."

I glanced at the ever-present forms around us. "What about them?"

"They will only act on her orders, so while she does not realise what we're doing they are essentially harmless."

"And as soon as we get the rune?"

Andras flashed me a grin. "Then we need to run. Very

quickly." He held the pocket watch to his ear and then nodded. "Clever, clever," he breathed.

"What is?" I asked.

He ignored me, bending down to examine the stone at the base of the building. "Joshua, touch the mausoleum."

"Where?"

"Anywhere; it does not matter."

Joshua did as he was told and immediately let out a low gasp. "It's incredible," he breathed. "The power…"

Andras grinned as he straightened up. "The mausoleum *is* the rune," he announced. Stepping to Joshua he asked: "Can you sense what she is doing in there?"

"I can feel them and see them," he replied with awe in his voice. "She is still freeing the Wraith from Kate. It looks like she is nearly there; I can sense the creature resisting, but the power from this place is too strong."

"Then we have very little time," Andras said. "As soon as the Wraith is free, I want you to focus all of your energy on the mausoleum. You need to concentrate on bringing it into your hands, all of it. It does not matter what form it takes, as long as it is small enough for you to handle."

"What are you scheming now?" asked Byron.

"Do you want to save both Kate and Pearce? Then let us do what needs to be done."

"You are going to steal the rune before she has a chance to use its power to possess Pearce," I said.

Andras grinned. "All being well."

Joshua shouted: "It is gone."

"Do it, now," Andras barked. "And be ready to create a portal out of here as soon as I say."

I stepped back as the building started to glow under Joshua's hands, knots of muscles and blood vessels standing out in stark relief on his neck and arms as he performed Andras' mad task. I felt the sword at my back vibrate once more and looked at Byron, seeking some reassurance from him that we were doing the right thing, or at least a hint of what we should be doing instead. He just stood there, looking as confused as I felt.

A breeze played at my face, growing stronger so it became a gale blowing out from the walls of the building. And then it was gone, revealing Kate, Pearce and the crone in the middle of an empty space, looking around in bewilderment. The crone was on her knees with her back to us, with Kate slumped in Pearce's arms. Something rushed past us, something cold, white and angry.

Joshua turned and beamed at Andras, holding a large disk-like object in his hands.

"Now," said Andras. "We need a portal, now."

"Where to?"

"I do not give a shit where to, just not here!"

I drew my sword as Joshua started the now familiar incantations, looking around in anticipation of the chaos that was doubtless about to follow. Sure enough, the crone whipped round to glare at us.

"You," she hissed. "You dare…?"

Andras ignored her. "Come to me, now," he shouted. Pearce lifted Kate and ran towards us, giving the furious crone a wide berth.

"You have no idea what forces you are playing with, the consequences of your actions," she shouted, her face twisted with rage.

"I am only too aware," replied Andras. "For I am—"

"I was not talking to you," she snapped. She raised her hands above her head. "The deal is now forfeit, as are your lives and your world."

My sword was vibrating madly in my hands in response to Joshua's magic, such that I feared it would be precious little use to me as a weapon. The shuffling hordes around us had been sparked into action by the crone's fury and they advanced on us, adopting recognisable forms as they did so.

It was as though we had been in a protective bubble all of that time, a bubble that the crone had swiftly burst. The stench of death and decay seeped over us, whilst the once-silent creatures now erupted in a chorus of moans and yells. Dark eyes twinkled at us from deep sockets within faces, the skin on which—where there was skin—was stretched tight over angular bones and pulled back from yellowing teeth. As I stared at them I imagined the lives they had led: a miner here, a young chimney-sweep there, a schoolteacher, a soldier…

"Come, now," shouted Andras. "We cannot hold this open much longer."

I spun round to see the swirling vortex of a newly created portal in front of Joshua. Pearce and Kate were already stepping through, with Byron and Andras not far behind. I rushed to join them, stepping aside to let Gaap go through and then wondering for a fleeting moment at the stupidity of my manners in such a situation. I looked at Joshua, his face twisted with the effort.

"Go," he said through clenched teeth. "I will be right behind you."

I stepped backward, our eyes meeting before he glanced up and beyond me in surprise.

*

I emerged into the familiar crepuscular landscape of the place we knew as the Red Desert, that place where we had lost Kate all those days before. I staggered away from the portal before collapsing in a heap onto the cold sand, squinting into the light of the three over-large suns looming low on the horizon as I looked back at the portal, willing Joshua to emerge.

"Where is he?" asked Andras.

"He said he would be right behind me," I said. "He seemed distracted by something though."

"He needs to come now," snapped Byron, starting for the portal, "before those creatures—"

A form appeared in the centre of the portal, growing larger

until it exploded towards us, blasting the portal into nothingness as it did so. I flinched and covered my face with my arms in anticipation of a gale that never arose.

I lowered my arm and blinked to see Joshua staggering forward, his arms round a large bundle. Andras darted forwards and grabbed the disk-shaped object from his hand, the rune Joshua had created from the power emanating from the mausoleum in the afterlife. He stroked and examined it as though to check that it was real and undamaged.

Byron snatched it from him. "I think it best that someone else look after that," he said.

Andras started towards him with a snarl but I was at Byron's side, my sword ready. Andras glared at the point of my blade, then at each of us before shrugging. "Just wanted to check he'd not left it there," he muttered.

Our attention was yanked back by Pearce. "What have you done?" he shouted at Joshua.

We looked up and realised that the bundle he had brought with him was in fact a person.

I looked over in shock at the sight of Lexie Bradshaw, blinking at us in confusion.

Chapter Fourteen

It took a few moments for my eyes, brain and mouth to coordinate properly in the face of this fresh insanity.

"That's… that's… what?" I stammered.

Byron and Andras were rounding on Joshua, although I noticed they were keeping a wary distance from him. In turn, the young man was clutching his sister close as though he feared that we intended to snatch her from him.

"What have you done?" asked Byron. "This goes against all laws… it should not be possible."

"As you always said," replied Joshua. "But I knew that I could get her back."

"Do you realise the implications?" asked Andras. "Not only have we stolen their rune, but now you have taken one of their own."

"What implications?" I asked.

Andras glanced back at me, a look of helpless exasperation on his face. "We are dealing with beings of immense power. There is no telling what they could do."

"But we have their rune," said Joshua. "Surely that makes them a fair bit less powerful."

"Granted," said Andras. "But you do not know anything about that… creature." He pointed at Lexie.

"She is my sister," said Joshua defiantly, holding her tighter. "Isn't that right?"

"That's right," croaked Lexie, as though she had not used her voice in a long time. "Where are we? What happened?"

"You're safe," said Joshua.

I walked forward, ignoring the hissed warning from the others as I knelt down in front of her. "What do you remember?" I asked her gently.

"We were in St Albans," she said slowly, "at the portal, after the demons had tried to invade. I was working on Maxwell's device to contain the portal and needed to activate one final lever and then…" She frowned. "…I do not remember anything else until just now."

"And you remember your name?" I asked.

"Lexie Bradshaw."

"Where were you born?"

"Sheffield."

"Do you remember who I am?"

"Gus Potts," she said. "Really, is this necessary?"

Andras chuckled. "Well, she certainly talks like Lexie."

She glared at him. "I remember enough to know not to trust you, demon," she spat.

I allowed myself a grin.

"By the way," said a voice from behind us. "I'm fine, in case any of you was wonderin'."

I gasped and spun round, running over to Kate. "You're…?"

"In one piece, if a bit sore," she said, her defiant glare giving way to a grin as I hugged her. "Good to see you 'n all. Thanks for comin' for me."

We huddled round her, hugging and patting and smiling while Pearce loomed in the background, her guardian angel.

"How do you feel?" I asked. "Are you…?"

"As far as I can tell, I'm demon-free," she said.

"Are you sure?" asked Joshua.

She raised an eyebrow at him. "Trust me, when you have one

154

of them things in your bonce, you know about it."

"Of course. Was it…?"

"Like somethin' was trying to pull my insides out through my skin while rummagin' round my head with a hot poker. Not fun, let me tell you. Right now I'd kill for an ale and a good meal." She pulled her arms tight round her body, shivering.

I chuckled and then looked up to see Byron beckoning me away. When we were out of earshot he said in a low voice: "We need to keep an eye on her. What she's been through would be enough to break the strongest person."

I stared at him. "That's not the only reason you're worried, is it?"

He took a deep breath. "I'm not convinced the Wraith is gone," he said. "Such things are incredibly tenacious; expelling it seemed far too easy."

"He's right," said Andras, appearing at our side, the gagged and bound Gaap still trailing miserably behind him. "That was suspiciously easy. But Kate appears to be relatively free of any demon possession."

"Such things can hide very well."

"Granted. But sooner or later it will need to show itself. As you say, we need to keep a close eye on her."

"And if it's still in there?" I asked. "What then? Do you mean to say that we went through all of this for nothing?"

"Well, not quite for nothing," said Andras, jiggling the rope around Gaap's neck. "We have stopped Kate turning into a Mage, at least for the time being. Although we have managed to make some pretty formidable enemies."

"Meaning?" I asked.

"We're not going to be very popular in the afterlife when we finally do die. If I were you, I'd take a leaf out of my book and avoid that outcome for as long as possible." He turned and looked at the others. "And then there's the question of our new stray spirit."

We both followed his gaze to Lexie, who was still standing

close to her brother.

Kate looked up at us, sensing our eyes on them. "What you lot cookin' up? And what's with the new pet?"

Andras chuckled, pulling Gaap along with him. "You remember Gaap? Lackey to the Four Kings and general pain in the arse?"

"I remember him well," Kate said. "Why's he still alive?"

"It suits my purposes for the time being," Andras said.

"What purposes would them be, then?" she shot back.

Andras chuckled. "I have missed you, young Kate."

"It is a fair question, though," said Byron. "You have kept us in the dark at pretty much every single point of this endeavour. Not that I would expect anything less from you, but the time has come for you to tell us exactly what it is you have been plotting."

Andras shot him a cold look. "You are always so keen to see the worst in my motivations."

I stifled a chuckle and Andras turned to glare at me. "Please," I said. "Do not presume to think that any of us trust you. You have always acted in your own interests."

"And you would not do the same? Are you trying to tell me that your actions have been all been purely in the interests of charity?"

"What do you mean?" I asked.

He gestured at Lexie. "Bringing her back from the afterlife is the most egregious act of stupidity, and incredibly selfish. It was her time to die; what gives Joshua the right to subvert the ways of the universe? And as for Kate, the safest thing to do would have been to kill her outright, but there is no way you would have accepted that. Do you have any idea of the risks if we had not managed to get Pearce away in time before being forced to fulfil our side of the bargain?"

"What do you mean?" asked Kate, staring at a sheepish-looking Pearce. When he did not answer, she looked back at me. "Gus? What have you buggers gone and done?"

"There was a price for healing you, for expelling the Wraith,"

I said. "The... whatever she was... wanted a vessel to possess, through which the dead could visit the land of the living."

She turned and glared at Pearce. "And you thought you'd just offer yourself up, eh? Like some bloody stupid knight wanting to save every bloody damsel in distress whether she bloody well wants it or not? No, I know what it is: you were thinking of makin' some grand sacrifice, so you could be all noble and stuff." She shook her head. "You made a deal and then you all broke that deal. Anyone think that's goin' to end up well for us?"

"Especially given that we stole the source of their power into the bargain," pointed out Byron.

"Exactly," said Joshua. "We took away their ability to get at us when we removed that thing." He pointed to the disk in Byron's hands.

Pearce cleared his throat. "Actually, about that," he said. "I am not sure that you did remove their powers just in time."

"What do you mean?" asked Andras.

He tapped a finger on his forehead. "I don't think I'm quite alone in here."

"Are you positive?" Andras said. "How can you be sure?"

"I know my own mind," Pearce replied. "And I know that I should not be experiencing what I am right now."

"But we took away her power," Andras yelled. "She should not have been able to..." He turned and let out a stream of curses whilst Gaap watched from the end of his leash with an amused wrinkle to his eyes.

"She did something immediately after the spell she cast on Kate and before you all appeared," said Pearce. "I cannot quite recall, and it is no doubt beyond my understanding, but..." He shrugged.

"How do you feel?" asked Byron.

"Perfectly fine, although I have the distinct feeling of others around me; almost like those creatures we were surrounded by in the afterlife. As though they were standing just beyond my line of sight, whispering to each other and waiting."

I gestured to the others and we retreated a few paces from Pearce and Kate. "Could it be the Wraith?" I asked in a whisper.

Andras frowned. "He does not appear to be demonstrating the symptoms. You see, a Wraith is a rather violent creature. They are not a parasite as such: they invade, rather than inhabit. If the Wraith was in there, we would know about it." He shook his head. "It appears that they were faster and smarter than I gave them credit for. Shut your mouth, you," he snapped at Gaap, who appeared to be enjoying Andras' rage and grinning behind his gag.

"What do we do?" I asked. "We can't allow them to go back to Earth, surely?"

"Absolutely not," said Byron. "We have no idea as to their intentions, or indeed what they are capable of."

"That creature said they just wanted to observe the land of the living," said Joshua slowly. "What is so bad about that?"

"In and of itself, probably nothing," said Andras. "But then we attempted to double-cross them and stole something of huge value…"

"By 'we' you of course mean 'you'," Byron pointed out. "As with so many things, all of this could have been avoided if you had not chosen to act precipitately."

"If I had not chosen to act, she would now be a Mage, or dead," snapped Andras, pointing at Kate. "Time and again, my actions have saved you all."

"Aside from when you tried to kill us, steal our souls or invade our world," I muttered. As he rounded on me I held up my hands. "We need to calm down; this is solving nothing."

"You are right," said Byron. "So are we agreed?"

"What are you lot muttering about over there?" Kate called over.

"They are debating whether I should be allowed back to Earth," said Pearce. "And I agree that I should not; I will not allow these creatures to invade our world. We have enough problems with the Almadites. I will remain here."

I nodded, relieved that his sense of duty and propriety had spared us any further fighting.

Byron turned to Joshua. "You realise that this means that Lexie cannot come with us either," he said.

Joshua turned on him and for a moment I feared he would strike our friend. "No," he said quietly. "I am not leaving her; not again."

"The Pooka is right," Andras said. "She does not belong this side of the afterlife. Just her very presence could give them the way into your world that they crave. Who knows: she could have inadvertently been responsible for Pearce's possession."

"No!" shouted Joshua. "I will not have her taken away from me. If you want me to create a portal back to Earth, then she comes with us."

As he stomped away, Lexie turned to face us. "I am not a threat to you or our home," she said. "I just want to be safe with my brother once more, to get back to my old life. Just think how much use I would be if I could work with Maxwell once more."

I frowned at her, my resolve weakening as I considered the sense behind her words.

"Lexie," said Byron softly, "we have no way of knowing the consequences… you were dead…"

"And maybe I still am, or perhaps I am something else. Somewhere in my condition, in what has happened to me, could be the key to winning the war against the Almadites. The best person to consider all of this is currently sitting on Earth: surely you owe it to all of us to take me to Maxwell, so he can consider how I might be able to help?"

Joshua marched back over to us, grabbing Lexie by the arm. "I am creating a portal back to Earth and Lexie is coming with me; there is nothing any of you can do to stop me."

"Joshua, please," said Byron, but the young man had already turned and walked away.

"Well?" I asked the others.

Andras was watching them depart. "Young Lexie has recovered

her poise remarkably quickly, don't you think?" he mused.

"He's right that we can't stop him," said Byron, ignoring him. "All we can do is keep as close to them as possible, in case Lexie's presence does something."

"The risk may not be that high," said Andras. "We are out of the afterlife here, in the land of the living as it were, even though it is a different land of the living to the one you are accustomed to. The point is, that we are already out of the afterlife and she is acting perfectly benign. Maybe she is not a threat to your realm after all."

"You could extend that logic to Captain Pearce," pointed out Byron.

"Granted," shrugged Andras. "It was just a thought."

We joined Joshua and Lexie, watching as they made the arrangements for the portal spell. Andras grunted his approval. "Clever," he said. "You are going to use the power of the rune to create two portals close together."

Joshua nodded, tight-lipped, and so I looked to Andras for an explanation.

"We have previously used vehicles to protect ourselves from the worst excesses of the Aether whilst travelling through it, something that we are lacking at the moment," he said. "One cannot punch directly from one realm to another, but young Joshua here has come up with a solution: creating a portal to the Aether and then another portal right in front of that one, which will go to Earth, thereby limiting the amount of time we need to spend in the Aether itself."

"I did not realise that was an option," I said. "Why have we not done that before?"

"Because it requires two things that were missing before," said Joshua, unable to resist showing off any longer. "The knowledge of the exact location of the realm that we need to create the second portal back to Earth, and the power to do it. Earth is one of the few places I can easily find in the Aether, and the runes we have in our possession give me the power I need to create both portals simultaneously. Now, stand back please."

We did as we were told, shuffling backwards as Joshua began the incantations. Byron grunted in surprise as the rune in his hands started glowing and vibrating. Not to be outdone, I felt the sword strapped to my back also resonate in sympathy with the magical forces. Gaap started to shuffle around, as though he wanted to be as far away as possible.

The now-familiar sight of a portal spun into existence in front of us, the vortex showing the loathsome blackness of the Aether beyond. Joshua's chanting increased and, a moment later, the portal revealed a second vortex within, showing the familiar green grass and blue sky of home.

There was a sound like vomiting from behind us, followed by a bellow and then a scream. I turned to see Kate backing away from Pearce, who was standing erect and somehow suspended a foot or so in the air. His face was stretched and contorted, his mouth and eyes wide as a dark mass pulled itself from his body.

"Close it!" shouted Andras but, before Joshua could respond, the black mass shot towards and past us, through the portal. We were thrown backwards by the force of its passing, watching as the portal popped shut behind it.

"What happened?" I shouted as I pulled myself to my feet.

"It—something—the creatures that possessed Pearce," said Byron, staring at where the portal had been just a few seconds beforehand. "They have gone across to Earth!"

"Get the portal open again, now," said Andras.

Lexie looked up at us from where Joshua lay, a few feet from where the portal had disappeared. "He is unconscious," she said. "The force of the blast must have knocked him out."

"We need him awake," Andras said, kneeling next to Joshua. "We need a portal back to Earth right now."

She glared back at him. "You lay a finger on him and I will make you suffer," she hissed.

I looked from that standoff to where Pearce lay slumped on the ground being tended to by Kate. "This does not look good,"

I commented quietly.

"That," said Byron, "would be an understatement."

*

Pearce groaned as he woke up. "What happened?" he asked.

"You puked black," said Kate.

"You were somehow purged of whatever it was that possessed you," I said. "The bad news is that whatever was inside you has managed to escape to Earth, and we are still trapped here."

He sat up quickly and then slumped back down again, putting a hand to his head.

"Take it easy," said Kate. "You'll need a few moments to get over havin' that thing in your head. Trust me, I know."

I felt a pang of jealousy as I watched them share a look of understanding and sympathy. After a moment, Pearce looked over to me. "We need to get back to Earth," he said.

I gestured to where Andras, Byron and Lexie were gathered round Joshua. "We are doing our best," I said. "Unfortunately our only method of getting there was knocked out in the process and is still unconscious."

"So… we wait?" he asked.

"We have little choice," I said. "Which is a problem in and of itself. You see, I have finally realised what was so familiar about this place."

Kate looked around. "Looks like where we were when that demon snatched me," she said, letting out a little laugh. "Like I've never been away."

Pearce groaned. "You mean…?"

"Yes," I said. "Not even time is on our side."

Kate looked from one to the other of us. "What is it?"

"When we were here last time, it was only for a few hours," I said. "However, when we got back to Earth, quite a few days had passed."

She frowned. "So every second we waste here is a lot more

back on Earth?" We both nodded and she pulled herself to her feet. "Then we really do need to get a move on, don't we?"

I jumped up to support her as she swayed on her feet. "You should also take it easy," I said. "You have not yet recovered from your own ordeal."

"Sod that," she said. "Take me over there, I'll get laughin' boy woken up. And by the by, don't think that all this lets you off the hook for what you did. I'll be dealin' with you later."

"Me?" I asked. "What do you mean?"

"Later," she said with a determined look on her face.

*

I paced the rock-strewn landscape as we waited for Joshua to summon up the energy to create a portal back home. He had finally woken up, thanks in no small part to Kate's rough treatment that had in turn earned the simmering wrath of Lexie. However, he was still weak and disorientated, having caught a hard blow to the side of his head when he had fallen to the ground.

"How are you?" asked Byron, wandering over to join me.

"I am stuck in some vast desert on a nameless world with a pair of Almadites of uncertain motivation and a young sorcerer who seems to have been driven mad with grief. But at least he has his dead sister here to comfort him. Meanwhile there are spirits doing who-knows-what to my home and, to top it all off, the girl we went to save is blaming me for everything having gone so disastrously wrong. Not that I can blame her." I flashed him a tight smile. "So you could say that I have had better days."

"Kate does not blame you; she knows we are all equally at fault for what happened."

"In my experience, she has a very effective method of apportioning blame quite violently as a way of motivating people to set things right post-haste."

"Then we make it right," said Byron, sitting down on a large rock. "Moping around never helped anyone, eh?"

"Are you adopting the role of my tutor again?"

He laughed. "I don't think I ever stopped, did I? Come on, let's think all of this through. You and me, while Andras is distracted."

I looked over at where the demon was bent over Joshua, helping him to prepare for the process of getting us back to Earth. "You still do not trust him, do you?"

"No, and neither do you," he said. "That is the healthiest state of affairs for all of us. Remember: he is still an Almadite, even if he fights with us against the Four Kings."

"What is it that he wants?" We had both instinctively lowered our voices; probably a futile effort given the demon's acute sense of hearing, but it at least gave us the delusion of privacy.

"What he has always wanted: power. The question is, what is the extent of his ambitions? To rule Almadel once more? Or does he want to continue their conquests throughout all the realms?"

"He has reassured me that he has no designs on Earth," I said.

"And you believe him?" Byron raised an eyebrow at me.

I ran my fingers through my hair. "He says that he has been changed by what he has experienced on Earth, including the time he spent with us when he was N'yotsu. He says that he has been 'infected' by our emotions," I grinned at the use of the word, "and that they would stop him from carrying out the sort of atrocities he used to commit. Or at least make him think twice before doing so."

"Emotions are a two-sided coin though, are they not?"

I nodded. "And so is Andras; he is a particularly spiteful and vicious creature, but he has also fought on our side a number of times now."

"Let's consider this in the light of selfish acts, given how he accused us all of acting in that manner," said Byron. "Yes he fights with us against the Four Kings, but their overthrow would also serve him, because then he would be able to seize power for himself."

"In that case, why help us with Kate?" I asked. "To ensure that there was one less weapon that they could use against us?"

"Maybe. Or maybe it was a useful opportunity for him to return home and cause trouble; do you remember how he made a pact with Mama? And all that talk of helping to start a revolution in Almadel? We still do not know everything he agreed with her."

"And now he also has Gaap, and so has a valuable bargaining tool to use against the Four Kings: their right-hand man."

Byron nodded and then held up the disk that Joshua had brought back from the afterlife. "This also troubles me. The five runes were scattered across the realms as a way of protecting the rest of us. If one being, or even a race, were to get hold of the supreme power they provide when unified…"

"Is it really that bad?" I asked.

"Oh yes." He jumped down and drew a dozen circles in the dust at our feet, each one spaced a hands-width apart from its nearest neighbours. "Imagine that these are the different realms in existence, with the space between being the Aether. At present, it requires an individual of great power and ability to create a portal that can link from their realm through to the Aether."

"Such as Joshua," I said.

"Yes. Him or the Warlocks. Of course, some realms are harder to puncture than others: such as Earth before the Fulcrum weakened the barrier to the Aether." He drew a line from inside one of the circles out into the empty space of the Aether. "Once in the Aether, one then needs to find the realm that one wishes to travel to and create another portal to it." He continued the line straight into another circle. "Which again requires great power and effort, as we are seeing right now." He nodded at Joshua.

"If one has enough power," he continued, "and knows exactly where the two realms are, it is possible to build a bridge that constantly links those two places. This has been done in the past, but only for short periods of time, given the sheer amount of energy needed to maintain it. This is why the Almadites, while they have been a scourge on the worlds they have invaded, have only managed to spread intermittently across the realms."

"Where do these runes fit in?" I asked.

He placed his finger in one of the circles. "The holder of the power of all five runes would no longer be limited by any of the laws I have described." He moved his finger out to another circle, then another and another. "They could move about the realms at will, taking whole armies with them. They could build everlasting bridges or even merge realms. They could rule all creation."

I shuddered, looking down at the line he had drawn, linking and jumping to every single circle. "That seems pretty… terrifying."

"Which is exactly why we need to ensure that no one is able to unite all of the runes."

"What do we do with that, then?" I asked, pointing at the rune in his hands, the small, disc-like object that until not long ago had taken the form of an entire mausoleum in the afterlife. Until, that is, Joshua had intervened and transformed it into its current, more portable form. "Should we hide it somewhere here?"

He shook his head. "There is every risk that the Almadites will be following us. We cannot risk it falling into the Four Kings' hands; they already have two of the runes."

We both looked up at a burst of activity from the others. "Ah, it looks like Joshua may now be about ready to do the deed."

*

I stepped through the portal, experiencing the now-familiar disorientating swirl that accompanied travel through the barrier between worlds. This was amplified by the fact that I was doing so without any form of vehicle to transport or protect me.

As my eyes adjusted to the dim light of dusk, I looked round to see a dozen rifle barrels pointed at us. "Not again," I moaned, dropping my sword and raising my hands above my head.

Byron cleared his throat. He was standing at my side, having passed through the portal straight after me. I looked at him quizzically and he nodded to the sky. I looked up.

At first glance it was night-time; however it was not just the darkness of a night sky that loomed over us, but a complete absence of sky. With a groan I realised where I had seen such a sight before: the afterlife.

Chapter Fifteen

"I demand to see your commanding officer," bellowed Pearce at the firmly bolted door. "I am an officer in Her Majesty's armed forces, and I should not be treated this way!"

"I'd save my breath if I were you," said Andras from the corner of the cell. "I don't think they answer to the same superiors as you do."

"We are in England," he panted, dropping to the ground, his limited reserves exhausted.

"You saw the sky," said Andras. "I think it's safe to say you've been invaded."

We were crammed into a windowless box room, a makeshift cell in the remnants of the old mansion house at the Yewfields Estate where the demons—spearheaded by Gaap—had first broken through to our world. We had been escorted there by the guards who had met us on our arrival through the portal, none of whom had cared to speak to us save to relieve us of our weapons and effects and lock us in a cell.

Unfortunately, they had also removed Gaap's gag and restraints.

"You have lost," he crowed. "Soon the Four Kings will be here and you will all die!"

Andras smashed his elbow into the demon's face, and he

slumped to the floor.

"Thank you," I said. "But I fear that he may have a point. We need to do something. Joshua, can you create a portal for us yet?"

He shook his head from where he was propped against the wall. Lexie glared at me from next to him. "He needs a bit longer," she said.

I looked over to Byron, who shrugged back at me. "If we had your sword and the other runes with us then Joshua could draw on them; the fact that he is still struggling to find the magical wherewithal would suggest that they are being held far enough away to stop him making use of them. Or they are being shielded to stop him being able to draw on their powers."

"What about the Fulcrum?" I asked. "We're practically on top of it; can he not draw on the power from that?"

"Ordinarily, yes," said Joshua in a low voice, "but it is not enough on its own. The runes, though, they were the strongest medicine…"

I puffed out my cheeks and slowly exhaled as I considered what we should do next.

"What now?" asked Kate. "Earth's mightiest heroes defeated by a box room and a bunch of badly-dressed soldiers?"

"They weren't soldiers," said Pearce. "At least, not soldiers attached to any regiment I recognise."

"They did seem quite rag-tag," I said. "But I thought I recognised some uniforms there?"

"They did not match," said Pearce. "My guess is that they looted their uniforms from dead bodies or army depots."

"Which is worrying enough in itself," pointed out Byron. "That would suggest either some large battle that the regular troops lost, or a widespread collapse in law and order."

"And we're stuck in here," muttered Pearce. "Damn my stupidity. This is all my fault…"

"Don't be so—" started Kate, her words cut off by the sound of shouting and gunfire from outside. We listened to the cracks of rifles and then the pounding of feet around the walls and above our heads. After a few minutes a key turned in the lock and the door banged open to reveal an incredibly welcome sight.

"Good day, sir," grinned Sergeant Jones. "Was wonderin' where you'd got to." He rushed in and helped Pearce to his feet. "All of you need to come with me, right now."

"Sergeant," beamed Pearce. "Does that mean that the regular army are here to rescue us?"

"Yep, we're the authentic article," said Jones, "unlike these rag-tag lunatics who captured you. But there'll be time for questions and answers later; I've got a company of men harryin' them from the treeline to buy us some time, but I don't know how long they'll be able to hold out."

We followed him out of the door and up a flight of stairs. "Wait," shouted Lexie. "The rune!"

"And my sword," I said, turning to Jones. "They took our weapons and effects; we need to find them."

Jones looked at Pearce, who nodded. "I am afraid we cannot let those items fall into the wrong hands, Sergeant."

"All right," Jones said. "Any ideas where they are?"

Andras held up a hand. "I am sensitive to their emanations. This way." He was carrying Gaap's inert body over his shoulder and hefted it into a more comfortable position before moving off up what appeared to be a servants' staircase. It was steep and narrow, and Gaap's head collided with the wall on a number of occasions as we climbed them.

"Why'd you bring him?" Kate asked. "It's going to be harder to make a quick getaway with that waste of space. We should get shot of him."

"I would prefer to keep Gaap where I can see him," said Andras. He reached the top of the stairs and turned left, leading us down a narrow corridor and to a locked door, in front of which stood a panicked-looking guard.

"Keep back or I shoot," shouted the man, the barrel of his rifle wavering as he looked at the crowd of people and demons bearing down on him.

Jones cocked his rifle, aiming it at the man. "Son, you look like a smart man. I don't know what they've promised you, but you can work out the odds right now. I'd put my weapon down if I were you. Just tell 'em we overwhelmed you and you had no choice: you don't need to get hurt."

He stared at us for a moment and then dropped his rifle on the ground, raising his hands above his head. "Good man," said Jones, rushing forwards to take the weapon and ushering him back against the wall. "Now where are the keys?"

"I don't have them," he said. "Promise."

"It's all right, we don't need one," said Andras. With one swift kick he took the door off its hinges, sending it flying into the room beyond.

I stared at him, remembering the preternatural strength he possessed. "You could have done that when we were in that cell," I said. "You could have freed us a lot earlier."

"To what end? An unknown number of armed men outside, with nothing to distract them. We would have had all of them on us in minutes. Besides, I wanted to see what would happen next."

I glowered at him as he fumbled his way into the room, clearly struggling with Gaap's bulk in the confined space. Byron, unencumbered, pushed past him and reached the central table on which were held the objects they had taken from us.

"I'll have that," he said, grabbing the rune as Andras glared at him. "And I believe this is yours, Gus." He threw the sword to me and I caught it one-handed, a smile spreading across my face at the weapon's familiar weight and warmth.

I turned the sword on the guard, noting with satisfaction as he cringed away from me. "What is happening here?" I asked. "Who are you people?"

"We are the anointed ones," he said defiantly. "The followers of Satan. All of you unbelievers shall die."

"Pretty ballsy words from the one with the sword pointing at his head," commented Kate.

"Where did you get those uniforms?" I continued. "Where are the regular army?"

The guard laughed hysterically at me, spittle flying in all directions.

"You're mad," I muttered.

"Trust me, sir," said Jones, "you'll get no sense out of him. Me and my mates have got all the answers you need, so if we've got everything we need then let's get out of here."

*

The scene outside the mansion house was chaotic, the battle lent an otherworldly air by the lack of sky above. The bulk of our captors were focused on repelling an attack from the woods and grounds around the house and so we were able to surprise them with our own miniature offensive from behind. After a few moments of being overwhelmed from both sides, they turned and fled.

We ran to join Jones' comrades in a massed charge away from the estate and towards the road to Hatfield, where a stable of horses awaited us. We hastily mounted while the soldiers kept guard, occasionally firing a volley at the treeline to discourage any would-be pursuers.

Satisfied that we were all ready, and after waiting for Gaap to be bound to Andras' horse, Jones led us all westwards.

We rode hard until we were safely past St Albans, at which point our pace slackened slightly to allow the horses to recover; our destination was Hughenden Manor, Disraeli's country estate in Buckinghamshire, which was still a good half-day's ride away. We had left behind us 20 or so soldiers on foot, tasked with delaying and hopefully deterring any pursuit by means of skirmish actions before melting into the countryside and following us in their own time.

We were accompanied by a dozen soldiers on horseback,

each of them looking as though they had been through a score of battles. Above us, the black void persisted, uninterrupted by neither star nor cloud nor celestial body. Just as in the afterlife, the blackness seemed to suppress all sounds and sensations, as though we were wandering through a dream world. All around us was quiet, with even the birds, animals and insects holding their counsel and awaiting the return of a daytime that may never arrive.

"What I want to know is," said Kate, reading my thoughts perfectly, "if there's no sun or moon or stars, how come we can still see?"

"It is a fair point," said Andras, "as long as you assume that the usual physical laws apply. I rather think that your world has gone beyond such things now."

"Max must be having a dicky fit," she muttered. "He hates it when stuff happens that his science can't explain. Do you know if he's all right?"

"You'll get to meet him very soon," said Jones. "He is safe and has been keeping an eye out for signs of your return. In fact, it's him you need to thank for tipping me and the lads off that you were back."

"He must have been monitoring for Aetheric disturbances," said Joshua as Lexie nodded in agreement behind him.

"Yes, sir," said Jones. "When the sky went like this, we knew something was up. Mr Potts has been hard at work ever since."

"How long has it been?" I asked. "Since the sky…?"

"Nigh on three weeks, give or take. At least I think so; without the sun or moon it's been hard to tell the passage of time."

Byron and I shared a look of dismay. The amount of destruction that could have been wrought in that length of time did not bear thinking about.

"Now that we are moving slowly enough to be able to talk," Pearce said to Jones, "you should fill us in on exactly what has been happening in our absence."

Chapter Sixteen

After taking us from the Tower of London to the safe house where we met Disraeli all those months ago, Sergeant Jones had gone on an extended tour of the country. This was partly to try to wrong-foot anyone who was attempting to follow him, but also to keep himself out of the hands of the authorities—technically he was now a deserter.

Shortly after our departure to the Aether, Jones had made his way back to Hughenden Manor to offer his services to Disraeli, arriving just in time to accompany him on a trip to Paris disguised as his manservant.

Disraeli had been tight-lipped about the reasons for their visit but Jones had just been happy to be doing something useful while keeping out of the reach of the English army. His initial intention had been to act as bodyguard but Disraeli's nature meant that worrying about the man's security was a pointless act. Disraeli did not do anything by half-measures, insisting on making a prominent entrance to every room and eschewing any attempts at caution in his arrangements. After a while Jones settled into the role of under-used manservant, albeit one with a pistol always to hand and a wary eye on his surroundings.

Disraeli had seemed pleased with his meetings in Paris and they had then set about a miniature grand tour, taking in Berlin and Saint Petersburg before returning home via London. In each place, Disraeli did not share the purpose of his meetings, although Jones gained the distinct impression that they were with some impressive 'higher-ups.'

On their trips across the Channel, Jones was struck by how differently Disraeli and his entourage were treated compared to the common people who were segregated and refused entry to the Continent. Some of these refugees called out to Disraeli, trying to seek assistance from him or benefit from the sway that his status had with the officials guarding the gateways to Europe. Jones had found these the most taxing parts of his grand tour; not only in terms of needing to be on a heightened state of alert in case Disraeli was attacked, but also the pain of seeing ordinary men and women, who in other times would be merrily going about their business in the towns and cities of England instead reduced to the status of bedraggled refugees.

Little had he known then that this was only the slightest foreshadowing of what was to come.

Jones had become understandably skittish on their return to England and as a result had decided to not accompany Disraeli to London, lest he be recognised and apprehended. Instead he had decided to take a diversion around the south coast, agreeing to meet up with Disraeli back at Hughenden Manor a few weeks later.

The first few days were highly enjoyable, seeming to mainly involve him drinking his way through the many taverns he encountered on his progress from Dover to Folkestone and then sweeping northwest towards Maidstone with a view to skirting London and its environs. It was around the third or fourth day of this alternative and altogether earthier grand tour, when he had taken a stop at a coaching inn on the road between Ashford and Maidstone, that things started to change.

He awoke one morning to find his head feeling like it was stuck in a box filled with nothing but the distant sound of a woman screaming. It took him a few moments to haul enough of his addled senses back into the land of the living to realise that he was in fact lying on a hard mattress in an inn, with what he had assumed to be a box instead the effect produced by the still and claustrophobic darkness of night. Grumbling, he had pulled himself out of bed and to the window, ready to shout at the woman to be quiet.

It was only when he reached the open window that he realised a few things. Firstly, the inn had been pretty crowded when he had passed out the night before, and so it was odd that no one else had yet taken it upon themselves to hush her. Especially as Jones was a very heavy sleeper after a few drinks. Secondly, the screaming was unnaturally loud. Thirdly, the sound of the carry-on seemed to be a lot louder and shriller in part because of the lack of any other noise. And lastly, surely it must have been morning by then, so why was the sky still dark?

He looked outside to see a crowd of people gathered in the courtyard, all staring up at the sky. Jones angled his head to follow their gazes to see… nothing. No stars, no cloud, no sun or moon, simply the complete lack of anything above them. At first he did not comprehend what was happening, mistaking it for a total eclipse of the sun. However, as the minutes ticked by with still no change, he realised that something more sinister and permanent had taken place.

He hurriedly dressed and made his way through the darkened corridors of the deserted inn. He heard a woman sobbing in one of the rooms and paused, knocking to see if there was anything he could do to help. Her crying continued unabated as though she had not heard him, and after a moment's pause he decided to press on.

Everything outside was hushed, as though the world had been converted into one huge cathedral, the only sounds being a whispering from some of the people standing around and the distant howling of dogs.

Jones approached the nearest man, who he recognised as the innkeeper. "What's going on?" he asked.

"Beats me," said the innkeeper. "One moment the sun was coming up, then all of a sudden everything up there just disappeared. It's damned peculiar, don't you think?"

Jones frowned as he stared upwards. "That's not a night sky," he said. "There should be stars or something."

"There's nothing there," the innkeeper said. "What does that mean?"

Jones turned in a full circle, taking in all aspects of the heavens. "There's no sun or moon but we don't need torches," he said. "That's pretty queer, don't you think?"

The innkeeper shrugged. Like the others in that courtyard, he seemed to have been lulled into a strange lethargy by the lack of sky, almost as though the void was sucking away his ability to think and exercise willpower.

Jones made his way through the sea of unmoving bodies, his mind abuzz with the implications. Such a thing could only be demonic in origin, he reasoned, and therefore it was imperative that he found Benjamin Disraeli and Maxwell Potts as soon as possible. That meant he needed to urgently make his way to London.

It is likely that this sense of purpose was what saved him from the lethargy that appeared to have overcome so many poor souls around the world. Whilst at first thought the lack of a sky may seem trivial to the casual reader, it is only when you lose such a thing that you realise just how integral to your life that thing is. The ever-changing features of our sky is something that we all take for granted. After all, it is always there; a backdrop that, even on the greyest and most overcast day, still shows gradations, gaps and variations of colour. Our moods and motivations are affected by the sky and the weather that it foretells, and it can also be a source of so many other emotions: the awe and wonder of a clear and starlit night, the sheer lazy pleasure of a sunny day or the terror and oppression of a thunder and lightning storm.

What the world had woken up to on that fateful day was a complete lack of all of these inputs, meaning that everyone and everything dwelling beneath it suddenly found themselves bereft of direction or motivation. This extended beyond humans to include birds and animals, for all of those creatures relied on the sky for navigation or other means, so they too were suddenly bereft.

Jones immediately decided to set off, pausing only to gather his belongings together. Passing by the sobbing woman's door he noted that she had now subsided into a low moan, still refusing to respond to his knocks. He muttered some words of reassurance before moving off, realising that if he stopped to try to comfort everyone upset by what had happened then he would never reach London.

The inn sat at a crossroads just outside of Smeeth, a small village on the road to Maidstone, and it was in this direction that Jones set off, relieved to note that his horse was largely indifferent to what had happened to the sky. As he walked he noted that people were reacting in markedly different ways to the phenomenon above their heads. Some simply stood, mute and staring at the sky, as though by sheer willpower they could bring back the sun. Or maybe they were looking for some form of direction from an unseeable deity. Others were distraught: screaming, shouting and wailing at the loss as though it heralded the end of the world. Jones wondered if these were the ones who were most dependent upon the idea of a God above them for their sustenance and sanity, and therefore saw the blankness overhead as a sign that all they had believed in, the very basis for their faith, had been torn away. Indeed, some he passed were rocking in frantic prayer, tears streaming down their cheeks and tearing at their hair as they pleaded with their God to bring them salvation in this, the End of Days.

Making his way along the road, Jones passed a ruddy-faced

squire dressed sloppily in fine clothes. One glance at him made clear that the man had been driven quite mad, his eyes swivelling left and right as he muttered to himself. This was to be the first of many such sad creatures Jones encountered on his journey, as the loss of the sky seemed to be too much for the sanity of some poor souls.

As he made his way towards Maidstone, Jones was surprised by a shout: "Oi, you!" He twisted in his saddle to gaze back and saw a swarthy-looking man stepping out from the bushes at the side of the road. Slowly and carefully, Jones slid his hand down to the pistol hidden in the depths of his coat as he eyed this newcomer with practised suspicion.

"Good to see another face," the man said as he approached. "At least one that's not just standin' around starin' at the sky." He was wearing a long coat, under which was the remnants of what appeared to be an old infantry uniform. Slung over his back was a Snider–Enfield rifle, the standard issue for the British Army. Jones was in plain clothes and in no mood to reveal his status as a deserter and so decided to pretend ignorance of these details, for the time being at least.

"Aye," said Jones. "Where are you headed?"

"London, I guess," the man said. "Not much goin' on around here apart from people giving up and going mad. I figure there's better chance of some action up there in the big city. You?"

"Same."

"Mind if I accompany you? Right now everything's quiet, but I'd rather be travelling with people if others start getting violent on account of all this. Safety in numbers and all that, eh?"

Jones had to agree with the man's logic. He nodded. "Of course."

"Great, thanks," grinned the man as he trotted over to Jones' horse. "Don't say much, do you?"

"It's been an unusual day so far. Let's just say I'm sizing everything up right now."

"Includin' me." The man held up a hand. "Don't worry, I

totally agree. A man like you's right to take precautions, especially at times like this. We'll find me a horse in the next town and I can ride alongside you, we'll make better progress that way. If you don't mind keepin' a slower pace until then I'd be much obliged. By the by, you can take your hand off that pistol; I promise I won't do nothin' stupid."

Jones glanced at him, but kept his hand on the weapon. "What makes you think I'm armed?"

"Because you clearly aren't a stupid man. Dressed like you are, with a horse, the way you talk and sit. You're an army man, aren't you?" When Jones did not reply the man continued, opening his coat: "I am as well. I would ask if you were an officer, but by the way you talk, I'd say you weren't. Am I right?"

"Sergeant," said Jones after a pause. "At least I was."

The man clapped his hands together and let out a whoop. "A deserter too? My luck must be changin' finally! Here I was worried I'd end up meetin' a hopeless civilian and have to waste my time protectin' them. Or worse, a bunch of soldiers all a-huntin' for deserters. This is great: two of us'll be unstoppable."

"Against what?" asked Jones.

"Against whatever this madness throws at us next. I were there the first time the demons started opening portals back at Greenwich. I saw what they could do and I said to myself, never again. Never again would I let myself be on the losin' side. That's why I ran from my regiment, see? I knew things would be going south, but my commanding officer's more concerned with sitting and doing nothing. That's not for me: I want to be where the action is."

The man's bragging continued nonstop as they made their way to Maidstone, such that Jones seriously contemplated leaving him behind. But there was a lot to be said for keeping company with like-minded people, although he was determined not to let the man in on his own plans.

At Maidstone they set about procuring supplies and a horse, a task that was complicated by the lack of any open stores whatsoever. The residents they did encounter seemed to follow the pattern of others elsewhere: either overwrought, insensible or just purely insane. A large crowd had gathered in the main square, but none of them displayed much interest in the two newcomers.

They found a coaching inn and knocked on the door, receiving nothing but silence in return. "Ah well," shrugged the deserter. "I'm guessin' it's every man for himself, then."

He headed round the side of the inn, and after a moment's hesitation to hitch his horse to a post, Jones followed. Half a dozen horses milled around in the stables and yard to the rear, snorting and whickering, clearly slightly agitated by the lack of any food or water. The kitchen door was open and the two men entered, calling out a cautious greeting as they did so.

A quick inspection found the building to be empty save for a drunk who was sleeping on one of the tables in the bar, having seemingly taken it upon himself to consume all of the alcohol in the premises. The deserter stepped round him, examining the bottles until he finally found one full of more than just dregs. He took a long swig and then offered it to Jones, who accepted gratefully.

"Looks like everyone's takin' the end of the world pretty badly, eh?" said the deserter.

"Maybe they'll come to their senses when the novelty of the absent sky runs out."

"I doubt it," said the deserter. "You see, I have a theory." He grabbed another bottle, testing it for weight before taking a swig and wincing. "What do you and me have in common over all them others out there?"

"We're both ex-army?" shrugged Jones.

The deserter nodded. "But not just that. Yes, we have the training and stuff, and we've no doubt both seen some terrible things on the field of battle, but we've also got purpose and direction. We're both moved by earthly things like a chain of command, the need to take action, planning and reconnaissance.

Not like them sheep out there, who care so much for their God and precious little else. They're returning to their natural state, waitin' for someone to lead them and show them the way."

"What way would that be?" Jones asked. "You fancying yourself as some kind of preacher?"

"Oh no, not I," he laughed. "But someone'll step up at some point, mark my words. Or all them out there will die."

Jones shuddered at the thought, but also knew from what he had seen that day that there was little he could do on his own. He needed to find Disraeli as soon as possible. "Let's gather what supplies we can and make our way," he said. "There's nothing for us here."

The deserter waved his bottle. "We have plenty to occupy ourselves here. Why don't we rest a while?"

Jones gestured to the dribbling drunk. "And wind up like him? You help yourself. As you said, I have a purpose and it's not served by getting insensible here."

An hour later they were back on the road, the deserter having reluctantly agreed to Jones' logic but still insisting on bringing as many bottles with him as he could carry. While in the circumstances Jones found the thought of getting drunk highly appealing, his sense of mission was even stronger and it was this that he clung on to as they made their way along the road to London.

Time was a difficult thing to measure under that never-changing sky, especially as neither man had the advantage of a pocket watch. The clocks they passed were meaningless: was it midnight or midday?

They rode until they felt the fatigue so intensely that they had to stop. By that point the deserter was merrily sloshed and Jones settled down to sleep in a hollow a little way from the road, not really caring if the man followed him or not.

He was woken by shouting in the distance and sat up, straining to hear over the sound of the deserter's drunken snoring. The noise appeared to be drawing closer, coming down the road towards London. Jones crept forward, keeping himself as close as possible to the ground. He checked back, relieved to note that the horses were hidden from the road by the hollow.

He watched as a group of men, heavily armed and intoxicated, appeared from the southeast. There were about a dozen of them, all on horseback and some carrying bundles trussed across the saddles of their horses that, on closer examination, transpired to be the bodies of women. Some of these passengers were kicking and struggling feebly while others had clearly resigned themselves to their fate.

Jones bit back the urge to intervene: there were too many of them and it was apparent that they would be in no mood to welcome an intercession.

He watched them disappear over the horizon and, satisfied that no others were likely to appear for the time being, stood and made his way back to their makeshift encampment. He had no idea how long he had been sleeping, but felt strong and rested enough to get back on the road; with any luck they could be in London before they needed to rest again.

The deserter very reluctantly woke up, grumbling and groaning at Jones as he did so, and it was only the threat of leaving him on his own that galvanised him into action. They gnawed on hunks of bread and meat as they rode, Jones keeping a wary eye out for any other travellers. He had decided against telling the deserter about the group of men for fear that that would only spur him into doing something foolish, such as try to find them and join in their debauchery.

The deserter was considerably less talkative after his sleep, although Jones could not decide whether this was due to a hangover or the reality of their situation having finally hit home. Regardless, Jones was glad of the quiet, giving him a chance to make his own sense of what was going on. Frustratingly, he was able to focus on little other than the rocking motion of his horse, as the blankness overhead would time and again press down on his thoughts.

They were a few miles from Greenwich when Jones felt a familiar tingle on the back of his neck, a warning sign that they were being watched and pursued. He twisted in his saddle and then cursed.

"Go!" he shouted to the deserter, spurring his own horse into a gallop.

"What is it?" called the other, struggling to keep pace.

"Soul-less," replied Jones, not caring if his voice reached the other man or not. He cursed himself; he should have realised that if anyone was well placed to take advantage of the current situation, it was those beasts.

The Soul-less. The remnants of humans who had been tempted by the demons and lost their souls in the process, as a result reverting to little more than bloodthirsty beasts united only in their hatred of humanity. Following the Battle of Greenwich they had become a large problem across swathes of the countryside, although the army had taken steps to eradicate as many of the creatures as they could over the following years. The one benefit was that they always seemed to take care to not get too close to any populated areas, and it was this that Jones was keen to take advantage of.

As they entered the outskirts of Greenwich, their horses panting hard, Jones looked back to see that the Soul-less were still closing on them. He cursed; they were showing no signs of slowing down. Could it be that they were emboldened by the new situation enough to lose their previous reticence?

They galloped through streets that were largely deserted, aside from the occasional prone body. They did not have time to pause and check whether these unfortunates were dead or merely unconscious, for the Soul-less were still hard at their heels.

They rounded another corner, the sounds of pursuit drawing ever closer, and Jones considered turning to fight as a preferable—albeit suicidal—option to being cut down from behind.

The pop and crackle of gunfire from around them focused his mind on the present, causing his horse to rear in terror. He landed hard, rolling away from his gelding's hooves and towards the nearest wall in the hope that it would afford some protection from these new attackers. Pulling himself up onto one knee, he drew his pistol and scanned around for someone or something to shoot.

He paused as he realised that these new assailants were targeting the Soul-less. With a roar, Jones swung round to join in the attack and managed a handful of rounds before those godless creatures still standing turned and fled, screaming in frustrated rage.

"Wait there," someone shouted from a window above them. Jones looked around in the sudden silence and saw the deserter lying on the ground near where his horse had thrown him, his head resting on a rifle pointed out in front of him.

"Are you all right?" Jones asked, scrabbling over to him.

The deserter looked up and flashed a weak grin. "Landed awkwardly on me ankle but I weren't hit. Reckon I'll live."

Jones helped him to his feet and they looked around as people started to emerge from buildings. All were armed and cast suspicious glances at the two newcomers.

"You'll drop them weapons," said one man, pointing a rifle at them.

They complied and watched as a tall, grey-haired man stepped out from a building to their left. He looked them up and down and then nodded. "Come with us," he said. Jones looked around at the wall of gun barrels and realised that they had precious little alternative but to comply.

They were escorted to a large town hall building that had been turned into a storage space, the once-ornate and ordered rooms and corridors now stacked full of food, weapons and blankets. Clearly these people—whoever they were—had not wasted any time in taking the sky's disappearance as a call to action.

They were led to the council chamber room and ordered to sit in a pair of chairs placed in the middle of the room. They looked around, halfway between bemused and nervous, at the sea of hostile faces around them. After a few moments a tall, dark-haired and well-dressed man entered the room, pausing to talk to a few of the men standing by the door who had escorted Jones and the deserter to that building, before walking over to the two seated men in the centre of the space.

"Who are you?" asked the man.

Jones regarded this man impassively, glancing around at the others as well to determine how much of a threat these people really were. However, it was the deserter who answered first.

"We're just normal folks like you lot," he said. "Just tryin' to survive, wonderin' what's been goin' on, you know?"

The man stared at them for a moment, and then turned his attention to Jones. "And who are you?" he asked again.

"Ex-soldiers," said Jones slowly. "Just like some of you lot by the looks of things." He glanced around. "So who exactly are you then?"

"What regiment?" the man asked, ignoring Jones' question.

After a moment's thought, Jones decided that the truth was the safest option. "The Royal Welch," he said. "But I'm not welcome with them right now."

"You're not an officer," the man said. "So I guess you're either a Sergeant or a Corporal."

Jones nodded. "Sergeant. Jones is the name. Who are you, exactly?"

The man stared at them for a moment. Then a small smile played across his face. "We have a couple of deserters here, do we?"

The deserter nodded rapidly. "That's right," he said quickly. "We're no friends of the army. Oh no, not us. By the by, I love what you guys did back there, and we haven't had a chance to thank you lot for savin' our skins, have we?"

Jones ignored the man, instead focusing his attention on their interrogator. "You still haven't told us who you lot are," he said. "You're not the army, that's for sure. I take it you're deserters too?"

The man sneered at him. "Some of us might be, some of us ain't. Point is that things have been changing over the past few years and now it's finally time for the likes of us to seize our chance while we still can. Seems to me that you boys have a choice to make: you're either with us and a part of the new world order, or you're against us."

"With you. We are with you. Definitely," babbled the deserter, his head nodding so rapidly that Jones half-feared it would fly off his shoulders altogether.

Their interrogator ignored this show of sycophancy, keeping his gaze focused on Jones. "What do you say?" he asked, a thin smile playing across his lips. "Where do you stand?"

Jones shrugged. "Seems to me I'm on the side of anyone who stops me being torn to pieces by those demons back there," he said slowly. "But I always like to know who it is I'm fighting with and for before I nail my colours to any masts."

The man laughed. "I like you," he said, clapping his hands together once with a sharp crack that made the deserter jump. "I think you and me are going to get along famously." He rose to his feet and beckoned for them to follow. "I'll show you boys what it is we're about."

They followed the man warily out of the room, Jones noticing that the others around them still had not relaxed their gazes or lowered their weapons. As they had spotted when they first entered the building, all manner of supplies had been raided from the nearby homes, stores and warehouses, and were stacked in the rooms and corridors they passed.

"We've been waiting for a sign for a long time," the man said as he walked. "That sign finally came when the sky disappeared. The old ways weren't working, not for the common man, not for anyone who wasn't one of the chosen few."

"Chosen few?" asked Jones, looking around and keeping a mental tally of what he could see, the numbers of people and any potential threats or weaknesses.

"Yeah," said the man. "You know, the toffs, the officers, all those who gave orders. Well," he waved an arm around vaguely, "they're not in charge any longer."

Jones frowned at the man. "What makes you so sure? It's only been a few days, surely, and anyway there's still plenty of time for the government or the army to clamp back down again."

"How far have you travelled since the sky disappeared?" asked the man.

Jones shrugged. "From just past Maidstone," he said. "Couldn't tell you how many miles, but I can tell you I didn't see much apart from a load of scared and confused people."

"And how many soldiers or policemen did you see in all that travelling?" asked the man. "How many people in so-called authority did you see taking charge and helping to bring order?"

Jones shrugged again. "Well… none, I guess."

The man clapped his hands and spun round, pointing a finger at Jones. The man's eyes were aglow with zeal, a passion that lit up his face with an almost boyish mania. "Exactly," he hissed. "They're all gone now, and it's down to the likes of us to seize our chance while we can."

Jones raised an eyebrow, fighting to maintain his composure in the face of this strange man. He was unsure whether to be scared, alarmed or amused by the way he spoke and acted. "And who are you exactly?" he asked again.

The man shook his head as he led them into a long hall that had been converted into a makeshift canteen. "All in good time, my new chums," he said, sweeping his hand to gesture expansively at the room. "All will become clear when you've proven that you can be trusted. In the meantime, you're welcome to stay as our guests. We have food here, more food than you would ever have seen in the army. Eat your fill and rest well, and soon you will be given the chance to prove exactly whose side you're on."

The other people in that canteen were similarly evasive when it came to explaining their purpose or identities. While the deserter continued to persist with his inane mix of compliments and questions, Jones satisfied himself with simply observing and keeping his own counsel.

All of the people around them appeared to be united by some form of common purpose, that much was clear. As Jones and the deserter had noticed over the previous days while travelling, it seemed to require an element of focus and direction to avoid falling prey to the aimless fugue that had overcome so many people. However, the purpose that united their new hosts was not readily apparent. What was it they wanted?

After they had eaten their fill of sausages, steak and mashed potatoes, they were led to another room filled with hammocks, mattresses and rugs. One of the ever-present guards gestured for them to choose a bed and make themselves comfortable. This they did, watching as the guard retreated to the door and closed it behind him.

"So," grinned the deserter. "Looks like we've landed on our feet here doesn't it, matey?"

Jones resisted the urge to snap at the man's idiocy. "I'll be a lot happier," he said, "when they tell us exactly what's going on here, who they are and stop having us followed around by guards all the time."

The deserter giggled. "Don't know what you mean," he said. "You heard him yourself: he likes us."

"Yeah," said Jones slowly. "But he never did tell us who he is exactly, did he?" He lay down and rolled over without waiting for the deserter to reply.

*

While Jones had been determined to remain alert, at some point he must have dozed off because he was shocked back into wakefulness by the door slamming open and two armed men marching in and shouting at them to get up. Jones complied, following them out of the room and down the corridor towards the outdoors.

"Time to make yourselves useful, gents," said a man in front of them. His looks and manner reminded Jones very much of his old Sergeant Major back when he had first signed up with the army. "We are all going on a foraging party," the man continued. "You'll come with us and gather what you're told to gather."

They were taken by horse and cart along the roads westwards and then across the river towards London. Everywhere was eerily quiet as they made their way, something that Jones remarked on to the guard who was sitting next to him.

Free from the stifling atmosphere of the headquarters, the man seemed happy to talk. "Yeah," he said. "It's been like this ever since the sky went away. Seems that most people just decided life weren't worth living no more. Them that's still of a mind to do something at all upped and joined us. But the rest, well…" The man shrugged.

As they moved further through the city, heaps of rubbish lined their path. With a shock, Jones realised that these were in fact the bodies of people lying slumped on each other as though they had just decided to stop and give up on life there and then. As he watched he saw one or two move, stirred into a dim form of consciousness by the sound of their passing.

"We should help them," Jones said.

"Nah," sneered the man next to him. "They're all goners. Anyway, we've got a higher cause to work for now."

Jones stared at him, wanting to do something but knowing he was powerless without a weapon against their numbers. "And what cause would that be, exactly?"

The man stared at him for a moment, clearly trying to decide whether Jones was being idiotic or just difficult. A look of shock flashed across the man's face as he realised that these newcomers had not been inducted into whatever secrets the others shared and he looked away, his jaw clamped shut.

Jones' days settled into a routine of foraging followed by food and sleep, all the while staying under the watchful eye of the guards. He had no idea how many days were passing, his only way of marking the passage of time being the periodic changes in activities. The trips themselves proved to be incredibly depressing, with them encountering very few people alive as they travelled despite Jones' keeping a watchful eye out. The few people still living that they encountered were as still and insensible as those he had passed on his way towards Greenwich in those early days after the sky's disappearance.

All through this, the guards steadfastly refused to allow him any form of weapon for even a moment. The foraging trips themselves, aside from the terrible helplessness he felt at not being able to help those poor souls who lay or wandered around the streets, were for the most part a backbreaking monotony of lifting and carrying.

On the third such trip, Jones was in the process of trying to manoeuvre a crate of ammunition into a wagon when a shout rang out from the next street over. Without thinking, he let go of his load and ran towards the sound of the cries, instinctively recognising the sound of someone in trouble.

He rounded the corner to see one of his fellow foragers backing away from a demon that was advancing upon him with murderous intent.

Jones looked around as he ran towards the monster, trying to spot something that could be used as a makeshift weapon. He settled on a length of wood that had been discarded in the street, clearly once part of a costermonger's barrow. Kicking it into the air, he caught it one-handed as he ran, swinging it around his head and yelling as he advanced on the demon. The creature started to turn at this noise and Jones caught it hard across the head with his bludgeon, sending it flying to the ground.

"Come on! Run!" he yelled to the man who was still cowering helplessly against a wall. When the man did not reply, Jones grabbed him by the arm and propelled him out into the street and past the demon, which was now getting to its feet with a snarl filling its face.

Jones looked down at the length of wood in his hand, noting with dismay that the impact with the demon had had broken it in two. He threw the remainder at the demon's face and used the brief distraction it afforded to make a run for the safety of the others who, he noted with incredulity, were just standing around watching.

"One of you bastards fire at the thing!" he shouted to them as he ran at full speed.

For a moment they gaped at him before starting to back away. Jones glanced backwards to see that the demon was still tearing after him, all bright red eyes, sharp teeth and grasping claws.

This sight spurred Jones into a sprint the like of which he had never before managed, and he barrelled into the nearest guard, snatching the rifle from his hand. He swung round and swiftly discharged the weapon straight into the demon's face. He followed this up with a succession of hard strikes of the butt of the rifle to its head.

He shouted as he struck at the creature, finding an outlet in the mindless violence for all of the pent-up frustration that had built up in him over the past few days. After a few moments he was grabbed roughly by the shoulders and pulled away, the rifle snatched from his grasp.

"It's done," said a guard, throwing the bloodied rifle disgustedly back to the man who had surrendered it so meekly.

Jones sank to the floor breathing hard, but there was a part of him that enjoyed the newfound respect he could see in the others' eyes.

The next day he was just getting ready to settle down to another meal and rest when he was summoned away from the canteen and into a chamber. The room he found himself in contained a large table that had been laid out for dinner, with meats and bread dotted invitingly around. At the head of the table stood the man who had interrogated them on their arrival all those days ago.

On his urging, Jones sat opposite him, watching as three other individuals took up the remaining seats. Jones noted with a slight degree of satisfaction that the deserter had not been invited to this gathering; he had been very keen to ingratiate himself with any and all of their new companions and had soon been whisked away to join some other party. Jones had been pleased to see the back of the man and his idiotic rantings.

"How are you finding our hospitality?" asked the man at the head.

Jones placed his hands on the table, looking around as he tried to ascertain the reason for this invitation. "I'm not sure you could call it hospitality," he said slowly. "No one will talk to me, I still don't know any of your names or your intentions."

The others around the room chuckled and the man looked around before nodding to Jones. "We appreciate your patience and your hard work over these past few days," he said. "You have proven yourself to be a good worker and we are keen to test you in other ways too. In particular I'm very conscious of the fact that your more... specialised talents appear to be going to waste."

Jones could resist his hunger no longer and grabbed at a nearby hunk of bread, tearing it into chunks and pushing them into his mouth. He looked at the man opposite as he chewed on a large mouthful.

"I heard about how you handled yourself with that demon," said the man. "I fear that many of our people would not be as quick-thinking as you appear to be."

Jones shrugged. "Had to do something," he said through a mouthful of food. "Couldn't just stand by and watch someone get torn to ribbons."

"We have need of men of action, people like you," said the man. "Your kind will be extremely valuable in this new world that we are on the cusp of creating."

Jones raised an eyebrow. "New world?" he asked through another mouthful of bread.

The man nodded. "The old world is over; even a fool can see that."

Jones shook his head. "It's only been a few days. There is

still time for the government, the authorities to re-establish themselves. And yet you are acting as though—"

"How many days or miles did you travel after the sky disappeared?" asked the man. "How many days have you been with us here, scavenging around London?"

Jones opened his mouth to reply but before he could do the man interjected. "In all that time, how many aimless, mindless imbeciles did you come across, driven to despair by what has happened?" He did not wait for a response, instead slamming his fist down hard on the table, making the glasses and plates chink together, an audible exclamation point emphasising his point. "Exactly! There is a reason why we alone have survived and are the lords and masters of all we survey."

"And that reason is…?" asked Jones.

The man spread his arms wide. "All of those sheep, all of those imbeciles who now line the streets and aimlessly wander about, unable to fend for themselves, they were all united by one thing." He held up a finger, his eyes shining with the bright zeal Jones remembered from when he first met him. "God: that's what. They were all so beholden to their God that they could not cope when He finally abandoned them."

Jones' chewing had slowed down as he took in this diatribe. He grabbed a nearby glass of wine and took a sip in the hope that it would help to lubricate the mass of food now stuck in his cheeks. He did not like the way this conversation was heading.

"We are the messengers for a new world," said the man. "We have been delivered here to prepare the way for His coming. That is the work that you have been helping us with and that is the work that we would have you play a key role in."

"And when you say 'He'?" asked Jones.

"I mean of course the one who has made all of this possible," said the man, waving his arms vaguely about him.

"All of this…?" Jones instinctively pushed another chunk of bread into his mouth, if only to give him an excuse for not replying straightaway.

"The sky, the demons, the portal at St Albans, the coming of the new world," said the man, spittle flecking the tablecloth as he spat out the words. "He who will deliver us from the old world of so-called elites with their precious gods. Satan himself!"

Jones fought hard to not laugh in their faces as he considered this, for looking round the table he could tell that they were completely sincere in what they were saying and what they believed. He realised that he was in an incredibly perilous situation, for to make a wrong move at this point could not only end his life but also any chance of his superiors being warned of this new threat until it was too late. Whatever this threat was. He frowned, trying to make sense of the man's words. "By Satan do you mean the demon Andras?" he asked.

The man barked a dismissive laugh. "No, not that usurper," he spat. "We serve the one true Lord. He is coming and He has told us to pave the way. There are many others like us, and our time has finally come. The question is: are you with us or against us?"

The bread in Jones' mouth had taken on a rock-like quality as he struggled to digest this turn of events. He took a long swig of wine, draining his glass and using the liquid to flush the food down his throat. Swallowing hard he looked up at them and forced a grin. "In your new world, will I still have to be a Sergeant?" he asked.

The man looked at him for a second and then emitted a short, shrill laugh that was taken up by the others around the table. "That is one of the reasons why I appreciate you," said the man. "You have a very direct and earthy sense of events. No, you do not have to be a Sergeant. You can be whatever you want to be; why not be a Major, or a General?"

"In that case," said Jones, "I figure that the old world didn't work too well for me. As long as there's food, beer and women then your new world is fine by me."

The man stood and walked round the table to Jones, picking up a bottle of wine and refilling Jones' glass, placing a hand firmly on his shoulder as he did so. Putting the bottle back down on the table, the man gathered up a glass of his own and raised it in a toast that was joined by all the others. Jones raised his own glass and downed the contents, feeling a burning sensation run down his throat as he realised exactly what it was that they were toasting.

Whilst they did not immediately bring him into all of their confidences, Jones saw and heard enough to realise that their insane plans needed to be stopped as soon as possible. He learnt that a large proportion of men and equipment had the previous day been sent to St Albans, the reasons for which he could only guess at but knew they would not be favourable. Each day, more and more people came to join the group, mostly aimless souls simply looking for sanctuary, but there were also far too many people already sharing the same zeal as the man and his Satan-worshipping colleagues.

The following night, Jones was placed on sentry duty outside the headquarters building. Whilst this was no doubt a test of his reliability, it was a test that Jones was determined to fail. He waited until an hour or so had passed and all seemed silent around him before slipping off into a side street and running as fast as he could westwards towards Whitehall.

Chapter Seventeen

I stared at Jones during a break in the journey from St Albans to Hughenden as we tried to come to terms with all that he had said. "Satanists forming an army in London?" I asked incredulously.

"I know," said Jones. "I barely believe it myself, and I was right in the thick of it. However, it's true, and they're not only very well organised they also have widespread support too. Since I left them they've been nothing but trouble."

"Completely insane," muttered Pearce. "The world is going mad…"

"I wish that were the case," muttered Andras.

We turned to look at him. "What you not tellin'?" asked Kate.

Andras sighed. "This turn of events is certainly not helpful," he said, "but I'm afraid that those people are no more insane than the rest of you."

I took a deep breath. "I really have neither the time nor the patience for another one of your protracted riddles," I said, keeping my voice low and level. "Just tell us exactly what you mean."

"I mean that the higher power that those people said they

follow is in fact a very real one," said Andras. "Certainly as real as I am."

"You mean to say that they are worshipping one of your people? An Almadite?" asked Byron.

Andras nodded slowly. "And I think I know exactly which of my people."

"The Four Kings?" asked Byron.

Andras nodded again.

"So we have another demon invasion on our hands," said Kate. "I guess it's that time of year already."

I allowed myself a wry smile. "In which case, we should definitely make haste. You say that everyone is at Hughenden?"

"That's right," said Jones. "Disraeli, your brother and what's left of the army and police. Plus a load of refugees we gathered up on the way."

"You said that everyone had just sat down and given up?" asked Kate.

Jones nodded. "Certainly most people, at least at first. After a while, a lot seemed to snap out of it before it was too late. Them that didn't..." The rest of his sentence hung in the air between us, the silence implying much more terrible things than words could ever portray.

I shuddered. "How many people...?"

Jones shook his head. "Impossible to say, sir. Based on what I've seen, I'd say thousands or even millions across England. If this is also happening around the rest of the world... well, it don't bear thinking about."

*

We huddled in the cover of a line of trees, looking out at the army of howling, screeching monsters before us. My heart sank as I contemplated the sheer numbers in our path.

"I have never seen so many Soul-less together in one place," Pearce muttered.

"It appears that your Sergeant was correct in saying they have become emboldened by the changes up there," said Andras, nodding towards the sky.

"What now?" asked Joshua from just behind us, as always hunched close to Lexie.

"There are too many of them for us to attack," said Pearce. "Going round them would cost too much time and just opens us to the risk that we would be discovered." He scratched his chin. "They never tend to spend more than a few hours in one place, they are probably just regrouping here before moving on. We will remain here for the time being and wait them out. Hopefully they should be gone by morning."

I barked a short, mirthless laugh. "Morning?" I asked. "You still believe such a concept exists?" I nodded up at the blank canvas stretched above us.

"Fair point," he said. "In any case, I think that discretion is the better part of valour right now, and in any case we could all do with a rest."

"I second that," said Byron, and we shuffled backwards away from the treeline. Pearce left a line of men to stand guard while we found a clearing to wait out the foul creatures.

The intention was for us to get some rest, which we all attempted with varying degrees of success. Gaap was tied to a tree and, after checking that his bindings and gag were secure, Andras retreated back towards the treeline. Gaap, for his part, very quickly closed his eyes and appeared to fall into peaceful sleep, as did Lexie. Joshua sat next to her and absentmindedly stroked her hair while he stared into the middle distance. Byron and I watched him from the other side of the clearing, sharing a collective unease as we tried to fathom what was going on in the head of this insanely powerful young man.

Kate had lain down under a rug that had been wrapped tenderly around her by Pearce, who had then gone back to guard duty. We sat in relative peace until suddenly Kate jerked awake with a shout.

She sat up, breathing hard and looking around her as though she expected to still be in whatever nightmare she had recently escaped. I rose to my feet and went over to her, sitting by her side and putting an awkward hand on her shoulder.

"It's all right," I said softly. "We're here."

She glared up at me, about to snap some flippant comment. Then her face softened and her shoulders slumped as she nodded. "Yeah, I know," she said in a quivering voice. "Just can't shake them bad thoughts."

I looked at her. "How much sleep have you actually had since we rescued you?"

She shrugged. "A bit," she said, a defensive tone creeping into her voice.

I resisted the urge to answer back, instead letting the silence stretch awkwardly between us as I stared at her. After few moments, she relented.

"All right," she sighed. "It's just… every time I close my eyes or things go quiet all I can see is that… thing and I can't shake the feelin' of something inside me growin', trying to eat up everything in my body until there's nothin' left but some empty shell." She shivered uncontrollably.

I hesitantly put an arm out and around her shoulders again, gently touching her body; not so firm that I could not snatch it away if she resisted, snapped at me or tried to strike me. Instead, she welcomed the embrace, folding into it and pressing herself against my arm and side. I felt my heart skip a beat as I realised that we had broken through some sort of invisible barrier that had always stood between the two of us; in spite of all our time living, working and fighting together we had never shown any form of physical intimacy towards each other until that moment.

I gently rubbed her arm. "It's understandable, you know," I said softly. "After all you've been through I'd be more worried if you didn't show any ill effects."

She chuckled. "You're a physic now, are you?" She frowned and shook her head. "I don't know. I just can't shake the feeling that I'm damaged goods somehow."

"What, even more than before?" I asked with a smile.

She playfully punched my leg. "You know what I mean. That thing was there inside my nut doing God knows what, and even though it's cleared off I don't know what it did, what it took away or what it changed. None of us do. I might be better off not being here at all. You all might be safer without me…"

I shook my head. "You know that's not true; we need you. You're the one true warrior among us. If anyone is going to beat what happens, then you will. We all need you: me, Max…" I took a deep breath before adding the final words, my heart almost fighting its utterance. "…Pearce."

She looked up at me. "Is that a bit of jealousy I sense there, Augustus Potts?" she asked, a smile playing across her lips.

I shook my head far too quickly. "No, no, not at all. Nothing of the sort. I just… I have noted how he has been with you recently."

"After all I've been through," she said. "Fightin' demon invasions, being kidnapped and possessed, then off to the spirit world to get cured, not to mention runnin' all over the place trying desperately not to get killed. Do you really think I'd have had time to fit in romancing around all that?" She dug her elbow gently into my side.

I chuckled. "I suppose not."

"What about him, though?" Kate asked, nodding at Joshua, whose face was a bliss of half-dozing contemplation as he toyed with the slumbering Lexie's hair.

"That is an altogether different worry," I said softly. "The power he has is quite breath-taking… and yet I have no idea what his motivations really are."

"Come on, it's obvious what he wants," said Kate. "He just wants to play happy families, to have everything as it was before we all waded in and ruined his life."

"I just worry about Lexie," I said. "It's astonishing that he's got her back but everyone has been very clear that her being here is against the natural order of things. What if she causes yet more damage without even realising it?"

Kate shrugged and I looked at her, noticing how tired she appeared. Her eyelids fluttered as though they were too heavy for her face to keep open and then they slid shut as she slipped into what I hoped was a dreamless sleep. I sat there for a while, gently holding her and enjoying the warmth of her body against mine before feeling self-conscious and deciding to get up and do something else.

Ignoring the knowing glances of the others around the clearing, I slowly extricated myself from around Kate, taking care to rest her head and shoulders gently down on the ground before covering her with the blanket again. I stood and stretched, looking around before deciding to venture over to the pickets stationed at the treeline to see if there had been any activity.

I joined Pearce and Andras, surprised to see them both kneeling almost companionably together. Squatting next to them I muttered: "Any change?"

Pearce shook his head. "The majority appear to be resting, as I suspected," he said. "The others are either fighting among themselves or have been killed by their comrades."

"That's very obliging of them," I said as I looked out at the mass in front of us. They truly were a barbaric bunch, reinforcing every prejudice I had had about the Soul-less. There appeared to be no leadership amongst them whatsoever, with the group instead seeming to have adopted a herd-like, almost animalistic mentality. My first thought was that they were akin to a mob of sheep but I revised that to the more suitable comparison of a pack of wolves. Each seemed concerned solely with his or her own status within the group—for there were women there as well as men. Those who slumbered had proven themselves worthy of whatever position they held within this weird social ranking, while the remainder sniped and snarled at each other to establish their relative standing, much like rival lions battling for supremacy over a pride.

It was hard to imagine that these creatures were, in most respects, no different to myself and my friends, for such was their savagery it was almost as though we were staring back thousands of years in time at an earlier state of humanity. With a flash I wondered if this was what the demons truly wanted of us; to send us back to a less threatening and cohesive state, so they could rule supreme over us.

"I did not realise there were so many of them still in existence," I muttered.

"Nor did I," said Pearce.

"I don't think there were," said Andras. When we both glanced quizzically at him, he added: "I would not be surprised if the phenomenon that has taken over the sky has had some bearing on the numbers here." He pointed out a group of Soul-less close to us. "See how those ones seem to be dressed in relatively fresh clothing and are not as decayed as the others?"

I stared at where he was indicating. The group did look remarkably normal in comparison to the Soul-less, although such a thing was relative. Whatever turned a person from a human into one of these things, it degenerated their bodies as swiftly as their minds, with their muscles standing out in stark relief to their skeletal anatomy and their heads taking on an almost skull-like aspect. The creatures also seemed to care little for clothing, with naked Soul-less not an uncommon sight.

Those nearest to us, however, did not appear to be as far advanced in their transformation and could have been mistaken for normal, independently minded human beings. Save, that is, for the fact that they shared the same snarling mindless looks on their faces and were behaving towards each other like little more than rival dogs.

"Do you mean to say that they are more recent creations?" asked Pearce.

"But who could have created them?" I asked. "I thought the majority were a by-product of your—"

"Yes, yes," Andras said quickly. "We don't need to go over

all that again. However I would wager that these creatures were either created by another like me, or, more likely, something inherent in the changes to the sky that has fundamentally affected humanity."

"But then why have we not all been affected in the same way?" I asked.

Andras sneered at me. "You are always so keen to tell me how different you are to each other, so why should you all be uniformly affected? You heard from Sergeant Jones that some people were reduced to a near catatonic state shortly after the sky disappeared, whilst others started raving about worshipping Satan. It is sensible to assume that either or both of those states of mind were a precursor to ending up like this." He waved his hand at the field before us.

I shuddered. "And yet we are fortunate enough to not be affected."

"Maybe there was something that took place at the same time as the infection spread across our world," said Pearce, "the infection that turned the sky this way. Perhaps as it spread it touched everyone in its path. We were in the Aether at that time, so it makes perfect sense that we would not have been affected."

Andras chuckled. "Such perfect scientific reasoning. Maxwell would be proud of you, Captain."

A thought struck me. "You created these creatures," I said to Andras. "Could you cure them?"

Andras shook his head. "Maxwell and I tried on countless occasions while I was stuck as N'yotsu, but to no avail. As far as I can tell, the changes are irreversible."

"Just like Kate's changes were irreversible?" asked Pearce, staring straight ahead.

Andras raised an eyebrow at him. "To cure her we had to break through into the afterlife, bargain with the undead and in the process cause all of this. Probably. Just to cure one person. Imagine what we would have to do to cure thousands or perhaps millions of people."

Pearce stared steadily ahead. "There must be a way."

"The more pressing matter," continued Andras, "is the question of what we do with our little undead hitch-hiker back there."

"What do you mean?" I asked, staring at him.

"The creature that Joshua is deluding himself is his sister," said Andras. "Surely I'm not the only one who can see it?"

"See what?" asked Pearce.

"Have you managed to have a conversation with her since he brought her back?" Andras asked.

I shrugged. "She answered my questions perfectly well."

"That's not what I meant," said Andras. "I meant a real conversation; not just a few stock answers that she could have plucked from any one of our heads."

I stared at the demon, trying to decide whether he was being sincere or just seizing on one more opportunity to divide us.

Andras shrugged back at me. "Just think about it," he said.

I frowned, but my mind was already running over my interactions with Lexie. Joshua seemed not to have noticed, maybe because he was keen not to look a gift horse in the mouth, but she showed no curiosity at all in what had happened since she had been killed, or in her life before that point. Furthermore, she was unable to answer anything beyond the most basic of questions about her past. Could Andras be right? Was she constructing her responses and interactions with us from the contents of our own minds? And if so, what did that mean she really was? Indeed, was she actually real at all? Such a thing seemed ridiculous, but far more fantastical things had happened to us over the years.

Pearce rubbed his eyes and stretched.

"You should get some sleep," I said to him. "We can keep watch here. I can't see much happening for a while in any case."

"I cannot sleep," he said softly. "Not any more." Under the weight of our combined stares he reluctantly continued: "Every time I close my eyes I can sense them, hear them pounding away at my skull. I daren't try to sleep in case I never wake up."

"That's very common," said Andras. "It'll pass; nothing to worry about."

"How do you know?"

"I've possessed my fair share of people in the past, and suffered a good deal of exorcisms into the bargain. Don't worry: it's an all-or-nothing arrangement. There's no part of the creatures left inside you, you just need a bit of time to recover."

"Time we don't have."

I sighed, thinking about our group of so-called heroes. Kate and Pearce were in danger of being incapacitated by the after-effects of their possessions. Joshua was displaying every sign of being unhinged while none of us were sure of what to make of his sister. That left me, Byron and Andras to defend humanity: and two of us definitely did not trust the third. My heart sank as I considered the prospect of this rag-tag bunch facing a real battle.

Chapter Eighteen

It felt like days passed under that unchanging sky before the Soul-less began to move away from their makeshift camp. At first the migration was barely perceptible, a few creatures deciding to wander off in a north-easterly direction. Then, after a few moments, more and more joined the flow, like leaves caught in a stream.

By this point we were gathered at the treeline, watching with bated breath as the creatures shuffled off, occasionally pausing to attack each other. We crouched with our hands on our weapons, watching for signs that any of them would decide to venture towards our hiding place. Thankfully none did, instead preferring the open spaces afforded by the fields and hills.

"Maybe they're fed up with always being in hiding," mused Kate. "If I were them, I'd take full advantage to parade around wherever I wanted."

After around an hour only a handful of the creatures remained, excepting, of course, the bodies of those Soul-less strewn around the ground, abandoned where they had fallen or been murdered by their associates.

I glanced at the others, clearly sharing my unease at how reluctant these stragglers were to follow the horde. Pearce scanned the skyline to the east, where the bulk of the Soul-less had disappeared. Satisfied that none remained within seeing distance, he nodded to us. "If they won't leave," said Pearce, "then we should rid ourselves of them. With me!"

We followed him as he charged out from the undergrowth, his sabre whirling as he ran. Kate stayed behind, a gun trained on Gaap to ensure that he did not succumb to the temptation to run while we were distracted. As I ran I felt the runic sword sing in my hand as it welcomed the exercise, having spent far too long without being wielded in anger. The others followed suit, enjoying the opportunity to do something other than run or hide. None of us used guns or rifles in case they alerted the other Soul-less to our actions but even so the violence was over in a matter of moments, the creatures being no match for the ferocity of our attack or our numbers.

Satisfied that we had cleared this obstacle, we struck off at once towards the west.

Half a day later, we passed through a sentry gate and then cleared a rise to be confronted with the welcome sight of Hughenden Manor, Disraeli's country pile. The building's squat yet imposing bulk was in turn surrounded by an army waiting for the orders to move out and attack, trampling the once-majestic gardens into a brown and red mass of mud, tents, men and horses.

As we entered through the manor's main doors I realised just how bedraggled we were. After all, it had been many, many days since any of us had had the luxury of a wash or a change of clothing. As a result I felt even more of an impostor in those stately surroundings than I would normally have done.

We were led directly to a study on the ground floor in which stood the welcoming figure of Benjamin Disraeli.

"My dear fellows!" He shook each of our hands vigorously in turn, touching his lips to the hands of Kate and Lexie. He glanced at Gaap. "Is that…?"

"It is," I said. "You may remember Gaap from the battle at St Albans last year."

"How could I forget," muttered Disraeli. "The fiend manipulated the Queen and I to act against our wishes, and nearly caused all our deaths. Is there a reason it is here?"

Gaap leered at him. "My time will come again, you just wait until—" He was silenced by Andras' elbow meeting his face with some force.

"We took Gaap prisoner when we were in Almadel, and I am keen to ensure he remains safely incapacitated," said Andras. "As a result, I am afraid he must remain with me."

"Indeed," said Disraeli, casting a cold eye over the two demons before turning back to the rest of us. "In any case, we have been awaiting your return with much trepidation. And, of course, there is one who is particularly keen to see you." He beckoned towards the door behind us and we turned to see Maxwell being wheeled in by a butler.

"Max!" Both Kate and I said, rushing to his side.

As uneasy as ever in the face of physical displays of affection, Maxwell waved away our greetings, although he did flash a broad smile at each of us. "I knew my calculations would be correct," he said. "Tell me, Sergeant, how accurate was my estimation as to the timing?"

"Very accurate, sir," said Sergeant Jones.

"It was very much to the good that Sergeant Jones and his men arrived when they did," I said. "No sooner had we managed to make our way back to this world than we were apprehended by a rather unusual regiment of soldiers."

"They were not soldiers of the type I would recognise," snapped Pearce sniffily.

"I am afraid you are correct, Captain," said Disraeli. "But you must all be famished after such a long journey. My housekeepers will arrange some refreshments and we can all share stories as to what has happened over the past few months."

*

Further warm greetings ensued when we were joined in the dining room by General Gordon, the military leader who had been as constant a presence in the battle against the demons as any of us. I was particularly relieved to see that he had not been affected by the fugue caused by the changes in the sky; but then again, if someone with as redoubtable a character as Gordon had been incapacitated, then surely the rest of us would have been doomed as well.

Disraeli and the others listened keenly as we told them of our exploits in Almadel and beyond the Aether. When we had finished, the statesman clapped his hands together.

"Sergeant Jones has told you of his journey to meet me?" he said.

"Aye, sir," said Jones, "although I didn't get to tell them of when I actually met you."

Disraeli nodded. "Well, after having had a highly successful trip around the continent, which I shall tell you all about at a later date," he nodded to Andras as he said this and I noted that the demon nodded back. I narrowed my eyes as I wondered just what Andras was up to this time. In the meantime, Disraeli continued: "I was in London when the sky went missing, although I suspect it took rather longer for the natives there to notice that than in most other parts of the world. After the constant fog of pollution, a bit of a void was no doubt a welcome relief to some." He paused to allow all those listening to chuckle at this. Ever the showman, even in the midst of a crisis. "I also witnessed many people falling into the strange catatonic state that Jones has no doubt already told you of. Those of us who were unaffected tried our hardest to help those who were, but to no avail."

"Gladstone…?" I asked, wondering if maybe the Prime Minister had also been affected by this condition.

"Alas, no," said Disraeli. "Mr Gladstone retained all of his faculties. Not that one would necessarily notice the difference, that is."

Kate tutted at him in mock reproach and Disraeli held up his hands in apology. "I could not resist," he chuckled. "In any case, as would be expected, Gladstone lived down to my every expectation as to how he managed the crisis. It took very little time and only a small amount of lobbying before the Queen invited me to take charge of an emergency government."

A smile spread across Pearce's face. "So you are the Prime Minister again?" he asked.

Disraeli nodded. "Not that I find much pleasure in our situation, you understand. That said, I find myself more invigorated by being able to properly shape results rather than being forced to stand by and watch as that jumped-up preacher ruins everything."

I could not help but smile; in spite of everything that had happened, Disraeli still could not shake the animosity he felt for his old political adversary. "And so why are you here, rather than in Downing Street?" I asked.

"Shortly after Sergeant Jones found us, we came under attack from his former Satan-worshipping comrades. We fought a rear-guard action to get as many people out as possible, but London is for the time being lost."

"The Queen?" asked Pearce.

"Is perfectly safe," replied Disraeli. "She has gone to Balmoral with her Household Guards. Given that the majority of the trouble is centred around St Albans and the southeast, for the time being at least, I felt it was the safest course of action."

Pearce nodded. "And it looks like you have been gathering together quite an army here yourself, sir."

"Yes," said Disraeli. "Word has been spreading far and wide that the main centre of operations is here, for now, anyway. In the meantime, we need to determine a way to stop the Satanists, Soul-less and demons and reverse whatever it is that has happened to our world."

"I assume, then, that this is not just a phenomenon limited to England?" I asked.

Disraeli shook his head. "I have already had word from Europe and the Americas that they are all experiencing the same issues that we are. Whilst our Continental cousins were previously content to cut us off and pretend that the Fulcrum was a peculiarly English problem, they have now been forced to recognise that we are all in it together, as it were." He raised those bushy eyebrows at us. "Not that I take any pleasure in the fact, you understand."

I looked over at Maxwell, who had been scribbling away at various pieces of paper whilst we had been talking. "Well, Max," I said to him. "I am assuming that you have a theory or two about what has been happening here?"

"I do, I do," he muttered absentmindedly. Then, looking up: "There are a great many variables at play right now."

I took a deep breath and steeled myself for another endless session of meaningless scientific babbling.

"I have missed this," Andras grinned, throwing himself into a chair next to Maxwell. "What are your thoughts old chap?"

Maxwell blinked at him before glancing down at his papers. "As always, the Fulcrum is at the heart of what has happened. It has provided the power to enable the various portals to and from the Aether to open, disgorging the residue that has infected our world."

"Tell them your theory about the sky," prompted Disraeli.

"Ah yes. I have run several tests over the past few weeks, trying to ascertain what exactly it is that is obscuring our view of the heavens. The results were somewhat perplexing, until now."

"What do you mean?" I asked.

"I had expected to find some form of matter or barrier but in fact I found nothing at all." He looked round at us expectantly and then scowled. "Do you not understand? There is nothing there. No barrier, just a complete absence of anything at all."

"Which must mean…?" prompted Andras.

Maxwell rifled through his papers, tutting as he discarded one and then another before he finally reached the one he was looking for.

He turned and beckoned towards the butler just behind his left shoulder. "I need you to bring me the pile of books stacked on the Aethereal research side of my study," he said.

"Of course," said the butler. "Which side would that be, exactly?"

"As you enter the study," Maxwell explained slowly, "you will see my mechanical research papers to your left, then the demonic research, then the memoirs and diaries that I have compiled, then there are the grimoires…" He shook his head as he realised the impossibility of what he was asking the poor man to do. "It would be easier if we were all to go to my study. Shall we?" He waved to the butler to wheel him out of the room.

I shot an amused glance at Disraeli, who nodded and ushered us forwards to follow my brother.

The study that Maxwell had appropriated in Hughenden Manor was reassuringly similar to every other study and laboratory he had had over the years. What had once clearly been a fine room decked with glorious furniture was now a mess of papers and apparatus, with the no doubt highly expensive pieces being used as little more than shelves and worktops.

"You managed to bring so much with you," noted Joshua.

"Yes," said Jones, a tinge of irritation touching his voice, "Mr Potts was very insistent that we bring as much as we could, even in spite of the advancing enemy forces and the need for speed."

I chuckled as I found a spare space to stand, leaning myself against a wall in preparation for the lengthy conversation to follow.

Maxwell had stationed himself in the midst of his papers and set about working his way through them until he finally held one aloft with a broad grin. "This is the one, just where I said it would be." He shot a reproachful glance at the butler.

"You were saying," prompted Andras, "about the results of your testing?"

"Yes," said Maxwell. "As I said, I saw nothing in those

213

results. Literally and precisely nothing." He looked around at us expectantly before continuing. "Don't you see? Such a thing is just not possible. There always has to be something there; nature abhors a vacuum, after all."

"But when we were in the afterlife," said Pearce, "the sky there was an exact replica of what we're seeing here; there was certainly nothing up there."

"How could you be so sure?" Maxwell fixed him with a questioning stare. "You certainly may have perceived it as being nothing, but surely you had no way of knowing that."

"I just knew..." muttered Pearce.

"Such a place was beyond anything that you could comprehend," continued Maxwell. "You had managed to transport yourselves to another reality completely removed from this one, and so the laws we are accustomed to in this world cannot even be said to come close to applying there. By the by," he turned to Joshua, "when all of this is over I really must pick your brains on everything you learnt, encountered and did in that place."

Joshua looked up from where he had been sharing a whispered conversation with Lexie. "Hmm? Oh yes, of course."

"In any case," continued Maxwell, seeming to either not care or not notice Joshua's lack of interest in proceedings, "I think that we can safely discount the possibility that our whole world has been transported to the afterlife. For one thing, the evidence does not support it: you saw a black smoke," he consulted another set of notes, "seeping through the portal between the Aether and this world, having left Pearce's body, that would suggest more of an infection rather than a wholesale transportation spell. And notwithstanding that, the amount of power and energy required to move an entire world into a separate realm or beyond all realms would be...?" He gestured to Andras expectantly.

"Unimaginably huge amounts would be required to even consider such a thing," Andras said, nodding.

"...therefore we should assume that there has been some

form of infection that has caused these changes to our physical environment as well as precipitating all the other changes we have witnessed since that point."

"But you said that your tests showed no results whatsoever," said Byron. "How could that be?"

"It could only mean one thing: the shift between science and magic that was precipitated by the Fulcrum is much further advanced than I had anticipated. I had always predicted this happening, that there would come a point where magic was more prevalent than science—meaning that my old scientific methods and tests became redundant. I always assumed that that would be a gradual process as our calculations seemed to suggest, did they not Lexie?"

Lexie looked up at him blankly and I again wondered what she and her brother were whispering to each other. After a moment she blinked and then nodded. "Yes, there was a graph; it was a bell-shaped curve. I remember now."

"Indeed. However it appears that the change has happened much more rapidly than anticipated, and the evidence would point to the mysterious black smoke you witnessed having acted as a catalyst for that final push."

"So the sky is still there, it has simply been obscured?" said Disraeli.

"In a manner of speaking, yes," nodded Maxwell, rifling through his notes.

Andras was frowning. "But if that was the case, it would still take an extraordinary amount of power to achieve this. In order to do so you would need..." We all watched him expectantly as he stared into space, his eyes widening. After a moment he noticed our eyes on him and quickly added: "Great power." I noted that his gaze flickered over me, Byron and Gaap as he said this.

"It would," agreed Maxwell. "But the evidence seems to point in that direction, would it not? The only question is, what could create and sustain such power?"

"The Four Kings?" asked Byron.

Andras shook his head "No, no. They would not be able to do so without Gaap here."

I raised an eyebrow. "But I thought you always said he was just a lackey?"

I was not sure if my eyes deceived me but it appeared that Andras almost squirmed under this questioning. "Yes, well, every demon has their place and their assigned task."

"And that is why you wanted to bring him with us?" asked Pearce, a rare smile touching his lips. "I may have to revise my opinion of you, demon. We have not only gained ourselves a hostage but a valuable one that the Four Kings will want to get their hands back on, as our custodianship frustrates their plans. Good thinking."

I looked over at the bound figure of Gaap, who Andras had still refused to let out of his sight. The demon seemed almost confused by this turn of events.

"Yes, indeed," agreed Andras quickly.

"The question remains," continued Maxwell, glaring at everyone as he fought to bring the room's attention back to himself, "if this was some form of infection then why has it been as selective as it has?"

"Those of us who were in the Aether at the time were free from any exposure at all," I said. "We have already established that."

"But the rest of us… what is so different about us and the soldiers around this room compared to the multitudes out there who swiftly degenerated into an almost dreamlike state?"

"I suppose we know there's something what's worth fighting for," observed Kate.

All the eyes on the room suddenly turned to her, including an increasingly agitated Andras. "What?" she asked, clearly surprised that such an offhand comment could have warranted so much attention.

Everyone seemed to be missing something very obvious. "But

was it not the case that Pearce was possessed by the creatures from the afterlife?" I asked.

"Yes," said Byron slowly. "What's your point?"

"The black smoke that infected this world came directly from him," I said. "And Andras said that they would all be gone from his body now, is that not correct? Possession is an 'all-or-nothing deal', I think you mentioned?"

"I did," nodded Andras.

"Where did the creatures from the afterlife go? We've not seen any of them in this world so far."

The resulting silence was broken by Andras tapping his clawed fingers on the surface of a table. "We have seen them. They are everywhere. Don't you understand? They are the reason that so many people have been acting differently, lethargically, insane or simply turning into Soul-less. They are possessing everyone who does not attempt to fight their influence." He frowned. "But it would require huge amounts of power to even attempt that…"

He started to pace the room, dragging Gaap with him like a recalcitrant puppy. After a couple of turns he spun round to face Maxwell. "Do you still have the objects that were found in that other realm? When Kate was kidnapped?"

"Yes," said Maxwell, pointing to a table against the far wall. "Over there." Andras darted over to it, pausing only to hand Gaap's leash to Pearce. He picked up the various objects, scrutinising them before tossing them back down onto the table. Spinning back round, he marched over to Jones. "What did that man say to you? The one who talked about a 'new world order'?"

Jones shrugged. "He said that the old gods hadn't worked out, that it was time for others to rise up against politicians and the ruling elite. That they were preparing the way for the coming of Satan."

Andras clicked a long finger in front of his face. "Are you sure that that was the exact name they used? Satan?"

Jones frowned and then nodded. "Definitely."

"What's going on? What is it?" I asked.

Andras paced a little while longer and then stopped, rubbing his head. "I am so very, very slow," he muttered. Then, looking up as though he had made up his mind to confide some terrible secret, he said: "I told you that there were five runes that were once used to control all the realms, and that these runes were, many, many millennia ago, scattered across the various domains."

"And the afterlife," said Byron, patting the rune that he was still storing in his jacket.

"Exactly," said Andras. "Well, the device that the Warlocks were using when you surprised them was intended to seek out the rune that was secreted in the Aether. And by the looks of the inscriptions on it, they were very close to finding it."

"How do you know?" I asked.

"Because the markings on those objects there," he indicated the items we had stolen from the Warlocks, "are very similar to those required to seek out that object. I did not know what those runes looked like until I saw them for the first time: in the afterlife."

"But you examined that before we went to Almadel," Maxwell said. "How have you only just realised this now?"

"Because they very closely match those on the rune that we rescued from the afterlife," said Andras, pointing at Byron.

"Then that means…?" asked Disraeli.

"That the Four Kings have more of the runes than we thought," said Maxwell. "Which means that they could have used that power to help facilitate this infection."

"But how did they manage that, assuming you're right?" asked Pearce. "They were nowhere near us when we were in the afterlife."

I looked pointedly at Gaap. "No, but one of them was," I said. "That creature has been with us all along; could he have somehow communicated with them?"

Pearce started to drag the demon towards the door. "Get this creature out of here and locked up," he shouted to a guard by the door.

"No," said Andras "he's too dangerous to be left unattended and away from me. I have a better idea." He swung his fist at Gaap, catching him hard across his jaw and sending him slumping to the ground, once more knocked unconscious. I almost felt sorry for him. Almost.

"Well, now that that has been dealt with, what does all this mean? asked Disraeli.

"It means that we have been dancing to the demons' tunes. Again," I spat, glaring at Andras.

Andras raised his eyebrows. "Don't pull faces at me," he said. "I have been duped just as much as the rest of you. In any case, it is not the Four Kings we need to worry about. The people Jones spoke with referred only to Satan. That implies only one person, and the one person who has meddled even more in human affairs than I have over the years: Belial, who also likes to call himself Satan, or the Anti-Christ."

Disraeli frowned. "You mean the Devil? Like Lucifer?"

Andras shook his head. "Lucifer was on the side of light until he fell. No, Belial is pure... what you would term 'evil.' He always has been."

Chapter Nineteen

We rode with General Gordon at the head of a vast column of men, horses and ordnance, by our reckoning the largest army to traverse across English soil since at least the Civil War. Our job now was to make sure that there remained a human civilisation to record this achievement for the history books.

We rode in silence, each one of us still replaying the contents of the conversation at Hughenden Manor in our heads, as well as the terrifying implications of what we had learnt.

"The Four Kings have always operated together, as a unit," Andras had said. "Each of them brings a particular skill and set of powers to bear. Such a state of affairs was necessary while they were all evenly matched, while none of them possessed the runes that they needed to rule supreme. However, that is not to say that they have all just rested on their laurels and been content to let the status quo continue. I know that Belial in particular has been very active in certain worlds, yours being the main one."

"What do you mean?" Disraeli had shifted around at the mention of this new threat.

"Ever since the dawn of man you have been obsessed with your gods, the mythical battles that supposedly maintained the balance between 'good' and 'evil.' Many of your religions sought to delude you into believing that such a balance had been tipped in favour of what you call 'good'." He barked a short laugh at the stupidity of this. "The truth, as I have said so many times before, is a lot more complicated than this, but that is a discussion for another day. The fact remains that many of your mythologies, religions and stories do actually have their roots in reality."

"I am struggling to see how this relates to our current situation," Disraeli said.

"As Maxwell already realised," continued Andras, "the tales of demons infecting this world were based on actual events involving myself, my kin and creatures from other realms dotted throughout the Aether. Some of these creatures were summoned temporarily to this world by sorcerers or the like, while some," he gestured at Byron, "took refuge here because they had nowhere else to go. Others visited of their own accord, seeking to influence and manipulate events to their own advantage."

"Such as Belial?" said Maxwell.

Andras nodded. "Exactly. When I was a citizen of Almadel I knew that he had plans, but I was never able to ascertain what they were. It was only when I ended up in this realm by happy accident that I realised he had been coming here for some time. It became apparent that Belial had already laid claim to your world, writing himself into your stories, your cultures and your cognitive and social development ever since you climbed down from the trees. One can only assume that everything that has happened here is a part of his grand plan."

We had all stared at him, trying to comprehend just what the demon had told us. Every aspect of my being wanted to rebel against such a thought but I also knew from bitter experience just how capable the demons were of shaping our history and development; after all, Andras himself had managed to influence both mine and my brothers' lives, killing our parents and sending us down the paths that led to us serving his purposes, not least of which was Maxwell creating the portals to the Aether.

Disraeli, on the other hand, was much more reluctant to accept such a thing. "I refuse to believe that the whole of humanity can have been played for such pawns," he said. "It just cannot be possible."

Andras shrugged. "I do not much care what you do or do not believe." Ignoring our looks of horror at his insolence, Andras continued. "The fact of the matter is that Belial has had a plan for many millennia and I strongly suspect that it is now coming to a head. But it is not just Belial who has used us as pawns, is it Joshua?"

All our eyes turned to Joshua, who frowned up at us in confusion.

"It was not just a happy accident that we found ourselves in the afterlife, was it?" continued Andras. "Mama warned that there was a price in return for her helping us."

"That's right," I said slowly. "We promised to help them overthrow the Four Kings. We still need to do that, don't we?" A chilling thought tickled at my brain. "Or is all of this, what has happened to the sky, her way of getting her revenge on us for not helping them yet?"

"No, but you're on the right lines," said Andras, almost effecting the air of a schoolmaster as he paced the floor. "Mama is very much dead by now; no one would have been able to survive being the focus of that number of Wraiths. But the movement she was a part of, that lives on. And what would their revolution need in order to succeed?" He pointed a clawed finger at Pearce, clearly expecting an answer to the question he had posed.

"They would need to tip the balance in their favour," Pearce said. "Orchestrate some form of distraction that would lure the Almadite army away from their home for long enough for the Slaves to rise up."

Andras nodded. "Which is what we did. It turns out that Mama was much more devious than I gave her credit for."

"You made a deal," I said. "A deal that got us to the afterlife so that we could rescue Kate and also bring back Lexie. But you and Mama knew that the afterlife would demand their own price, a price that would tie up our world here in this Hell. And so all of this… is your fault?" I turned to Joshua. "You said when we were in Almadel that you had managed to also read Mama's plans, before you disappeared to get the Juggernaut. You knew all about this as well, I take it?"

Joshua blinked back tears. "We had no choice. It was the only way. But we'll be able to fix it; we always do."

Maxwell let out a short laugh. "Your faith in my abilities is touching, although it might be misplaced. We surely have more to worry about than just what is happening to the sky and our people."

"What do you mean?" asked Disraeli.

"Weighing up all of the evidence, it is obvious is it not?" Maxwell frowned at us and then ticked the points off on his fingers. "Firstly, this world has been infected by something from the afterlife, which has effectively paralysed large parts of the world's population. Secondly, my scientific methods are now useless, irrelevant, meaning that the Fulcrum's effects are stronger than ever before; magic is now as prevalent here on Earth as in other realms. Thirdly, the other realms around the Aether will no doubt have felt this shift happen, or at least those who are sensitive to such things."

"Such as the Almadite Warlocks," said Byron.

"Yes, exactly," said Maxwell. "Fourthly, the Slaves on Almadel needed a distraction to lure the Almadite army from their world. Fifthly, Belial has been creating mischief behind the scenes here on Earth for thousands upon thousands of years. The fact that everything is coming to a head right now means…?"

"That we need to act, and act quickly," said Andras. "Belial is coming, and I would wager that he is now much more powerful than I have ever given him credit for."

From that moment, we wasted little time in moving out, although that act was not instantaneous, given the large amounts of people and equipment that needed transporting. My body was feeling the strain of the past days of activity and I took the opportunity to rest for a while.

I dreamed that I was adrift in a vast, milky sea. With a shock, I realised that this was something akin to the Aether, but I was not alone. A form flickered and flowed around me, always just out of my field of vision.

Abomination, hissed a voice as old as time itself. *You will be unmade.*

I knew that creature, I knew that voice. I had encountered it before, when Maxwell had used the Compound on me, and again when the Warlock had attacked me in that other realm. It was the voice and creature that had tried to tear me apart from the inside-out on both those occasions.

I woke with a shout and in a cold sweat, looking around to realise with relief that I was back in the real world and in one piece.

"You all right?" asked Kate.

"Yes, just a bad dream," I replied shakily.

"Understandable, given the circumstances," said Maxwell. "Ah, it looks like we are now ready to move out."

Half a day later, we reigned in our horses as we approached the Fulcrum, taking in the scale of the vast army in front of us. "It appears that our friends have been busy," said Pearce. "And they do not appear to be fussy as to their choice of comrades-in-arms."

The group of soldiers that had captured us on our return to Earth had grown substantially, clearly bolstered by the likes of the Satanic forces Jones had encountered in London. They formed the core of a mess of discordant sounds, shapes and colours. Demons and humans—as well as those very much in between—seemed to be, for the most part, coexisting albeit not necessarily peacefully, for every so often altercations would break out in their ranks. One thing, though, was very clear: they were all united in a common purpose.

Staying concealed, we gathered our forces together and considered our next move.

"We should attack immediately," said Andras. "We need

to overwhelm them before any more arrive to bolster their numbers."

General Gordon nodded. "For once I agree with the demon," he said. "It would appear that they are gathering together all of the various creatures that have invaded our world. There is every chance that the longer we wait, the bigger their numbers will grow."

"You are thinking of demons arriving through the portal?" asked Disraeli.

"Not just them," said Andras. "I'm thinking also of the Soulless." He nodded at the scene before us. From our vantage point we could tell that more and more of those moribund anomalies were straggling towards the makeshift army around the portal from all points of the compass.

"So it is agreed," said Disraeli. "We advance forthwith. Are you comfortable that we have the numbers?" he asked Gordon.

Gordon nodded. "Assuming no more are hiding anywhere, then we are relatively evenly matched for the time being. All the more reason to strike now."

The order was shouted along the lines and the soldiers busied themselves in a frenzy of checking weapons and gathering themselves together. I made my way to the front of the lines and hefted my sword, testing its weight once again and looked up to see Byron's eyes on me.

"Once more unto the breach, dear friends, once more?" he asked.

I grunted. "Hopefully for the last time."

Joshua and Lexie stood by Andras and Disraeli, receiving their own orders. "I don't like it," Byron said. "Lexie should not be so near the action. She is too much of an unknown factor."

I nodded. "Did you hear Andras' argument with him on that? I think that if we want to keep his cooperation then we're going to have to put up with this for the time being at least." Joshua's reaction had been particularly vehement when Andras had suggested that Lexie remain at Hughenden rather than come with us. During their argument Lexie had remained mute with that same far-off look on her face that she had worn ever since we had found her. Eventually Andras had been forced to back down: after all, Joshua and his powers were central to our plans, and so he had us over a barrel.

"In any case," I said, nodding back to the wagons where Maxwell waited with Disraeli, "Joshua is not the only unreasonably stubborn one amongst us."

We both grinned as we remembered the battle of wills we had fought—and lost—with Maxwell. He refused to agree that he should keep as far away as possible from the battle, instead insisting on accompanying us to St Albans.

"Just because I am confined to this wheelchair," he had snapped, "does not mean that I am completely worthless. There may come a point when you need me."

It had been a minor victory of ours that he had agreed to remain at the command position with Disraeli and Gordon, rather than to join in the fight proper. He had eventually conceded that there were certain logistical problems with manoeuvring a wheelchair around a demonic battlefield of uncertain terrain.

As we watched, a commotion seemed to erupt from Maxwell's wagons. He twisted in his chair to bark out orders, and then people started to run in every direction.

Byron and I burst into a run towards them, meeting Maxwell, Disraeli and the others halfway. We watched as a mist curled out from the nearest wagon, licking at the air with malicious intent.

"Oh," said Maxwell.

"Max," I said, frowning. "That looks suspiciously like your Compound."

Disraeli shot him a sharp glare. "The substance that I ordered to be destroyed, you mean? On account of it being too dangerous and unstable? That Compound?"

"Well, yes," Maxwell refused to meet our glares. "I did destroy it. Most of it. I just retained a small amount for scientific purposes."

Any further discussion was cut off as the mist shifted and formed into something approximating a physical form, a vast head on top of a huge, undulating trunk of a body that pulsed with rage. It turned its head so that it was pointing straight at us and then, in an instant, it shot towards me and I felt myself being lifted into oblivion.

ABOMINATION! roared the voice from my nightmare, from the visions when I was attacked by the Warlock, from when I was near death the first time I had been touched by the Compound.

You are impure. You will be destroyed!

"Who are you? *What* are you?" I yelled into the maelstrom.

I am your doom. I am Almadel, the Purifier, the Unifier. I shall destroy you. You should never have been made. You should never have been exposed to the power of the rune!

I looked down at my sword. So that was it; this creature was outraged at how I had become part-demon thanks to the influence of this most powerful of artefacts, one of the fabled runes.

"Wait," I said, a distant part of me marvelling at how measured I was being. "You are Almadel? You mean…?"

"I always wanted to meet you," said Andras, appearing at my side. "The founder of my realm, the creator of all that my people grew to become." He frowned up at the flowing mass that loomed over us before sniffing. "Have to admit, I always thought you'd be a bit bigger, a bit less… misty."

You, my child, you stand with this impure thing?

"Look closer," grinned Andras. "I am an impure thing myself. I am Andras, Sire of Var. One of the greatest of your children, and I willingly created this 'abomination'!" He thrust out a hand and yelled an incantation, sending the mist spiralling away with a terrifying scream.

We landed hard on the ground. As I recovered my breath, I looked over to Andras. "Was that really…?"

"The very same," he said, brushing dirt from his coat. "Never meet your heroes, that's what I always say. He seemed like quite the tiresome bigot, don't you think?"

"I have encountered him before, like that. But I thought—"

"According to legend, when the runes were separated and sent their different ways, Almadel left to try and recover them. Some said that his essence actually lived on in each of the runes. It would appear that over the years he became incorporeal and seems to have been attracted to Maxwell's Compound as a medium for holding his essence. It appears that your impure state—neither human nor demon and, to make matters worse, created by the very runes that he revered—has attracted his attentions over the years." He grinned at me. "You have been stalked by a demi-god; congratulations!"

I frowned at him. "Where has it gone?"

Andras gestured to the Fulcrum, to where the mist angrily circled the Satan worshippers and their allies. "I believe he is seeking a host. We should attack before he secures one."

We advanced towards the waiting army, Pearce sending skirmishers ahead of us to engage the enemy and distract them from being able to mount too much of a coordinated defence. Surprisingly they did not seem too interested in attacking, instead redoubling their defences around the portal, backing away and forming a ring of sharpened steel and decrepit flesh around it.

I suddenly realised that Kate had fallen behind. Pearce and I turned to see her frozen in place and we both ran back to her.

"Kate," said Pearce, "you need to keep moving."

"I can't," she muttered, her eyes wide.

"We should take her back," I said to Pearce.

He nodded and took her arm but she struggled against him, her face ashen.

I looked back to see the cannons being wheeled into position, the artillerymen already hard at work calculating the angles that would give them the best chance of hitting the portal. Pearce nodded, relaying to us an order from behind and we watched as the cannons boomed as one, sending their projectiles hissing towards the portal.

We held our breath as the black missiles streamed over and past us in a perfect shallow arc. One landed amidst the defending creatures, scattering them with a satisfyingly bloody smear. The other headed directly for the portal itself but at the last minute it seemed to explode into dust, harmlessly drifting away on the breeze.

Andras cursed beside me. "They have managed to set up some form of protective barrier," he hissed.

"But you were expecting that, weren't you?" I said.

He nodded. "Part of me had hoped that they were less organised or more poorly equipped than I gave them credit for," he said.

I turned back to Pearce, who was still struggling with Kate. She was snarling as she pulled against him, refusing even to be taken to safety.

"The demons… they're everywhere… I can feel them…" she muttered, eyes wide.

"Let's pick her up," I said to Pearce. "The two of us can carry her away before the fighting starts."

He nodded his agreement, but before we could act on it I sensed a shift in the air. Andras clearly felt it too and held up his hand, signalling for everyone to stop and hold their positions. "Not good," he whispered. "Not good at all."

"What is it?" I asked.

Andras pointed at the portal. "It looks like we are about to have some unwanted visitors."

Even from this distance I could see the difference in the portal, the swirling inside growing in intensity before my eyes. My sword started to vibrate as a sickly familiar wind rose up from the portal and the creatures gathered around it started to howl in triumph, leering and gesturing at us.

I turned back to Kate, feeling a hot panic start to rise and swell inside me. "You need to snap out of this!" I shouted at her.

She stared back at me.

"Look around you," I screeched. "We are in the middle of a damn battle!"

Kate stared at me as though I were a part of some bizarre dream. "Things are not real," she whispered.

Pearce grabbed her by the shoulders. "I understand how you are feeling," he said with a calmness I envied. "I have felt it too; the feeling that the creature is still inside you."

She blinked at him, then her eyes lurched to me.

I forced myself to try to forget about the dangerous madness surrounding us; if Kate remained in that state in the middle of the battlefield, then she was as good as dead.

"Kate," I said, staring into her eyes. "Kate, we brought you back and we took that entity out of you, but these things always leave a hole. That will heal in time, trust me, but for now you need to fill it with something. Remember who you are and what you have done. You are Kate Thatcher, and you have been through so much worse than this. Just one last push and then we will be rid of these demons."

Kate started to hyperventilate, straining once more against Pearce. "We're going to die. We're all going to die here today!"

I racked my brains; what would she do if the positions were reversed?

In a flash I realised what I needed to do, although I did not relish it.

"Captain Pearce," I said, "I need you to hold her tight, and please resist the urge to hit me."

"What?" he asked.

I slapped Kate across the cheek as hard as I dared, the sound seeming to ring out in spite of the chaos around us.

She scowled at me, blinking back tears, which quickly snapped back into an angry glare. "Ouch," she snarled. "What did you do that for, you bastard?"

I looked to Pearce, willing him with my eyes to keep holding her back. "You were panicking," I said. "I asked myself what you would do if the roles were reversed."

She stared at me for a moment, then turned her head to speak to Pearce. "You can let go of me now. I've still got me senses: I'm not ready for Hanwell just yet. Or Hades." When he hesitated, she added: "And don't worry, I won't go for Gus."

He released her and she squared up to me, eye to eye. "You weren't quite right," she said. "I'd have really hit you." She patted me on the cheek, grinning as I flinched.

"What do you mean?" I asked. "I didn't want to hurt you."

"You slap like a little girl, Augustus Potts." She turned back to the action, but I could tell there was a wry grin on her face.

I looked out at the massing demons before us and the swirling vortex of the portal. The cannons were beating a steady rhythm, but the munitions failed to have any impact on the portal. "What now?" I shouted. "Should we attack?"

Andras shook his head. "It is too late," he replied, pointing at the portal. "They are already here. We are outnumbered."

The ring of defences around the portal had opened to admit a stream of new creatures, a river of effluence from the very bowels of Hell. Creatures from our worst nightmares roared at us: Warriors and Warlocks, Mages and Furies. They poured through with a furious intensity, bellowing as they advanced on us.

After a few moments the demon forces stopped, arranging themselves in a long line around 200 yards in front of our own. The line split in the centre to reveal a tall, terrifyingly beautiful figure riding towards us on a huge beast.

Andras growled next to me. "So, here…" he said, as much to himself as the rest of us, "…is Belial in person."

I turned to see Pearce and Byron next to me. "What now?" I asked again.

Before anyone could answer, Andras started to walk forwards. "Wait!" shouted Pearce, but Andras carried on marching regardless. With a deep breath, I started after him.

Belial was immense, even by demon standards. His height was massively boosted by the beast on which he sat, something that bore as much relation to our horses as a lion to a cat. The creature's body was at least eight feet high and it stared at us with piercing red eyes above a maw lined with hideously sharp teeth.

Belial himself was a sight beyond my wildest imaginings, even after all of the time I had spent fighting demons. When we had been in Almadel I had not had the opportunity to register too much of him or his fellow Kings, given how intent we had all been on escaping from that place as quickly as possible. In the sudden stillness in which we found ourselves, I was able to fully soak in his majestic yet evil countenance.

For that was what he was: in spite of everything I knew about him, all that I knew he represented, I could not help but wonder at the sheer beauty of the creature before us. It was almost as though he was surrounded by a terrible and yet alluring fire, a wondrous glow that bathed him and picked out his features in stark relief. As with so many of the demons, the particulars of his face shifted as my mind tried to make sense of what my eyes were taking in, finally settling on a classically handsome man, almost the spitting image of a Roman emperor or the statues of Alexander the Great from ancient times.

Andras had stopped in front of him and seemed to swell in size to match his adversary. "Belial," he called. "You will desist and leave this realm."

"Or what?" laughed Belial. "You managed to repel us with a rather elegant bluff last time, but I see even that has betrayed you now." He held up his hand and the mist of the Compound swirled in and around his fingertips, thankfully for the moment contained around Belial rather than reaching its foul tendrils out towards the rest of us.

Andras peered past the demon King. "Where are the other three?"

Belial smiled and narrowed his eyes. "I have no more need of them now," he said. "After all, I have the runes."

Belial held aloft a sceptre attached to which was a circular disc, not unlike the one that we had taken from the afterlife.

"So you have found the one held in the Aether," said Andras.

"I believe that is two to you, but three to me."

Belial gestured around him. "I have the superiority in numbers on the field," he said. "Once we have defeated you, I will take the remaining runes from your cold dead fingers."

Now it was Andras' turn to laugh.

Belial frowned at him. "Could it be that you have finally been driven insane?" he asked. "Look around—you and your pathetic army are vastly outnumbered and outgunned, so to speak."

"You should not believe everything you see," said Andras, turning and gesturing to Joshua, who had set up his various pieces of equipment just behind our lines, Lexie standing nearby holding the rune from the afterlife and Gaap's leash. Joshua started chanting and, one by one, portals started to wink into existence around the battlefield.

Belial and his army cast around as they watched dark shapes start to emerge from these fresh doorways. Slowly the shapes took human form as entire battalions started to pour through.

"Vive la liberté," came a cry from a nearby portal. The uplifting sound of soldiers shouting was echoed in several other languages: Prussian, Russian and even the twang of an American accent, as they all screamed their own war cries at these invaders. Andras turned and grinned at Belial.

"You see?" he shouted over the rising noise of these new armies. "It is not just us that you have to contend with, it is the whole of humanity itself!"

Belial looked around and then turned back to us, a grin spreading across his face. "Very good, he said. "I would thank you for making this so much easier for me." He held out a hand and the Compound containing the essence of Almadel seeped into his body. He leaned his head back, seeming to grow a few more feet in height and girth. "And now I am Almadel as well. I have his spirit and his strength, and you shall be ruined!"

I frowned and glanced at Andras, hoping to see some reassurance in his face or bearing. Instead I saw confusion and the beginnings of panic.

Belial laughed. "I see that the penny has finally dropped Andras. I will accept your surrender now."

"What…?" I asked.

"Stupid," muttered Andras.

We spun round at a cry from behind us. Lexie sprinted through our line of soldiers, holding the rune in one hand and pulling a newly released Gaap with her other. Before I could react, Gaap snatched the sword from my hand and ran over to his master followed by Lexie. Fear washed over me.

"And now I have all five runes!" shouted Belial. "Thank you so much for delivering them to me."

"Lexie!" shouted Joshua. "What are you doing?"

"I should have realised," snarled Andras. "I knew that something was not right, that there was a risk, but I was so distracted by everything else…"

"What do you mean?" asked Pearce.

Kate was staring at Lexie, her face ashen. "I know that creature now," she said. "I'd know it anywhere."

I stared at her. "What do you mean?"

"That's the thing that lived in my head," said Kate. "That monster…" She started to shake and Pearce put a reassuring hand on her arm.

"You see," said Andras, "the one question we never answered, was: what happened to the Wraith that we released from Kate's head?"

I stared at Lexie, unsure whether it was my eyes or simply this new evidence that suddenly made her take on a ghostly, demonic appearance. "But how could she do that? They never normally look human…"

"We were in the afterlife," said Andras gravely. "The normal rules don't apply there. It latched onto something that we wanted the most and made it flesh. Well, what one of us wanted the most, anyway—the most powerful one of all of us."

"This changes nothing," said Pearce. "We have the numbers now, we should attack." He waved his hand at the various commanders around the field.

The other armies remained motionless.

"What is this?" snarled Andras as he looked about.

Belial laughed. "You thought you had been so clever, didn't you? Sending your pet Prime Minister off around the world, gathering all of your armies together—the very best that humanity has to offer. But at no point did you stop to consider whether they were yours to command. You see, I have been here for millennia, since before these pathetic creatures were even sentient. At every step of their development I have been there, shaping and manipulating them, making them in my own image."

"Liar!" hissed Pearce.

Belial laughed, a sinister cackle that ran up and down my spine and made me want to run away and hide. He spoke to a base, almost primeval part of me and in that moment I knew that what the demon said was true.

"I admire your stubbornness," he said to Pearce, the focus of his gaze forcing the Captain to take a step backwards. "That is one element of your personalities that I have always tried to remove. But no matter, after today you will all be mine."

Andras shook his head. "Not today," he roared. "Not these creatures!" With a bellow, he threw himself through the air at the other demon. Belial met the swing of Andras' sword with his own, the two weapons colliding in a cacophonous clang that made my ears feel as though they would burst.

Andras' momentum unseated Belial, sending both demons tumbling to the ground. Belial twisted gracefully in the air and landed in a crouch, his immense sword held out to one side.

"This is a pointless exercise," he growled, straightening up to his full height. "If you are trying to stop me from using my birthright—my five runes—then you are sadly mistaken. You can only temporarily distract me, that is all."

"That'll do for me," growled Andras, charging forward once more.

The two demons seemed to grow in size as they fought, a vision straight from my childhood imaginings of the Titans from Greek mythology. It was hard not to be awed by the vicious elegance with which they attacked, parried and counter-attacked, a hideously mesmerising dance of death. I could not tear my eyes away from this breath-taking sight, almost as though we were watching two gods battling for our entertainment.

Andras at first appeared to have the upper hand, attacking with a power, passion and intensity that Belial could do little other than defend against. Andras roared as each blow landed, only to be met by Belial's sword and then, increasingly, by little more than thin air.

For while Andras was fast—preternaturally so—Belial was even faster; it was this speed, combined with the demon's beautiful ease, which soon began to tip the balance. I clenched my fists and breathed a warning as Andras miscalculated a blow and found himself exposed. Belial laughed and caught him in the side with a sharp elbow, veering away before gesturing for Andras to come at him.

"He is toying with him," I hissed.

My words seemed to shock Pearce back to wakefulness, having stood next to me as entranced by the battle as I was. "They both are," he said before pointing towards Lexie and Gaap. "Andras is buying us time; we need to get the runes."

We edged around the battle, noting that everyone else on that field—demon, human and Soul-less alike—were similarly frozen by the spectacle. Emboldened, we edged towards the creature wearing Lexie's face. After we had only taken a few paces it turned and glared at us, lifeless eyes boring into us and reaching for our very souls.

In spite of the adrenaline and courage that such a situation always provided, I faltered, turning to glance at my comrades to see that they were also thus affected.

"We need Joshua," said Kate, gesturing to the lines of soldiers behind us.

Pearce nodded and led the way. I backed away with them slowly, keeping a wary eye on the Wraith-that-was-once-Lexie, as well as the demonic gladiatorial contest before us.

Andras was wilting under Belial's attacks, forced back onto the defensive, twisting and turning so as to avoid being carved into pieces by the creature's greatsword. It seemed to be only a matter of time before Andras would be mortally wounded and then, with Belial in command of the five runes, surely all would be lost.

Joshua was staring at Lexie, tears running down his cheeks, his face a mask of pained disbelief. Around the battlefield, the portals that he had created spluttered their last and died, a sign of his waning interest in anything other than his sister.

As we approached he turned to look at us with pleading eyes. "Why is she doing this? What have the demons done to her?"

We all looked at each other, hoping that someone else would find the right words to say.

Byron was the first to speak. "It is not really her," he said gently. "It never was. The person we brought back from the afterlife was the Wraith that had infected Kate; it latched onto your thoughts and desires and made them flesh, showing all of us exactly what you wanted: your sister."

Joshua shook his head. "No. It can't be. It must be her."

Kate put an arm around his shoulders. "Me old chuckaboo, we need you. We need to get them runes from Belial before it's all over."

"But what about Lexie…?" Tears were forming in his eyes, his face desperate.

I squatted down in front of him, waiting until he raised his head to look at me. "Lexie is gone," I said as gently as I could. "She is resting, at peace, somewhere. Not that strange, hideous place you took us to; that was all just a trick, an illusion—a deception in fact. We have been played by Belial all of this time, don't you see? Once again they have been playing the long game against us. Kate's kidnap was just a way to get us to go where the demons had not been able to until then, so that we could retrieve the last rune for them."

"Although I only see four runes there," said Pearce. "The one from the afterlife, the one on Belial's sword, the one from the Aether and Gus' sword. Where's the other one? Lexie?" Then the realisation dawned upon him. "Gaap. That is why Andras was so keen to take him, why Joshua has suddenly had so much more power after the battle in the Citadel and why Andras would not let him out of his sight."

Byron nodded. "Yes. There is the small matter of why Andras did not feel it necessary to tell us all of this, but we will save that discussion for another day—hopefully once the concept of 'day' has been re-established. In the meantime, we have more pressing business to attend to." We all looked to Joshua.

"I'm sorry to do this mate," said Kate, before slapping him hard across the face. "You need to grow a pair, Joshua Bradshaw. Everyone needs you right now. There'll be time to wallow in pity later. We've all been through Hell, some of us a lot more literally than you. If I can snap out of it, then you bloody well can as well."

Joshua looked back at her with hurt bewilderment, his mouth opening and closing. When Kate lifted her hand again, ready to strike, he nodded quickly. "All right, all right. What do you need me to do?"

*

We made our way through the ranks of soldiers still transfixed by the demonic punch-up, towards the Wraith and the five runes that it was guarding. We shuffled nervously forwards, weapons drawn and ready, keeping a watchful eye on the combatants as well as the Wraith/Lexie creature in front of us. In my hand I held an ordinary steel broadsword, a crude weapon that Pearce had commandeered for me from an infantry officer. The weapon felt bulky and clumsy in my hand, a poor substitute for the finely balanced precision of my own sword, which was now clutched in Gaap's hand.

A desperate, foolish part of me had hoped that I would still be able to fight with as much power and precision as I had when in possession of the runic sword, although a niggling part of my own brain pleaded with me to not be so stupid as to try to put that to the test.

As we approached, the Wraith's head snapped round once more to face us. It turned its body, still recognisably Lexie but also so much more now that we could see through its veil of pretence. It seemed to billow and swell before us, a sickly white apparition that formed a gossamer yet formidable wall in our path. As one, the nearest demons turned to face us and we found ourselves surrounded on three sides by our enemies, countless numbers of them, whilst the final side of our prison was formed by the deadly battle between Andras and Belial.

We looked around at the hopelessly large numbers that encircled us, and past them at the unmoving figures of the human soldiers, still enthralled by Belial and whatever fugue he had cast on them.

"Don't know about you boys," said Kate, raising her pistol, "but it looks like today is turnin' out to be a good day to die after all."

Chapter Twenty

Andras was being thrown back again and again under the onslaught from Belial, the demon King laughing as he rained down blow after blow. Stumbling to one knee, Andras clumsily batted away one last swing, his sword arm crumbling under the weight of the attack.

Belial cackled gleefully. "I have been toying with you, enjoying our little game, but it is time for this to end. It is time for death; I can already feel the power of the five runes flowing through me. I am ready to reclaim my birthright."

Andras roared in anger at these words, throwing himself forwards in one last desperate attack, swinging his sword in a mighty arc straight at Belial's throat.

The demon King easily swatted the blade aside, as though Andras were no more than a slightly bothersome insect. The sword went flying from Andras' grasp and he landed heavily on the ground. Before he could recover himself, Belial followed up with a kick to his face before stamping down hard on his chest.

Belial held his own sword aloft, the point directed straight at Andras' forehead. "You know your problem, Andras? You have allowed yourself to grow weak in your new home. There once was a time when we were well matched, but this world and its people have infected you. It is your own weakness, you should not have allowed it; just like I did not allow myself to be infected, instead choosing to infect them." He raised his sword high. "And because of that weakness, you now die!"

Andras cocked an eyebrow at him and grinned broadly. "Do you know something?" he said. "I do believe you are correct." He closed his eyes and muttered a spell, his whole body starting to glow with the force of the incantation. Belial glared at him in confusion. "What's this?" he managed, before everything around him exploded in a flash of bright white light.

The demons surrounding myself and my friends were pressed back by this sudden force while Belial, having been closest to the blast, was thrown several yards away.

Andras rose to his feet, a hideous and demonic grin spreading wide across features that were even more angular than before. This was Andras at the height of his demonic powers, something far beyond that which we had become accustomed to spending time with. This was a creature from every living nightmare, a hybrid of legend and half-truths, the God of Lies. Andras flexed his arms and held out a hand, his sword flying into his grasp. "You are so right, my dear Belial," he said in a sibilant hiss that stretched to every corner of the battlefield. "I was weak for far too long. But no more!"

Belial roared in disbelief and charged towards Andras, an attack that was met with ease by the freshly revitalised and chuckling demon.

"What the…?" asked Pearce.

My attention had been drawn to a new, huddled figure hunched against the ground not far from where we stood. A dark creature curled up in a ball. Something about that form was very, very familiar. I ran over, for the moment completely unmindful of all the enemies around us.

I reached the figure, which was clothed in a long black greatcoat, and put a hand on its shoulder. The thing unfolded in front of me, uncurling and stretching out to reveal a very familiar face.

"N'yotsu?" I gasped.

He looked at me with those piercing dark eyes, a steely grin on his face. "The very same. It has been some time, has it not? Are you ready to cause one last act of mayhem?"

I laughed. "It would be my pleasure," I said. I pointed over to our friends. "We do seem to be in a bit of a pickle though."

N'yotsu nodded briskly. "I'm sure we can do something about that," he said. He raised his hands above his head and clapped once, a thunderous sound that echoed around the battlefield. As one the human armies seemed to wake up from their reverie, looking around at each other and then noticing the demons and Soul-less before them. Scattered shouts of disgust and anger erupted from around the field, quickly taken up until the demons were surrounded by an almighty wall of noise, a visceral yell of sheer unbridled release as all the human armies of the world converged on these unnatural foes.

"I should thank you for setting me free once more," Andras said to Belial, parrying a blow before twisting and then striking back with his own blade.

Belial met the attack in a shower of sparks. "You only delay the inevitable," he snarled before glancing up, momentarily confused by the change in focus of the battles around them. "What have you done?" Belial scowled.

Andras grinned. "You see, you are not the only one who has been playing a long game, moulding and shaping humanity, et cetera. While you were so keen to remove all hope, to create a race that are utterly subservient to your will, I also saved my greatest gifts for them: lies and free will." He batted away another attack before continuing: "That's not all. This world was never yours, but you have also lost Almadel as well. Even now the Slaves are rising against you, taking control of your own realm." He grinned even wider. "Before you die, know this: I, Andras, Sire of Var, have taken everything from you!"

Belial screamed as he swung his sword at him once more.

*

Back at our own small corner of the battlefield, the Wraith roared in frustration as its honour guard melted away, distracted by the battles they were now facing on so many different fronts. N'yotsu and I ran back to join Kate, Pearce, Joshua and Byron, sharing quick, wide-eyed nods before we faced up to the Wraith. It was a sign of the urgency of our situation that they all filed away the unexpected reappearance of someone we had thought long-gone, only to be discussed when—or indeed if—we survived this ordeal.

Joshua held out a hand to stop us and then advanced on his own.

He walked steadily, his hands outstretched in front of him to show that he was not armed. "Lexie," he said softly. "Lexie, I know there must be something of you left in there. It's me, your brother."

The Wraith stared back at him, this unexpected turn of events leaving it momentarily unsure.

"What's he doing?" hissed Kate. "I thought I'd snapped him out of this."

I held out a hand to steady her. Joshua was face-to-face with the Wraith by this point, staring steadily into its eyes. "Please, there must be something of you left in there, dear Lexie," he said.

Miraculously, the Wraith was transfixed by this display, staring back at him as he edged ever closer. "I just have one thing I wanted to say," he said. "I just… I'm so, so sorry." He took a deep breath and, tears streaming down his cheeks, muttered a series of incantations. The Wraith started to shriek and back away but it was too late—a brilliant blue fire shot out from Joshua's hands, engulfing the malevolent entity. It writhed and howled in the midst of this inferno before disappearing with an unnatural echo. Gaap had been watching this display in open-mouthed horror and turned to run, only to find Joshua's hand on his shoulder. He turned and looked at him, rapidly shaking his head. "No, no please," he said rapidly. "I don't… I did not realise… I can't be…"

Joshua's face was implacable as he muttered some more words, and in a flash Gaap was transformed into a circular runic plate not unlike the one that we had brought back from the afterlife.

I picked up my runic sword, savouring the reassuring weight and the flow of energy washing over me once more. "Now we can have some fun!" I said.

N'yotsu put a hand on my shoulder. "No," he said. "That needs to remain here," he plucked the sword lightly from my grip. "There is one more very important job we need to do."

I glared at him in frustration but the sense of his words cut through my anger. I watched as N'yotsu spoke with Joshua, muttering urgent instructions, laying out the runes in a pattern and scratching out instructions in the dirt at our feet. I looked around, picking up the heavy and clumsy infantry broadsword once more and standing ready to defend my friends in whatever task it was N'yotsu had set them. Kate and Pearce were at my side, occasionally firing rounds from their modified rifles.

"Looks like we're not really needed this time, don't it?" said Kate, a broad grin on her face.

"Everything still looks too evenly matched," I said, "and we have that beast to deal with yet." I nodded over to Belial, who was still locked in battle with Andras.

The two demons were perfectly matched in speed, skill, agility and ruthlessness. Every blow was met with a counter-blow, every attack was defended, no move was too quick that it could not be anticipated and blocked or evaded. They appeared tireless and I wondered if we were witnessing the beginnings of a battle that would rage on for all eternity.

N'yotsu appeared at our side, ushering us away from the circle in which Joshua stood. We looked over to see that the young man's face was aglow with rapt concentration, already reflecting the sheer power flowing through him.

"What's he doing?" asked Pearce. "Is it some sort of weapon?"

N'yotsu shook his head. "No," he said. "It is so much better than that. We are creating the most permanent prison ever."

There was a flash from above, as though we were at the heart of a violent electrical storm. We looked up to see a gaping red hole in the sky, a swirling mass as though we were staring up into the maw of a roiling volcano about to erupt.

"Now," shouted N'yotsu, his voice once more travelling to every side of the field, seeping into our very consciousness as though it had been there all of our lives. "Lie down now!"

Without thinking, every human on the field lay down. I glanced up at the sound of screaming to see the demons being plucked up and away into the heavens and through that hideous gullet. First a couple, then a handful, and then whole chunks of the battlefield were swirling, screaming up into that apocalyptic conflagration. The vortex pulled at the mask that had covered the sky, greedily sucking up the nothingness and taking it along with the demons.

Finally, Belial and Andras whirled up into the sky, still locked in battle and focused only on each other as they spun up and into the hole.

As the last shriek echoed away I looked back at Joshua as he lowered his hands.

With a pop, the hole disappeared, leaving behind a bright blue sky flecked with clouds: a perfect summer's day.

Chapter Twenty-One

We stood in the sudden stillness, looking at the confused yet slowly recovering human armies around us. Joshua collapsed in a heap and we ran to him, helping him to sit up and make himself comfortable. "I'm all right," he gasped, "just somewhat drained."

Pearce called for water and a nearby soldier handed over a canteen that Joshua drank greedily from, nodding his thanks as he returned it. Then he looked up at the empty place where the Wraith had stood, as though he expected to see his sister there. He burst into tears, his body convulsing as he finally gave voice to his grief. Kate put an arm round him.

"What exactly happened there?" she asked the rest of us.

"Do you remember when we first arrived in the afterlife and Gaap accused me of sending us all to a place called the Druj?" asked N'yotsu. Then, in response to our puzzled glances: "Well, not me—Andras. But I am one and the same person in many ways, even though I once again occupy separate bodies."

We shook our heads slowly.

"I suppose there was a lot going on at the time," he conceded.

"Ever so slightly," I agreed.

"Indeed. Well, Gaap did suspect that the afterlife was in fact the place we Almadites refer to as the Druj, a place that is beyond the Aether and any other realm for that matter."

"Like the afterlife?" asked Kate.

"Even more remote," said N'yotsu. "It is normally beyond the abilities of anyone to reach. It was the place that parents would threaten their children with, somewhere that has taken on an almost mythical nature over the centuries. Where we send our Gods to die."

"And yet you knew exactly how to find it," Byron noted.

"Do not forget that I have had millennia of wandering, exiled from my home realm, to explore and figure out the secrets of creation. I met many people over the long, long centuries who showed me more than even Belial knew. While he was fixated on power for its own sake, unable to see beyond Almadel and its petty squabbles, my horizons were broadened exponentially."

"Including playing with the development of the human race," said Byron. "To satisfy your own ends?"

"To frustrate Belial's goals," he said, a look of shame on his face. "Although I admit that at first there was a fair amount of sport and pleasure in what I did. However, you must admit that it worked out well for us in the end, did it not?"

I looked around. Were it not for his intervention, we would surely have been overwhelmed by the demons and ended up forever under Belial's control. However, it was bad enough when I had discovered that my family had been manipulated by Andras to achieve his own ends; to realise that the whole of the human race had also been the playthings of demons was a crushing blow. And now that they were gone, what was to become of us?

"You back, then?" Kate said to N'yotsu. "Are you really N'yotsu again?"

He smiled. "I—Andras—realised that to not lose to Belial, I needed to fight like him: without the more human side of my nature. And so Andras exorcised that part of him." He held his arms wide. "And here I am."

"Back full circle once more," I said. "But does this mean you will die?"

"Eventually, yes. As we discovered last time, I am not meant to be separated from my demon aspect for too long. Hopefully I have a few years in me yet, though."

I frowned. "You—Andras—whatever—sacrificed yourself for us…?"

N'yotsu shrugged.

"We could use the runes to bring Andras back and reunite you," said Joshua, wiping the tears from his cheeks. "I need a little while to recover, but…"

"No," snapped N'yotsu. "They will never be used again."

Epilogue

Bang! Bang!

I groaned as the noise continued with no regard for the effect that it was having on my already tender head. I buried myself under the bolster in the hope that everything would go away and leave me alone.

Bang-bang-bang!

I swam back to consciousness slowly and reluctantly through a thick fog. *It is all too hard,* a dim part of me whimpered. *Just drift off again; the noise will stop. Eventually.*

Bang!

It did not show any sign of abating.

Bang! Bang! Bang! Bang-bang-bang-bang-bang!

"All right," I croaked. Then, louder: "All right, I'm coming." I winced as the sound of my voice reverberated around my skull. Just what had I been drinking last night?

I levered myself out of bed and looked around. I did not recognise the room. "Must have been quite a night," I muttered to myself.

Having located the door, I staggered over after having reassured myself that I was fully dressed. Everything spun around me and I leaned on the wall for support before finally grasping the doorknob.

Kate and Byron stood there, staring at me with concern. "We heard you were back," Kate said.

I frowned, rubbing my head. "Apparently so," I muttered. "From where, exactly?"

"You don't remember?" Byron asked.

Kate shot him a look. "I thought that was the whole point of a forgetfulness spell?"

He tutted in reply. "Well, yes, but I just wanted to check."

"Wait," I said, my brain slowly catching up with my ears. "A forgetfulness spell? Why? What did you do?"

"Come with us," said Byron. "Now we're all back together we can have a proper debriefing."

I hesitated, feeling the strong pull of my bed.

"There's food," said Kate. "And plenty to drink."

This decided me and I followed them out of my room, along a corridor and down a grand staircase. "Where are we?" I asked, squinting at the fine decor and overly bright windows.

"Hughenden," said Byron. "Mr Disraeli kindly allowed us to recuperate here after our ordeal."

They led me to the main dining room, where an impressive spread had been laid out. N'yotsu, Pearce, Joshua and Disraeli were seated around the table, whilst Maxwell was off to one side, his nose stuck in a large, leather-bound book.

They all greeted me in an overly enthusiastic manner, as though we had not seen each other for months. I grunted, shook hands and generally did the minimum necessary to allow me to negotiate my way to the food, accepting a cup of tea from the maidservant in attendance and asking her to leave the pot by my place.

"How are you?" asked Disraeli as I grabbed at the bread.

"Fine," I said suspiciously, scratching at my chin and shocked to find a large amount of beard growth on my face. I ran my fingers over my cheeks and chin: there was at least a month's worth of facial hair there. Which surely was not possible, as I had shaved just the previous morning. "What the...?"

"Fascinating," muttered Maxwell, watching me closely.

I took a deep breath. "I don't want any long-winded explanations or theories," I warned them all in a steady voice. "I just want the truth, as quickly and in as few short words as possible: what have you done to me?"

"What is the last thing you remember?" asked N'yotsu. He held up a hand as I started to bridle. "Please, humour me: this is relevant."

I frowned. "I was with you all in the aftermath of the battle. Andras had just disappeared through the portal with Belial and the other demons and then..." I caught myself subconsciously running my fingers through my new beard. "We must have gone on to celebrate, although I don't remember where or for how long. Whatever I drank, I'm not having it again."

They shared a grin. "I am sorry to advise that what you are feeling is not due to alcohol," said N'yotsu, "at least not all of it and certainly not the memory loss."

"Don't worry," said Kate, throwing herself into the seat next to mine, "we've all felt it. You were just the last one to get back, that's all."

I drained my teacup and refilled it, considering whether I would in fact need something stronger. "Get back from where?"

"You remember the five runes?" asked N'yotsu. "How when they are united they grant ultimate power to the bearer? Well, I would not allow such power to be wielded ever again and so I decided that the runes should be split apart once more."

I looked at Disraeli, considering what the British Empire would have done with such an advantage. "You were happy with this plan of action?" I asked.

"I was not consulted," he said sternly. "Something that was probably for the best. Regardless, I believe the outcome is the correct one."

"You, Byron, Joshua, Pearce and Kate were each given one of the runes and sent to the furthest reaches of the known realms to hide them," continued N'yotsu. "Before you embarked on your journeys, you were subjected to spells of forgetfulness. These ensure that you cannot remember where you took the runes."

I rubbed at my increasingly throbbing head. "Which explains why I cannot remember a thing," I said. A sudden thought occurred. "My sword."

"…was the rune you took and hid," said Byron. "You agreed that it was too dangerous to remain in your hands, given that everyone now knows what it really is."

"Why would I do a damn fool thing like that?" I asked, my voice rising in panic. I felt my breaths starting to come in short, sharp bursts as though something was squeezing me.

"It was the right thing to do," said N'yotsu.

Kate put a hand on my arm. "Are you all right?"

"No," I said. "I am the very opposite of 'all right.' I have just given up the one thing that gave me my powers, the thing that created me, made me what I am. Without it…" I looked at Byron. "What becomes of me?"

"The changes the sword made are permanent," he said. "You are part-demon, part-human, remember? Just because it is not at your side, that does not change anything."

"As far as we know," chipped in Maxwell, my very own Job's comforter. "We will need to keep you under close observation to ensure there are no other ill-effects aside from the withdrawal symptoms that you seem to be currently experiencing."

Kate glared at him. "We're sure you'll be fine, and if not you've got your own little gang of geniuses right here to help you, yeah?" This last word was directed forcefully in Maxwell's direction.

"Yes, yes of course," he muttered.

"But the strength and speed it lent me," I protested. "And I can only really fight with that sword; all others just feel clumsy in compar—"

"Then it's about time you learnt how to fight without it," said Pearce with a tight smile. "But I'm not sure there will be as much call for that as there was before."

"Indeed," said Disraeli. "The Almadites are vanquished, banished to that other place—"

"The Druj," offered N'yotsu.

"Yes, there. Those who were not involved in the invasion are now preoccupied in other ways, I understand?"

"Indeed they are," said N'yotsu. "The Slaves and Workers have risen up, with a little help and encouragement from yours truly. Well, I had to do something to keep myself busy while you were all off gallivanting around the Aether or wherever it was you went."

"You did not help us distribute the runes?" I asked.

He shook his head. "Too risky. I still have too much of Andras inside me."

"Not even Andras trusts Andras," noted Kate with a wry grin.

"Regardless," said Disraeli. "We find ourselves in a new world. The likes of Maxwell now have a whole new set of physical laws to attempt to understand, given that the old ones no longer apply."

Maxwell grunted. "I have already made some interesting insights into the nature of the magic that now pervades our world, and I have some fascinating ideas for power generation. Not to mention the methods of transportation that I created so that you could travel through the Aether on your quests to hide the runes."

Disraeli nodded, speaking up quickly before Maxwell bedded into the details of his thoughts. "We have creatures from the Aether travelling here regularly, and some brave adventurers are already setting off to other realms to make their fortunes. There is much to be done, but I foresee a new age of peace and prosperity. That is worth a toast, do you not think?"

Everyone round the table raised their drinks, glasses and cups to join him in his toast, to a new world, a world of opportunity. I tried to ignore the hollow feeling inside as I followed suit, the sensation that in losing my sword, I had lost a vital part of myself as well.

THE END

Did You Enjoy This Book?

If so, you can make a HUGE difference.

For any author, the single most important way we have of getting our books noticed is a really simple one—and one which you can help with.

Yes, you.

Us indie authors and publishers don't have the financial muscle of the big guys to take out full-page ads in the newspaper or put posters on the subway.

But we do have something much more powerful and effective than that, and it's something that those big publishers would kill to get their hands on.

A committed and loyal bunch of readers.

Honest reviews of our books help bring them to the attention of other readers.

If you've enjoyed this book I would be really grateful if you could spend just a couple of minutes leaving a review (it can be as short as you like) on this book's page on your favourite store and website.

The Great Big Demon Hunting Agency

A NEW SERIES FROM THE WORLD OF THE
INFERNAL AETHER
By Peter Oxley

London, 1868. The streets are haunted by thieves, murderers…
and demons from beyond the Aether.

Spencer and Bart are the city's most incompetent crooks, and
they are in deep trouble. Hunted by both police and their
fellow criminals, they are forced to consider the unthinkable —
going straight.

Forming *The Great Big Demon Hunting Agency*, they think their
troubles are behind them, but they soon find themselves caught
up in a web far more dangerous than they could ever imagine,
pitched against demons, criminals and evil magicians.

Why are there so many demons roaming the London streets,
and can Spencer and Bart stop them before it's too late?

Who are the mysterious Tappers, and what are they doing with the women they abduct from the streets?

Can Spencer and Bart change the habits of a lifetime and not only stay on the right side of the law, but also save the day?

The *Great Big Demon Hunting Agency* is the new novel from Peter Oxley, the author of the Infernal Aether series. If you like dark gothic adventures with a light-hearted twist, then you'll love *The Great Big Demon Hunting Agency*.

AUTHOR'S NOTE

The beauty of writing about historical situations is that you get to delve into worlds which have been long-forgotten, live amongst the people there, marvel at how different things were (as well as how similar) and bring them to life for a new generation (or generations).

This sense of joy and wonder is amplified even more for the historical fantasy author, who also gets to create new worlds and fantastical creatures to play in.

This series started very much rooted in the late nineteenth century (1865, to be precise) and where possible I've tried to stick to the historical facts of the time in terms of geography and people. However, as you'll have noticed if you've got this far, certainly by the start of this novel (indeed, by three-quarters of the way through The Infernal Aether), I have troubled myself less and less with historical accuracy – after all, once you start to throw demons, spirits, golems, alternative dimensions and the like into the mix, I figure that people will forgive me for making stuff up…!

However, some bits of history are reasonably accurate.

Benjamin Disraeli certainly did say most of the more quotable lines he says in this book, and his animosity towards his rival Gladstone was very real. Of course, I've possibly been a bit unfair to Gladstone in this book, mainly because we've seen everything from the side of Disraeli and his friends. But again I figure that you will forgive me, as this is a work of alternative history/fantasy, rather than a political biography!

Many of the places quoted did and do exist, from the site at St Albans (although there's no Fulcrum that I'm aware of) to the Tower of London, Disraeli's pad at Hughenden House, and many more.

It won't surprise you to learn that Almadel is a figment of my imagination, inspired in part by the artwork in the 2000AD comic strips Nemesis the Warlock, which imagined a hellish future Earth known as Termight. Indeed, it was the Nemesis series The Gothic Empire which gave me, as an impressionable teenager, my first real taste of modern steampunk and inspired the ideas which were to grow into The Infernal Aether.

Will our heroes ride again? It has always been my intention to tie together in a trilogy the main story arcs which I started in the first book (although, with the addition of the novella A Christmas Aether, it's actually a trilogy in four parts, which pleases the Douglas Adams fan in me no end...!). But there are still plenty of stories to be told in this new world created by the Aether. If nothing else, surely Gus won't allow me to keep him parted from the runic sword for too long–and if he succeeds, then...?

I also have plans for other, minor characters to play a larger role in future stories–so do watch this space!

About The Author

Peter Oxley is an author, editor and coach who lives in the English Home Counties. He enjoys reading and writing in a wide range of areas but his main passions are sci-fi, fantasy, historical fiction and steampunk.

His influences include HG Wells, Charles Dickens, Neil Gaiman, KW Jeter, Scott Lynch, Clive Barker, Pat Mills and Joss Whedon.

He is the author of The Infernal Aether, A Christmas Aether and The Demon Inside.

He is also the author of the nonfiction book: The Wedding Speech Manual: The Complete Guide to Preparing, Writing and Performing Your Wedding Speech.

He lives with his wife, two young sons and a slowly growing guitar collection. Aside from writing and willingly speaking in front of large crowds of strangers, Pete spends his spare time playing music badly, supporting football teams that play badly, and writing about himself in the third person.

peteroxleyauthor.com
Twitter: @Peteoxleyauthor
Facebook: PeteOxleyAuthor
Tiktok: @peteroxleyauthor

About Burning Chair

Burning Chair is an independent publishing company based in the UK, but covering readers and authors around the globe. We are passionate about both writing and reading books and, at our core, we just want to get great books out to the world.

Our aim is to offer something exciting; something innovative; something that puts the author and their book first. From first class editing to cutting edge marketing and promotion, we provide the care and attention that makes sure every book fulfils its potential.

We are:

- Different
- Passionate
- Nimble and cutting edge
- Invested in our authors' success

If you're interested in hearing more about our books, being the first to hear about our new releases or great offers, or becoming a beta reader for us, again please visit:

www.burningchairpublishing.com

More From Burning Chair Publishing

Your next favourite new read is waiting for you…!

The Infernal Aether series, by Peter Oxley
    The Infernal Aether
    A Christmas Aether
    The Demon Inside
    Beyond the Aether
    The Old Lady of the Skies: 1: Plague

The Great Big Demon Hunting Agency, by Peter Oxley

The Casebook of Johnson & Boswell, by Andrew Neil Macleod
    The Fall of the House of Thomas Weir
    The Stone of Destiny

By Richard Ayre:
    Shadow of the Knife
    Point of Contact
    A Life Eternal

The Curse of Becton Manor, by Patricia Ayling

Near Death, by Richard Wall

The Haven Chronicles, by Fi Phillips
    Haven Wakes
    Magic Bound

Love Is Dead(ly), by Gene Kendall

Beyond, by Georgia Springate

10:59, by N R Baker

The Other Side of Trust, by Neil Robinson

The Sarah Black Series, by Lucy Hooft
    The King's Pawn
    The Head of the Snake

The Brodick Cold War Series, by John Fullerton
    Spy Game
    Spy Dragon
    Burning Bridges, by Matthew Ross

By P N Johnson:
    Killer in the Crowd
    Run to the Blue

Push Back, by James Marx

The Blue Bird Series, by Trish Finnegan
    Blue Bird
    Blue Sky

Baby Blues

The Tom Novak series, by Neil Lancaster
  Going Dark
  Going Rogue
  Going Back

The Wedding Speech Manual, by Peter Oxley

www.burningchairpublishing.com

9 781912 946365